LIVING WITH DEATH

Author, Richard Jan

Library of Congress Registration: TXu 1-668-624
Published by Richard Jan Hoekstra,
Copyright, 2010, Richard Jan Hoekstra, Grand Rapids, MI.
Edited 7/15/2024.

ISBN
Hardback: 978-1-964289-90-8
Paperback: 978-1-964289-89-2

Living with Death, is the title of the second book in a series titled **Dying to Succeed**.

Other books in the series include:

Book 1, Winds of Success
Book 3, Pretending to be Alive
Book 4, Presumption of Sanity
Book 5, Running from Regret
Book 6, Longing to Go Home
Book 7, Afraid to Hope
Book 8, Waiting in Infinity
Book 9, Chasing after Time
Book 10, Casualties of Words
Book 11, Traveling into Chaos
Book 12, Snows of Fear

And finally, as I wrote these books, I often played music. May I suggest that listening to music as you read these books may enhance the experience?

Thank you,
Richard Jan

NOTE: As a service to my readers, place, date, time and speaker have been placed at the beginning of each episode. Where only the time has changed, place and date may be omitted.

Business is the life blood of every civilization, the engine of war. Without business there is only starvation and fear. Wars are be fought in the trenches, but they are won in the boardrooms of business. Your job, the money in your wallet, your house and the bread on your plate comes from a business. Our cultures, our religions, and our countries thrive and die based on our ability to be productive.

> Time for Speaking
> Time for birth
> Time to build
> Time to laugh
> Time for peace
> Time to love
> Time to dance
> Time to hate
> Time for war
> Time to weep
> Time to destroy
> Time for death
> Time to be quiet

Contents

AUTHOR'S NOTE

Although I am familiar with the colored gemstone industry from having worked in it for ten years, I don't pretend to be an expert on any level. My knowledge can best be described as that of a man traveling through a city without ever stopping for an extended period of time to experience the living conditions up close. And yet, as I contemplated my journey after it came to an end, I thought it was interesting and perhaps worthy of being a wonderful subject for a book.

But what I discovered as I wrote was that the real story was not the gemstone industry but how the cast of characters reacted to the challenges they faced, challenges similar to what we daily endure. And it is my hope that knowledge gained from existing for a time in their shoes as you read this book; may encourage you to live a fuller, more purposeful life.

ACKNOWLEDGEMENTS

It is only fair that I acknowledge the help and encouragement that I received from New York Book Publishers. I went to them initially looking for guidance in editing, cover design, marketing, and distribution. They promised me that they could fulfill my needs. I accepted their proposal and began working with them virtually while living in the Midwest with their company's resources located in New York City. Our journey together has been an adventure; one not taken lightly, but traveled with some trepidation and concerns. Special thanks go to Victor Hughes, who guaranteed me they would not let me down. And thanks to my daily contact, Serena Hoffman for understanding my concerns and assuring me that everything was progressing as it should. And to Jim Bannister who took the time to talk to me when I needed a conversation. And to the many editors and artists who have contributed greatly to the final product. Thanks to them all for helping me achieve what I had hoped for when I first contacted this New York Book Publishers.

Page Left Blank Intentionally

CHARLOTTESVILLE, VIRGINIA, USA, JANUARY 23, 1997, THURSDAY,

4:30 AM, JOHN

A nightmare filled with cold, hard ice gathered me in her arms, wound her stiff fingers around my panicked body and held me tightly like a scorned lover.

Encased in a casket of pure white ice after being buried by an avalanche while skiing in the Alps, just enough light filtered down through the snow that I could see vague shadows above my head, nothing distinct. It was far worse when I closed my eyes. It got dark then, deathly dark, filled with shivering fear.

I remembered it all: the waves of panicked terror which racked my mind and body, heart racing, lungs gasping for air. I tried but could not dig out of the hard snow. Struggling only seemed to make the snow harder; my new lover was more determined to embrace me in her icy grip. Nothing... there was nothing I could do except scream for help in frustration and wait to die. And eventually that was exactly what I did. I died from hypothermia. My heart rate slowed until it stopped, and I died.

But not immediately.

Only after I gave in to the idea that I could not escape my icy tomb and live. Only after finally embracing death; nothing more, no more hassles, no demands, no problems. Only after one final, silent, cold goodbye to no one. Only then did my shivering panic stop as I lay quiet, eyes closed, resting in peace... accepting death's cold embrace.

Only after I accepted death was I allowed to die.

I did not die for long.

I was rescued, my heart was restarted by paramedics, and my breathing was restored before irreversible brain damage occurred. My cold-hearted lover who had embraced me, held me, and killed me... My new lover had also miraculously preserved me and saved me until I could be revived. And it was this miracle of new life which presented me with a mystery, an unanswerable question.

As I lay in bed, home in my comfortable Charlottesville apartment under warm blankets at night, I could not stop thinking about the question I could not answer. About why I had been willing to allow death to take me and why it had felt good... almost as if I wanted to die.

Why, why had I chosen death?

Was it because my cold-hearted lover was whispering in my ear as I lay in my icy tomb? Was she looking into my future? Was she telling me to accept her because she knew what I did not know, what lay ahead of me in my future? And this had been okay with me. I had struggled enough. I didn't want to continue. I was content to die, to embrace my new lover, death...

But does that make sense? Nobody wants to die. Nobody I know.

Over time, I have developed an irksome habit of waking up around four o'clock in the morning before dawn. By this time in the night, all the problems and confusions experienced during the previous day have had adequate time to process slowly through my subconscious and this is when my brain wakes me, alert and needy. It desires... no, demands solutions. It seems that all the problems which have reared their ugly head during the previous day must now be solved. My brain will not allow me to return to sleep again until it has presented a litany of complications associated with these problems, along with possible solutions to these complex difficulties. Only after I have decided on appropriate courses of action to deal with these problems, and my brain has filed these solutions neatly away on a mental shelf for use the next day; then and only then will my unruly brain allow me to go back to sleep... not before.

That is normally okay with me, except lately when the memory of my near-death experience in an icy tomb has been rearing its ugly head during this time of night, joining the parade of problems which must be solved. But this problem, or should I say this scene of frightening implications... my giving into death in a cold white tomb of snow which lives in my nightmares; this is a problem which has no solution because I don't think I will ever be able to understand it.

However, that doesn't seem to matter to my brain. My brain demands that this problem be solved.   And until I can solve the issue of my problematic death, why I accepted death, until my brain can wrap itself around all the implications of my embracing death and come to a solution... until this happens, the memory of my ill-advised visit to a compacted, bitter cold, snow tomb is destined to revisit me every night.

And it is like dying... over and over again.

3:35 PM, JOHN

The possibility of an early death was a new reality I had never contemplated when I put together a strategic business plan to form a company.

I never dreamed that all my planning would someday lead to my almost being murdered in an avalanche. But I believe that was exactly what happened. Even though there is no proven connection between my company and several attempts to murder me, I am convinced that the real motive behind these crimes is to take control of my company by eliminating me.

Six years of constant growth and success had vindicated my plans until several disastrous events occurred, all of them completely out of my control and seemingly random except for one, too obvious, common theme. They hurt my company in ways that only an insider would understand. However, none of them, not the robberies or the fire at our lab none, were more revealing or fearful than several attempts to end my life.

The company's successful years were based on the purchase, marketing, and sales of a majority of sapphires in the world. Unfortunately, that was no longer true. And as a result, my company was now on life support.

I am the CEO and it is a full-time job which normally requires long hours, seven days a week. I don't mind. I am a bachelor whose life was defined by my job. So, I wait, and I work, doing what I can while hoping for a break.

For several weeks now, my workload has been unusually low. This lull in my normally frenetic schedule was both unaccustomed and unwelcome. Everything physically possible which can be done, has been done to put product into our client's hands. This is my responsibility, but my resources are currently limited. Our operations are crippled until our lab can be rebuilt. Until this occurs, my company is relegated to selling only a very limited supply of naturally colored gemstones.

Most mined sapphires do not have good color. They fall into the category of needing some help from modern technology to finish what Mother Nature began. The process is called color enhancement, and special furnaces are required. It is these furnaces which are the weak link. They are still in the US being manufactured when they should have been on a plane flying to Australia to be installed and operated at our lab. As a result, rough sapphires purchased from mines around the world are accumulating in warehouse vaults, waiting to be treated.

Unfortunately, there is nothing I can do to change that. I am forced to wait for the furnaces to be delivered and operating.

My only hope is that the company will survive in the meantime.

5:30 PM. JOHN

As the sun set behind the plate glass windows of the clubhouse, evidenced by golden shafts of diminishing light streaking through wind-driven, wispy clouds washing through my mind, I absentmindedly listened to Monica order a shrimp salad.

Miss Monica Sorensen is my personal assistant, lawyer, lover and sometimes menace. During recent slow times in my work schedule, I have been asking her to spend time with me, anything to take my mind off the problems of the company. On sunny days, a drive through the hills or some shopping in town was suggested. And while these times away from the office were enjoyable distractions, they felt all wrong. I am a workaholic. Having large quantities of free time was not necessarily good for my mental health. Guilt and apprehension have dogged my conscience.

That evening, she agreed to accompany me to my golf club for dinner. Bodyguards followed us as we drove through the green hills outside of town because they were necessary. She understood. She had been with me on a few occasions when our lives were in danger.

I called her M because she preferred being called M rather than Monica. A fresh pink blush of sun-kissed color highlighted her high cheekbones. Her long red hair was casually combed back into a ponytail. Before leaving the office, she mentioned something about not having time to properly prepare; too much work to do. Could I please excuse her lack of cosmetic attention? I told her I didn't mind. Said she looked beautiful. And she did. Her pale lipstick matched the color of her fresh-air cheeks. She was gorgeous, drop dead gorgeous and smart; a lawyer who studied at the University of Virginia and graduated top of her class. Beauty and brains were a lethal combination if there ever was one.

After taking her order, our waiter turned to me just when my cell phone began to vibrate in my pocket.

Prior to the waiter's arrival, I had been digging myself into a verbal hole. M and I had been debating something. I don't remember what. I just remember thinking she was about to bury me so deep under the rubbish of my cocky brand of self-arrogant intelligence, so deep I would never be able to dig myself out. The waiter's timely arrival had fortunately rescued me from certain humiliation. And since cell phones are prohibited inside the clubhouse, I stood up from the table while waving my phone at M and suggesting she order something for me from the menu, I didn't care what; fish was fine.

'Yes, Bob.' I answered as soon as I was outside the clubhouse.

Bob Anderson was in charge of our New York Distribution House. Bob's business was one of our three sales outlets. His New York Distribution House sold gemstones to North and South America. Lin Hung-Chao manages one of the other distribution houses in Hong Kong. His company sells gemstones to clients in the Far East and Australia. While Arthur Wilson runs the third house in London, his clients are in Europe and Africa.

'John, Arthur is in New York,' Bob explained. 'We wondered if we could come to your Charlottesville office tomorrow and meet with you in the morning.'

'Of course ... I didn't know Arthur was travelling to the States.'

'He just popped in... spur of the moment trip. So... tomorrow morning, okay?'

'Sure. Want me to send a plane?'

'That would be appreciated.'

'Okay, I'll have my charter service call you. Tomorrow morning, then. Say around eleven?'

'Eleven is perfect.'

He hung up without another word; he didn't seem to want to chat. Now, that was odd for Bob. He was never at a loss for words and always liked to hear himself talk. Usually, I was the one who ended our conversations.

Before returning to the restaurant, I arranged the flight for my partners because I didn't want to think about business at dinner. Apparently, M had other ideas.

'Who called?' she asked after I sat down.

'Bob. He and Arthur are coming to the office in the morning.'

'Was this a planned meeting?'

'No,' I answered without further comment.

Something about the expected nature of the meeting was disturbing, something which I needed time to process, but not now.

Now I wanted to enjoy my meal.

JANUARY 24, FRIDAY, 11:06 A.M. JOHN

At approximately five minutes after eleven that morning, the large wooden doors to my office opened, and Helen, my dowdy but devoted office secretary, showed two gentlemen inside.

They walked in as if this was their first visit. It was not. They had been to my office many times in the past. I came around my office desk to greet them as Helen politely closed the doors behind her. My mood all morning had been particularly dour. I didn't know why. Just had the distinct feeling my buddies were not coming to town for my personal health and well-being. I feared they had something else in mind, something I would not like. However, I was determined to begin our meeting assuming they innocently wanted to discuss business, nothing more. To facilitate my hoped-for civility, I had dressed casually: long-sleeved blue polo shirt, sweater and khaki pants. They, on the other hand, arrived in a big city with power suits, white shirts and ties. I didn't mind, really. They always dressed this way. I sometimes wondered how I had ever connected with these two guys. In many ways, they were very different from me.

'Good morning, Arthur.' I extended my hand while noticing something slightly untidy about his appearance this morning. Like he hadn't slept well, his curly red hair was more than simply fashionably out of place. An air of dishevelment seemed to have permeated his normally tidy attitude, and his customary sardonic grin was sadly missing.

Bob, on the other hand, was his normal, unaffected self. He was a big, broad-shouldered man, and his hair was cut short like an ex-Army officer, which is exactly what he was. In contrast to Arthur, it was almost impossible for Bob to look untidy, given his strict dress code. A stern, tight-lipped expression always covered his face, highlighted by a permanent frown which was the product of years of disciplined behavior.

'Please sit down, gentlemen.' I motioned towards the leather couches in my office, normally used for informal conversations. 'Can I get you some coffee, a roll perhaps? This is Charlottesville, gentlemen, not New York. You're in the country. Loosen those ties.'

Putting on a happy face, I retrieved coffee mugs from a cupboard disguised by mirrored doors in one wall of my office.

I did not make a habit of requiring my secretary, Helen, to serve guests as did most CEOs. I suppose she would have if I had asked her, but I enjoyed doing away with certain assumptions of power, instead using the casual gesture of serving my guests as a symbol of my good intentions. Foreign visitors occasionally expressed genuine surprise when I served them. I didn't mind. This was my office, and this was how I operated.

After placing a thermos of coffee and a plate of sweet rolls on a table in front of my guests, I sat down. Goodwill only went so far; I never poured their coffee. They could pour their own.

'Past my coffee time, old chap,' Arthur said. 'I'm on London time. Don't bother.'

'Something to eat, then? I can have Arny prepare a sandwich.'

Arny was my friend and housekeeper after applying for a job. A bit down in his luck at the time, his African American heritage didn't serve him well in the South. I befriended him after spending time with him on the job and built an apartment for him next to mine. Although he continued to work for me as my housekeeper and cook, the truth was, I needed him more than he needed me, something which he clearly understood and constantly reminded me of. Fortunately, it was a relationship which served both of us.

'No, no,' Arthur responded with a flippant wave of his hand.

I took a sip of coffee from my mug. 'I appreciate you guys coming here. I would have suggested a meeting, but I thought you had enough problems to occupy your time without my dragging you out to my country office.'

Bob didn't immediately reply; instead turned to Arthur, who was studying the rolls as if something slightly odd was wrong with them.

'I'm afraid we're not here on usual business,' Bob finally replied, sounding like a sergeant at arms.

'I see.'

'Look, John,' he continued. 'Sorry, this wasn't my idea. Since the last board meeting, we've had numerous calls from members, past and present. Well, you can imagine. No one is happy. Everything is breaking down. And then with Vidu poisoned to death, and the London shipments permanently lost... well, you can imagine....'

'Stolen, you mean,' I interrupted, not wanting to allow our discussion to get out of control. 'I think we need to assume the shipments were stolen.'

'Okay, stolen. The point is the board feels something needs to be done.'

'Yes,' I replied, my jaw tightening, not liking the direction this conversation was taking.

Arthur chirped in at this juncture, his high-toned, affected English accent sounding unusually nervous. 'John, your office has been very quiet through all this. No real direction coming from Charlottesville, old chap. That's the message we keep hearing.'

I didn't respond, now wondering where this conversation was headed.

'Our clients are upset, naturally,' Arthur droned on. 'And miners aren't happy. Everyone is asking what we're going to do.'

'Why would the miners be unhappy?' I countered. 'Their payments have not been delayed.'

'Yes, yes,' said Arthur. 'But that's not the point, is it?'

'What is the point?'

'Something needs to be done.'

'So, you came here to formulate an answer for them?' I asked hopefully. 'Is that what this is about?'

'I'm afraid it has gone too far for that,' Arthur replied solemnly.

'What has gone too far?'

'Well, tell him, Bob,' Arthur exclaimed, his voice rising an extra octave.

Bob hesitated. 'Sorry, John, but we are here to tell you the board has voted an informal 'no-confidence' in your leadership. They all wish to express how grateful they are for the work you have done for the company. But now, in this time of crisis, they feel new leadership is required. You can stay on as a consultant if you wish, with full benefits for a period of time. In addition, you may continue to use your office suite as before, but the board is asking for your resignation as the CEO and Chairman of the Board.'

The word 'resignation' resonated like a bomb going off in my head. 'What are you talking about?' I demanded. 'I'm not aware of any vote.'

'It was taken in a private conference call,' Arthur explained nervously. 'Believe me, we have the votes,' he added quickly. 'Please don't make this any harder than it needs to be. We don't wish you any hard feelings. We simply need to get the ship righted. That's best for everyone.'

I sat back on the couch, amazed they had the balls to do this. I had made them very rich. Their fortunes were tied to a company I had built from scratch. Sure, they had helped, but the impetus came from me. They lived a very good life, with limousines and country homes and padded expense accounts. I never complained about what they earned. They were doing a good job. I let the excesses slide. But apparently, they now wanted more.

'Who will run the company after I step down?' I asked.

'The board has selected me,' Arthur said a little too proudly. 'I didn't want the job, mind you. But they insisted. I hope you don't take it personally.'

'Don't take it personally, Arthur? How would you take it? You come in here and tell me the board has, behind my back, voted to remove me from office. And you are my replacement. Wouldn't you take that personally, Arthur?'

'Look, John,' Bob stated in a conciliatory tone. 'Things are in a serious mess, and we need...'

I cut him off. 'When did this vote occur?' I asked, immediately feeling I had to get the facts on the table.

'Well, there hasn't been a real vote yet, just an informal poll,' Bob said, 'We thought it would be best to proceed on an amicable basis. Announcement to come after a formal board meeting. You know, a public announcement with everyone agreeing for the good of the company. Then some PR spin emphasising a turnaround;

everything positive, the company moving forward under new leadership.'

'I'm sure you see the wisdom in all this,' Arthur added. 'Put the past behind us, a new day and all that.'

'I see a lot in this. Wisdom is not one of them,' I replied bluntly.

'We were hoping you would be cooperative, John, for the good of the company.'

'Has Lin agreed to this?' I asked.

'We thought it would be better not to initially involve Lin,' said Bob.

'Why, were you afraid he would tell me? And with Vidu dead and out of the way, I guess this has been easy for you,' I shot back.

'That's not...' Arthur blurted.

'You're taking this all wrong.' Bob quickly interrupted Arthur, hoping, I guess, to get our conversation back on track.

My anger was ready to explode. I was trying to hold it in, but the audacity of these two incompetents was almost more than I could bear.

'How am I supposed to take it, Bob? You two waltz in here and announce you're taking over my company, something I spent years building. Not enough leadership, you say, not enough direction. What did you expect from me? If I knew how to fix our problems, I would do it. But I don't... And you don't either.'

They didn't respond.

'Do you really think this is my fault?' I asked, point blank.

'Nobody said it was,' Bob replied.

'And Arthur, you genius,' I said, ignoring Bob. 'How is your taking over this company going to solve anything? Do you know something I don't?'

'What are you implying?' Arthur's voice fairly squeaked in exasperation.

'Nothing more than what you are implying when you say your leadership can right the ship. Unless you know something I don't know, how can you make a difference? Will the fires and the robberies and the killings stop simply because you are CEO?'

'Of course not, I can't control what happens,' Arthur said, his face flushed pink.

'Then why will making you CEO help anything?'

'You're not thinking properly,' Arthur replied.

'I'm trying Arthur. Why don't you help me by explaining how you can make our situation better?'

Everyone was quiet for a moment. I breathed slowly, trying to calm down. Getting mad would solve nothing.

'Look, guys,' I said. 'We have been friends for a long time. In times of crisis, friends pull together, not apart. Why don't we all take a deep breath and try to rethink our situation?'

'I'm afraid it's too late for that. The board is pretty adamant,' Arthur said, trying to regain his composure.

Bob looked at Arthur before asking, 'John, I would like to talk to Arthur outside. Do you mind?'

'No, take all the time you want.'

They left the room.

My body was literally vibrating with nervous energy. I was so angry. And now I knew why my phone had been so silent. It wasn't because the phones in my company were not ringing. Phones were ringing, just not for me. These guys had been busy. I should have seen this coming. The seeds of deception were planted at the last board meeting. In fact, I had probably dodged getting sacked back then. Transcontinental calls must have been fairly flying back and forth across the globe in the weeks since then. Old Arthur was having a splendid time. It was just the kind of back door shenanigans he liked to wallow in. It fit his conniving British nature. And Bob, he liked to think of himself as a leader, but I doubted he had the balls to pull this off on his own. No, Arthur, the little weasel, he was the guy behind this coup.

I walked to a window in my office, expecting to see storm clouds forming on the horizon to match my mood. But it was a beautiful spring-like day. I wondered whether Bob was outside, attempting to talk Arthur out of it. Bob, for all his assumed self-confidence, never liked adversity. He probably went along with Arthur to placate him. I wondered how much real backing they had from the board. Maybe not that much. Maybe they just hoped I would step down without a fight.

My office doors opened.

I stood up, deciding it was time to get formal. Pull an Arthur, sit behind my desk, the kind of power play he would do; assume a throne behind a desk like some big shot. This meeting was no longer a casual conversation between friends. It had badly deteriorated. It was a contest between adversaries now. I motioned for them to take a seat in the chairs on the other side of my desk.

Bob began, 'John if you don't mind, I would like an opportunity to describe your proposed severance package. We failed to mention this in our conversation. Hopefully, the generosity of our offer will convince you that no ill will is intended here.'

I said nothing in response, curious about what he might offer, wondering just how badly they wanted to be rid of me.

Bob took his time describing a very lucrative offer which involved millions over a five-year period. As I listened, I was vaguely tempted to take their money. If I walked away now, I would never have to deal with these two idiots ever again. It was a thought.

'That's very enticing,' I said after he finished. 'It's quite obvious you guys really want me gone.'

'That's not how it is,' Bob persisted. 'It's meant to express our thanks for a job well done.'

'Just not lately.'

'You're not looking at this properly,' Arthur interrupted.

'I'm looking at it the only way possible. You two are firing me, and you want me to go away quietly.'

'No, this is about the good of the company. It may not appear this way to you now, but it's true,' Bob tried to explain.

'It's for someone's good,' I said. 'I'm not sure who. But sure as hell; it's not good for the company.'

'Look, John, we have tried to do this with as much civility as possible. But it will be done, one way or the other,' Arthur stated coldly.

'Thanks for being truthful for a change, Arthur.'

No one spoke. It was obvious we were at an impasse.

'We need your answer, John,' Arthur stated.

'You do, do you?'

'Yes.'

'Okay, how about this?' I replied. 'Tell the board I will take your offer under consideration.'

'No, we need your answer now.'

'I gave you my answer.'

'The severance package may not be offered later,' Arthur explained without expression.

'I'll take my chances.' I stared him down.

He looked away, refusing to meet my gaze.

Bob interrupted, realizing better than Arthur that our conversation was going nowhere fast. 'Let's all cool down,' he suggested. 'Why don't you take twenty-four hours and think about it, John? Then call me. I think once you've had a chance to reconsider, you will decide it is all for the best. You have worked very hard for the last six years, John. You could use a break. This could be good for you.'

No one spoke.

'Will you think about it?' Bob asked.

'I'll call you,' I finally answered, barely able to contain my anger.

Arthur started to speak, but Bob stopped him. 'Let's go, Arthur. I think we have accomplished everything we can for today.'

Bob looked at me again. 'Okay, John?'

'I think you had better go,' I said without emotion.

The big oak doors to my office opened and closed behind them as I sat fuming at my desk.

A full minute passed. I wanted to be certain my dastardly business partners were really gone before I left my office without saying a word to my secretary, Helen. On my way down to the garage, I fortunately didn't see M. I really didn't want to talk to her. I didn't want to talk to anyone.

Sitting behind the steering wheel of my BMW, I rested for at least ten minutes of solitude, allowing emotions from fear to anger to self-pity to race through my mind simultaneously. Eventually, when I had calmed down sufficiently, I turned the key. The motor started with a satisfying hum. The garage door opened. Sunshine and an open road beckoned outside.

I hit the accelerator hard in a vain attempt to escape.

2:10 P.M. JOHN

Any memory of driving through the countryside was quickly lost in a sea of mental turbulence. Eventually, for reasons unimportant, I found myself sitting in my car, staring at some mountains in the distance from a viewing area off the highway.

Everything in my world was different now. Apparently, I was destined to become the ex-CEO of an international business. And people who I thought were my friends were not. I wondered how many other illusions I normally mistook for reality were, in fact, not real.

I briefly considered quitting, letting Arthur and Bob have their wish. Let them struggle through long days and nights of worry in the future. Let them try to keep everyone happy, as I had been doing for the last six years. And in the end, let them feel the inevitable disappointment and betrayal which I was feeling today.

Why not walk away, I wondered? Walking would be an easy out. And it would have been except for one pertinent fact... I could not. I knew I would fight. As M had predicted when we last talked about my leaving the company. I was a fighter, not a quitter. So, what if I lost? So be it. I simply couldn't just walk away.

I took out my cell phone and called my friend Lin Hung-Chao who managed our Hong Kong Distribution House.

'We need to talk.'

'Are you okay?' he asked, expertly recognizing the anxiety in my voice

'I'm fine. Just need to talk... Please listen.'

I proceeded to give him the details of my morning's meeting. 'Yes, I know you didn't know anything about it. They admitted they left you out of the vote. I guess they figured you would be loyal to me and probably interfere with their plans.'

'I'm sorry, John,' Lin sounded genuinely remorseful.

'Don't be sorry. I should have seen this coming and been better prepared.'

'Did you think this would happen?'

'I had my suspicions.'

Lin was silent.

'Let's not dwell on the past. I didn't call for that reason.'

When he remained silent, I took the opportunity to move ahead. 'Let's look at the facts,' I said impatiently. 'It's pretty obvious they badly want to be rid of me.'

'Why do you think that?' Lin calmly asked.

'I can't see it any other way, Lin. Look at how organized they are. They know what they're doing. They offered me millions to go away quietly.'

'How much did they offer?'

'Twenty million over five years, but I'm thinking that's just a 'starter' offer. I got the distinct impression I could get a lot more if I really wanted it... As long as I agreed to go away quietly.'

'Do you want to take the money?'

'Lin, don't you know me by now?' I was exasperated. 'Why do you think I'm calling?'

'Sorry, John, but they are offering you a large sum of money,' he hesitated. 'Sorry, I ...'

'Forget it. I didn't mean to jump on you. I'm just upset.'

'What do you want to do?' he asked.

'I've been thinking. Perhaps we should talk to the board members, test their loyalty, and determine if Arthur and Bob really have the votes they say they have. It's the only way we'll know for certain.'

'Yes.'

'And think about this, Lin. The only way to get rid of me quickly, without my resignation, is to set an early date for a board meeting and call for a vote. Isn't this right?'

'Yes, if they want to force you out.'

'And a board meeting by teleconference would be the fastest method to accomplish this, right?'

'Yes.'

'Okay, first, we need to determine if Arthur has enough votes for a quorum. Without two-thirds of the board members agreeing, he doesn't have a quorum, and that means he can't call a meeting.'

'I will make the calls,' Lin volunteered, quickly understanding the situation. 'The board will be more honest with me than you.'

'Good,' I said, still wondering how it had come to this.

BANGKOK THAILAND, SUNDAY, JANUARY 26, 1:30 P.M. LUANG

The old patriarch received constant updates.

These memos, as they are called in Western business jargon, detailed the affairs of the family. Sent from his nephew's office, the privileged information had not been withdrawn from him, not yet. His nephew, Nue, was still keeping him informed. Even though Luang was no longer in a position to exercise influence over the family's businesses, he was still considered an important insider.

Not long ago, Luang Nue had retired from the chair at the head of a long conference table, the position he had inherited from his father. He decided it was time to enjoy what remained of his life. Because he had no sons so, when he retired, the head of the family council, the chair of power, was given to his nephew, his dead brother's son.

The family business was still profitable at the time of his retirement, established and operating as it had for more than a hundred years. He had no reason to assume this would ever change, but change it did, undermined by a company in America. Everything had gone downhill fast: jobs, money and connections; everything which made his family respected in his homeland of Thailand. The international business of selling sapphires, the core family business, was unceremoniously stripped from them by a young American and his company, little by little, until most of it was gone. Luang could not believe it had happened so fast. But the evidence was all around him, factories closed, men and women out of work. It had been a disaster.

Something needed to be done, and his nephew Nue was doing it. But the methods his nephew chose were all wrong. Luang was very concerned. Violence and death were not tactics he would have employed. His nephew had other ideas.

Recently, his nephew had changed course, revised his plans, and adopted a new strategy which was more in step with what the old patriarch might have done if he had been in control. His nephew was attempting to influence matters from the inside rather than violently destroying the structure of the American company from the outside.

The old man knew this new plan would take time.

He hoped his nephew had the patience to let it work.

JANUARY 29, WEDNESDAY, 3:40 P.M. JOHN

Over the weekend, I became more and more convinced that the solution to my problems was to return to a heavy work schedule.

By Monday morning, workaholic habits had been reinstated in my brain, and I was anxious to get started. It actually felt good to be active and productive again. By Wednesday afternoon, I was once again living in my office, leaving only to sleep for a few hours before returning again. I saw my friend and housekeeper, Arny, only once or twice during the next few days. And not much of Monica, no more sleepovers. It was as if I had once again assumed my former life as an isolated, workaholic bachelor. I guess my hope was that by returning to my old ways, I might somehow be magically transported back to my previous status. But the truth was, I was running as fast as I could in a vain attempt to hide from the pain and indignity of being fired.

M tried to relate, but I shut her out. Even when she was in my office, I was either on the phone or working. Dinners, if shared with her, were short on conversation. Breakfast and lunch were often eaten alone in my office as I worked.

Arny had seen it all before. He tried to help M understand, but he was helpless to do anything besides let it happen. And I was so preoccupied with my new-found obsession; I did not notice M slipping away. She seldom worked in my office as had been her previous habit. Instead, she spent her days in a small workstation near Helen.

But as I said, she was not my main concern.

Helping Lin with his calls to the board members was my number one priority. Once he started calling, Lin and I agreed he would remain on his phone until he had talked to every one of our members. And since they lived in almost every time zone around the globe, this promised to be a marathon. We also agreed he would urge each member to contact me. Therefore, I was obligated to be near my phone the whole time he was calling.

Because members of the board came from diverse cultural and business interests, we spent hours preparing special presentations tailored specifically to each of them. Our first priority was to get them to not agree to a board meeting via teleconference.

The company's bylaws required a quorum in order to have a board meeting by teleconference. A quorum requires a vote of two-thirds of the members. So, even if it was true, as Arthur stated, that a majority of the board had agreed to fire me, it wouldn't matter if he couldn't organize a board meeting to accomplish his goal. A majority would not do. All Lin had to do was to convince more than a third of the members it was only fair that I be given a chance to defend myself in an open, face-to-face meeting of the board. If he could do that, Arthur wouldn't have the quorum he needed, and any decision to replace me would have to be delayed until the next regularly scheduled board meeting.

Hopefully, this would allow me time to prepare a proper rebuttal.

This was our plan, a guerrilla styled, back-room action. Counter attack, fall back, hold, buy time, look for an opening.

It all sounded good when we were discussing it, but I wondered... worried it wouldn't work. However, in the absence of an alternative, we decided to go for it.

Lin handled the preparations for talking to the members from the Far East. They were his area of expertise. The other board members were my responsibility. I knew them better than Lin. I prepared their presentations.

We agreed to review each conversation before Lin made his call. It had to be right. And after he completed each call, Lin would call me with a 'post mortem.' Tell me what he had learned, anything which might be useful.

Our plan was to begin with those members we thought were most loyal to me. Lin would ask them to refrain from calling Bob or Arthur. We didn't want my two adversaries to know what we were doing. Hopefully, this would prevent Arthur from calling for an immediate teleconference.

I had purposely avoided talking to either Arthur or Bob since our last meeting. When Bob called two days after his visit to my office, I refused his call. And if he called again, I planned to give him only a brief reply, tell him I was thinking about his offer and I would have an answer for him in due time, when I was ready.

I knew Arthur and I knew he was becoming impatient. Several reports of his activities had crossed my desk. Apparently, he was already acting like he was the CEO, calling key business partners and dictating company strategy. We decided Lin should use his calls to emphasize I was still the acting CEO. We hoped this would counter Arthur's strategy.

One thought continued to nag me while Lin and I were preparing. I kept thinking about Phillip. I didn't know why. I just couldn't get that man out of my brain. I kept thinking he might have something to do with what happened. Not because I had a legitimate reason to suspect Phillip. I didn't. It was just because I knew Phillip. I knew he hated me. He didn't like the fact I had succeeded when he had failed. He could not understand how a man with no background in the field of colored gemstones could do what he, a brilliant geologist, had been unable to do. In his opinion I had cheated him out of a company which rightfully belonged to him. And it couldn't possibly be his fault. He was too smart to fail. He always put the blame on someone else, and in this, I was his convenient fall guy.

To make matters worse, he had previously been a friend. During that time, he and I worked for the same client; I was an aspiring advertising executive, and he was a geologist and a confidant of the owner; we discovered by accident that we came from the same hometown. That helped us establish a convenient friendship, a couple of bachelors having drinks together after work. He taught me about colored gemstones, something which helped me in my work. Initially, I was grateful, but over time, I became suspicious. Something about him was not right. I caught him in several lies, and when the previous company folded, I suspected he may have contributed to its failure, perhaps by misleading the owner. But I also knew he wasn't the only problem. They were a pair, he and the owner. I didn't trust either one of them.

Phillip came to me after my company was formed. Said he was looking for a job. But it quickly became evident he wanted more. He asked to be included as a full partner, demanded I give him stock, said this would be the smartest move I could make.

I said no, didn't trust him. After that he started his own competing company. It failed. He was not a good manager. He never accepted responsibility. Instead he blamed me.

I had not seen him or heard from him until recently when he appeared in London at a club where I was having dinner with Arthur. After our chance encounter, I couldn't get him out of my head. I kept wondering if his sudden appearance was no coincidence. Because everything began to go wrong at about the same time. I decided I needed to talk to him if for no other reason than to satisfy my curiosity and make certain, he wasn't involved. I assumed he was still living in Grand Haven, Michigan, our original hometown.

Helen raised her eyebrows skeptically after I mentioned his name, asking her to locate him for me. She knew about Phillip. I had told her his story. She confirmed his location when she found his telephone number listed in the Grand Haven directory.

I could simply have called him, but I knew Phillip. I knew he would avoid me if he was in any way involved in my company's problems. If I wanted the truth, I would have to find him and ask him to his face if he was involved. Then I had to hope he would give me some sign, something like a veiled smile of satisfaction which would tell me he was in the game. Because I knew he would never tell me directly. He would lie.

I made plans to fly to Michigan as soon as Lin and I finished our calls. And almost as an afterthought I decided to ask M if she would like to come with me. Fortunately, she was at her workstation near Helen's desk when I went to find her.

She hesitated at first.

'Look, you don't have to go,' I said, seeing her reluctance.

'Well, I ...'

'We haven't had much time together lately. I'm sorry. Maybe this trip would help us catch up.'

'Alright,' she agreed quietly.

'I can show you where I grew up.'

'Okay,' she smiled and then, as if a question had just occurred to her, 'Can I ask you something?'

'Later, we can talk on the plane,' I turned quickly to leave but stopped and said, 'By the way, Lin is preparing to make a series of calls to our board members to discuss Arthur's situation. I'll need to be available to take calls from board members who may want to talk to me directly. I'll be in my office most of the night.'

She gave me a funny look.

I didn't think much of it at the time.

Probably should have, but I was distracted, my mind into thinking about the calls.

6:30 P.M. JOHN

The telephone on my desk rang.

Prior to the calls, I had attempted a short nap. It didn't happen. I couldn't sleep, much less rest. My mind was too busy, my body full of nervous tension, too many scenarios whirling around inside my head, too many possibilities.

Helen had been informed of her role and held all calls except those from Lin and members of the board. Over the last few days, she had invented an excuse to contact each of the board member's secretaries to determine where the member would be today and when was the best time to call them. This information has been forwarded to Lin.

I sighed and picked up my phone.

'You ready, John?' Lin asked from Hong Kong.

His voice sounded calm, unruffled. I admired his composure.

'I'm ready. Vidu's brother first, right?' I spoke confidently.

'Right.'

Lin would make all the other calls, but we had decided this one was mine. I had a close relationship with Vidu. His brother had been appointed to take a seat on the board after Vidu was murdered on the streets of Chicago, killed by a lethal injection of poison. His murder was an open, unsolved case.

I assumed his brother would match Vidu's solid support for me, but I needed to ask. Fortunately, my call went as expected. I began by conveying my condolences. Then I told Vidu's brother that the company would continue to support him and his cutting operation same as before his brother's death. Nothing would change. He thanked me. After briefly describing the current situation involving Arthur and Bob, I asked him for his support. He agreed to help. Then he asked me a question, his voice laced with grief. Did I have any new information on who killed his brother? I told him the truth. Chicago Police were trying, but no new information had been discovered. He thanked me and hung up.

His call left me feeling empty. Even though I got what I desired from him, he had not received what he wanted from me. I called Lin and gave him a reply.

He listened quietly. 'Thank you for making this call, John. I'm sure it wasn't easy.' Lin paused. 'Now it is time for me to begin.'

'Thank you again.'

'No need to thank me, John. It's my duty,' Lin responded, 'and my privilege.'

'Thanks anyway,' I reiterated.

I called my charter jet service while waiting for Lin's first callback. A flight was scheduled for tomorrow afternoon. I was anxious to arrive in Grand Haven and confront Phillip, but the calls had to come first.

I poured a cup of coffee. It promised to be a late night. Helen had agreed to stay until nine. After she went home, I would handle the phone myself for as long as it took.

A few minutes later, my intercom buzzed. 'Lin,' Helen stated simply.

'Clarence is on our side,' Lin told me as soon as I answered his call. 'He regrets not talking to us lately. He has been busy getting the lab back into operation. He told me he had been conveniently excluded from any conversation by Arthur or Bob. This was the first time he heard they wanted my resignation. I'm quite sure he will contact you.'

'One more for our side,' I replied to Lin.

But then, I always knew Clarence wouldn't put up with Arthur's shenanigans. I expected his support. Still it was good to have my beliefs confirmed. Perhaps the board was far from the united group Bob and Arthur had described.

'Helen's buzzing me,' I said to Lin. 'It's probably Clarence.'

And so, my evening passed with the sun setting through my office windows behind distant grey hills. The sky eventually turned inky black as night spread over the valley when I wasn't looking, occupied instead with listening to voices speaking from distant rooms in other worlds. Some of the calls were quick and went as expected. Others took considerable time. Lin was a patient man, dealing calmly with each member, explaining our position, asking for time, and suggesting we wait for the next quarterly board meeting when the company's problems could be clearly and completely presented before any decisions were made.

A few board members expressed a reluctance to meet, but most admitted a 'face to face' board meeting was preferable to a teleconference given the importance of the situation. Some called me personally and expressed regret for not having talked to me before. Most said they assumed I had agreed to resign. Said this is what Arthur told them. They were sorry if they had known how I felt, well... perhaps.

We had a few surprises of course. Members who we thought would support me, but turned Lin down. I was hurt, but Lin did a good job of preparing me for this possibility. I tried to ignore them. My fear was these detractors might call Arthur or Bob, tell them what we were doing, but there was nothing I could do to stop them.

The evening progressed slowly. A half-eaten sandwich lay on my desk next to a cooling cup of coffee in my dimly lit office. The overhead lights were off. A chrome desk lamp cast the only light across a tally sheet on my desk, tracking each board member's name with a simple yes or no vote. So far, it looked good. We were closing in on having more than a third of the members agree not to participate in a quorum. On another sheet of paper, I kept a running commentary, including comments made by members. These notes could be important in a future board meeting, assuming, of course, I would be attending such a meeting. We hoped this would not be necessary, hoped we would learn who was trying to shut us down before the board convened, and hoped this would cast a more positive light on the situation. But in case that didn't happen, I needed to be prepared.

Sometime during the night, someone must have called Bob. Even though we had purposely timed our calls to the less supportive members during our night and their day, hoping these members would wait until morning to alert Arthur or Bob of our activities; apparently this was not a deterrent. It happened around eleven p.m. Helen buzzed me to say Bob was calling.

'Tell him I just left my office,' I paused... 'Say, why are you still here, Helen? I thought we agreed you would leave at nine.'

'I decided to stay,' Helen answered simply without hesitation. She was never one for long explanations. 'Are you sure that's what you want me to tell him?' she asked.

'Yes, and then go home.'

'You sure? I can stay.'

'No, you've done enough. Please go home. I need you here in the morning. Just take care of Bob before you lock up.'

'Okay, Monica is still here. She can stay to handle the phones after I leave. Is that okay?'

'What?'

'I said Monica is here. She's been helping me. There have been so many calls.' Helen hesitated. 'You don't mind, do you?'

'No... Okay, have Monica take over.' I rubbed my temples briefly. 'Just get rid of Bob. I don't want to talk to him. I don't care what you tell him. And then go home.'

I wandered out of my office to check on M, found her at her desk on the phone. In the background I heard Helen brushing off Bob.

'It's Paul Rogers,' M said when she saw me. 'Do you want to take his call?'

'Yes,' I replied, giving her a tired smile.

Night dragged on, filled with calls, mostly from Lin after each conversation, discussing how each board member reacted, plus calls from some of the board members. I answered each call or returned a call when I couldn't answer it immediately. Some callers were especially long-winded board members who wanted to know everything. I was patient. Each call was important. This slowed the process. Lin had to wait for me to finish my call before he could talk to me. And I had to wait for him to finish before I could talk to him.

Most of the board expressed some regret over the way Arthur and Bob had handled the situation. Many were surprised I was fighting as hard as I was. Some said it was nothing personal, for the good of the company only. They offered brief, meaningless apologies. I tried not to react, just listen. Some members didn't bother to call. They were firmly in Arthur's camp. I was amazed at how many members had turned on me, people I thought were my friends.

M must have heard the fatigue and melancholy creeping into my voice as the night progressed. A few times, she offered a few words of encouragement, but for the most part, she simply handled the phone lines like a professional secretary.

Towards the early morning hours, I got fewer calls. Even though Lin had encouraged each board member to talk to me, he doubted some would.   Shortly before dawn, Arthur called. It was mid-morning his time. By this time, he had received a complete rundown of our nocturnal activities. From the tone of his voice, it was obvious he was not a happy man. M took his call and politely indicated I was busy. She asked him if she could take a message. Arthur was not pleased. He didn't like being put off. He indignantly suggested she put his call through to me immediately, if not sooner.

'Sorry, Arthur, he's on another call. Would you like to wait?' M replied.

'No, I would not.'

'I'll tell John you called,' she answered like a pro.

'Not good enough. Please don't play games with me, young lady.'

Finally, M's personal secretary routine had worn down. She was tired after a long night. 'Look, Arthur,' she began. 'I really don't care what you want or what you think. I told you I would tell John you called. And maybe he'll call you back. But most likely, he will not. So please just crawl back into whatever hole you just crawled out of before I tell you what I really think of you!' With that, she slammed her phone down.

At the time, the doors to my office were open, and I could clearly hear her loudly annoyed response. I couldn't help but smile.

She immediately called me on the intercom and apologized. 'I'm afraid I got a little unprofessional with your Arthur. I'm sorry.'

I told her to stay where she was. I wanted to talk to her. Getting out of my chair, I went to see her. It had been a long night. 'It's okay, M.' I smiled as I poked my head into her office. 'I'm glad you told him off. I just wish you had said what was really on your mind.'

Her phone rang. 'It's Lin,' she smiled weakly after answering the call.

I retreated to my office. Lin's usually inscrutable voice actually sounded a little weary. He said he had been talking to a board member from Madagascar, a recent appointment.

'Firmly in Arthur's camp, just as you suspected,' Lin said. 'Didn't even want to talk to me.'

'Was he the last one?'

'Yes, he was last.'

'What's your count?' I asked.

'Nine are firmly for Arthur. Ten are on your side for now, and six told me they were undecided. Is this what you have, John?'

'Yes, and only a few indicated they didn't think it was necessary to wait for a formal board meeting. So, at a minimum, we have stalled a firing squad by teleconference.' I sighed, 'Good work, Lin.'

'You realize you have no guarantee of retaining the CEO position when the board meets,' Lin stated objectively. 'Perhaps between ten and fifteen board members expressed some level of indecision. Plus, a few members said they were not confident the company would survive long enough to require another board meeting. Some wondered if all this was really necessary.'

'I guess you heard more negativism than I did.'

'It was my job, John.'

'I understand... but for now, we have accomplished everything we hoped for. Let's try to be positive.'

'Yes, we have won an important battle, but I fear we may lose the war. Are you certain you want to continue?' he asked.

'Yes, absolutely. No way I'm giving up now.'

'I see.' The tone of his voice sounded clearly downcast.

'By the way, Arthur just called.' I said, hoping to lift his spirits. 'Monica politely told him to get lost.'

'Thank her for me. She certainly is a remarkable woman.'

'I will, and thank you again.'

'You're welcome, John.'

'Get some rest now.'

'Yes.'

My phone clicked off.

I turned my chair towards the distant hills outside my windows.

A hint of light in a grey sky was evidence of a new day. It had been a long night, filled with moments when I thought it might never end. But in retrospect, the night had passed quickly in a blur of frantic calls. We had won a battle, as Lin said, but we were far from winning the war. It was going to be a fight. Old Arthur had to know now it was not going to be easy. He had played his hand and I had not folded as he hoped. We would just have to sit back now and see how the cards fell in the future.

But something was irreparably lost. The innocence a new business experiences when everyone is friends and works together for the common good... This was gone now, replaced by greed and a rush for power. This downward slide in civility probably began months or even years ago; when the company became successful and rich, when no one was paying attention. Jealousy took over. Partners lusted for a bigger piece of the pie. Gemstones International had passed into the second stage of its life cycle. I wondered fleetingly if it may have already passed into its final stage, failure. Without pausing at the second stage, perhaps my company was already dead, and I just didn't know it.

I stood up weakly with a groan, more physically exhausted than I had felt in a long time. Without thinking, I headed for Monica's work station, hoping to see her, badly needing a friendly smile...

Her office was empty.

31

MUSKEGON, MICHIGAN, JANUARY 30, THURSDAY, 3:15 P.M. JOHN

Outside my cabin window, the cold, hostile waters of Lake Michigan reached out to the horizon.

Wind-swept whitecaps rode the dark green waters, agitated by a frigid winter storm. Mother Nature was apparently in no mood to offer me a warm welcome to my hometown.

It was late afternoon by the time the silver Gulfstream ride banked sharply over the lake on its approach to the main runway of the Muskegon County Airport, the nearest airport to my hometown of Grand Haven, Michigan, with a landing strip capable of handling a chartered jet. Prior to leaving, I spent the morning trying to get some rest. I was exhausted after staying up all night answering phone calls, but I couldn't fall asleep. Eventually, I gave up, got out of bed and packed a few items for the trip, mostly warm clothing. A weather report had indicated we would be visiting a cold and stormy West Michigan landscape. And the view outside my cabin window, as our plane taxied to the terminal, did nothing to deter that prediction. Freshly fallen snow whipped across barren strips of the cement runway in streams of white dust collecting against dirty brown banks of ploughed snow. Trees all looked dead, devoid of life; their grey branches were accented with newly fallen snow.

I remembered how, as a child, I used to hunger for spring through the long, dreary days of winter. A few warm days in the middle of the season would tantalize me into thinking spring had arrived. Then, it would turn frigid, windy, and cold again against a sky filled with dull grey clouds. New snow would fall from above, covering the ground. The winter coat was retrieved from a closet, and once again, I had to wait for warmer weather.

Turning from the plane's window, putting my memories on hold, it was time to focus on why I had come to this desolate place.

M was sitting quietly beside me at the time. Only a few words had been spoken between us during our flight. That didn't surprise me. I assumed she was as tired from last night's marathon telephone activities as I was. I had called her apartment earlier in the morning to warn her it would be cold in Michigan to pack warm clothes.

She said she didn't mind. It would be fun.

As our plane taxied to the terminal, I mentally questioned why I had asked her to come with me. I honestly couldn't remember. It must have seemed like a good idea at the time. Now, all I wanted was to be alone to concentrate on Phillip.

David Dykstra was a friend from high school. I called him on my cell phone while we waited at a rental car desk. 'I know it's short notice, but I'm in town. I wondered if you and Mary would like to join us for dinner tonight?'

'Us? Did I hear you use the plural form of the pronoun?' David asked, 'Did you get married since I last saw you? I don't remember getting an invitation.'

My friend could be a stickler for detail. Never could get anything past him. It's what made him a great lawyer. 'Not exactly, I brought a friend.' I glanced at M.

'A friend, really?' he chuckled.

'Back off, okay. Her name is Monica Sorenson. You'll like her. She's a pushy lawyer like you.' I winked at her.

She stuck out her tongue at me.

'Let me check with Mary and call you back,' he responded.

'Any Phillip sightings?' I asked.

'Saw him this morning at his favourite breakfast haunt. Why the interest?'

'Let's talk about Phillip at dinner. How about seven-thirty at the Kirby Grill?'

'Hey, this isn't the east coast,' he responded. 'We country folks eat a little earlier around here.'

'Okay, six-thirty then?'

David was a Yale-educated lawyer. He could have worked anywhere, but he chose to return to his hometown. He had his own practice with five associates. He liked it that way. He took on some big-time cases which forced him to travel. Once told me he turned down more cases than he accepted. Too much hassle. It wasn't worth the money. We saw each other on the road sometimes, or we kept in touch by phone. Every summer we got together when I

returned to my cottage on Lake Michigan for a working vacation.
He was my personal attorney.

And I guess if I had a best friend, it was David.

GRAND HAVEN, MICHIGAN, 4:50 P.M. JOHN

Mounds of snow bordered the driveway entrance under a forest canopy of leafless grey trees.

My cottage was located a few miles south of town on Lake Shore Drive. David took care of the place when I wasn't around. Thankfully, he had hired a snow plough service to clear the driveway. Otherwise, we wouldn't have been able to make it up the driveway.

This was the first time M and I had gone anywhere together without being accompanied by security guards. Arny did not approve. He had argued with me while helping me pack in the morning, telling me I was crazy. I responded by suggesting he mind his own business. This was my home town. Nothing ever happens in this sleepy little burg. Besides, no one knew where we were going and I was tired of constantly being stalked by a couple of impersonal extras.

Unlocking the cottage door, I held it open for M to pull her rolling suitcase inside. A musty smell greeted us. The cottage had been unoccupied for months. The heat turned down to a chilly fifty degrees and felt only a little warmer than a frigid breeze outside blowing off the lake.

I suggested we keep our overcoats on until it warmed up. After showing M the master bedroom and bathroom so she could unpack, I went into the living room to open the front drapes.

One of the first activities I always do when arriving at my cottage is to take a moment to simply drink in the panoramic vista of Lake Michigan. It is like renewing an old friendship. Opening a sliding glass door, I stepped outside on a snow-covered deck to be hostilely welcomed by a blast of cold air hitting me hard in my face. Undeterred by the incivility of my old friend, the lake, I shut the door and stood outside. I did not want to be denied an unobstructed view of the water in all its sensual glory, wind in my face, waves pounding in my ears, and seagulls screeching for attention.

Footprints in the shallow layer of virgin snow covering the front deck followed me to the edge of a bank. Built on the top of a sand dune sloping steeply down to the shore, the deck was a great place to view the lake in all its beauty. Snowdrifts covered stairs led down from the deck to a shoreline of frozen sand and snow craved by unencumbered winds off the lake, evidence of a Canadian cold front, blowing hard, perhaps twenty to twenty-five knots steady. The sleet-laden wind felt like cold metal pellets were stinging my face. Long lines of white-capped waves relentlessly rode the dark green waters, persistently ramming against tall ice dunes which had formed on sandbars near the shoreline. The crashing waves constantly collided with the ice dunes in an unbridled frenzy of unnerving mayhem. The noise made it impossible to hear M open a slider behind me. I didn't know she was there until I felt her move against my back. With her red hair blowing in the breeze, she huddled close to my body, which shielded her from the cold wind.

'It's beautiful, John,' she said loud enough to hear her voice above the din of crashing waves.

'It's also very cold. Let's get back inside,' I answered, finding little joy in the angry lake.

My cottage was decorated in what I liked to call Montana-cabin interior design with lots of wood and large glass windows. The furniture was simple blond wood frames upholstered with dark brown cloth cushions. Indian-style throw rugs covered with wood floors. Modern artwork and landscape photography hung on white walls.

Slowly, the furnace heated the cold hard surfaces of the cottage and it became tolerably inhabitable. I unpacked my suitcase, changing into a pair of jeans and a heavy sweater in preparation for driving into town to have dinner with David and his wife. He had called to say Mary agreed to have dinner with us. I thanked him for securing her approval.

'Dress warmly,' I suggested to M.

'I think I'll wear everything I brought,' she shivered.

After backing the rental car down the driveway behind some trees, I lifted the cover off my white Porsche Boxster which was parked in a garage. It was a great summer car. Top-down drives into town were a joy. However, we would not be driving with top down this day. Still, I loved this car and it would be good to get it out after sitting idle for months.

The engine turned over grudgingly when I turned the key before finally firing.

'Boys and their toys,' was all M said as she slipped into the seat next to me.

I smiled and hit a switch for her seat heater.

Dinner with David and his wife Mary was, for the most part, uneventful, except I laughed more than I had for months. Good friends, a pleasant restaurant. For long minutes, I actually forgot my reason for coming. We talked about old times and stories from high school and college. Somewhere into my third glass of wine after finishing dinner, I noticed M had become unusually quiet, almost as if she were sitting off to one side in a world of her own. She had tried to fit into our conversation but finally gave up. I understood. The three of us were old hometown friends while she was an outsider.

Our waiter approached. 'Any dessert folks? Coffee?'

I looked at M. She smiled stoically. I knew she was bored. Lack of sleep and too much wine had caught up with both of us.

'No, thanks,' I responded.

David nodded.

'Thanks for a great evening.' I smiled. 'It's always wonderful to see you two.'

'How long are you staying?' Mary asked.

'Kind of depends,' I replied. 'Which reminds me, David, would you mind calling Phillip's office in the morning? I want to talk to him. I would do it, but I don't want him to know I'm in town. I want it to be a surprise when I show up.'

'No problem.'

'I'm afraid Martha might recognize my voice if I call,' I added. 'She's still working for him, isn't she?'

'Yes, she is. What time do you want me to call?'

'Say, nine-o-clock.'

'So, this is about Phillip,' Mary commented, looking at me pointedly.

'I'm afraid so.'

Mary knew my history with Phillip. Everyone in town did. Grand Haven is a small town. Phillip and I had been the talk of the town a few years back. The failure of his company had been in all the papers. But the real reasons for its failure were not common knowledge. If you listened to Phillip's side of the story, you would assume it was someone else's fault. He could work as a reporter like no one else. David told me some of the town folks actually thought I was responsible. I assumed Phillip had something to do with this rumor, but I was too busy at the time to care.

Mary knew the truth. David had told her. 'John, you be careful,' she said with sincerity.

She didn't trust Phillip any more than I did.

JANUARY 31, FRIDAY, 6:55 A.M. JOHN

Phillip was on my mind; I couldn't sleep.

I quietly got out of bed early in the morning so as not to disturb M, who was sleeping soundly.

Last night's after-dinner activities were a bit blurry. M must have driven my Porsche from the restaurant to my cottage. Guess I had too much to drink. Probably dozed off in the car on the return trip and somehow dragged my weary body to bed, promptly disappearing under covers.

A dark, angry sky greeted my sleepy-eyed wandering into the living room. Strong westerly winds off the coast of Wisconsin were driving large waves over miles of open water. In a final act of desperate rebellion, the waves lashed out in frustration at immoveable ice dunes near the shore, washing up and over them, building the cold grey specters to new heights of grandeur. The waves were an awesome sight in the new light of dawn, like grey ghosts rearing their ugly heads out of the violent black waters of the lake, splashing high into the air.

It occurred to me that M must have been as tired as I was. She had stayed up the night before, just as I had. And yet, she had been the designated driver who got us back to the cottage after dinner, not me. That wasn't right. I owed her. When I heard some movement in the bedroom, I started breakfast. Thought it was the least I could do to make up for last night's obvious lapse.

Hot coffee was soon brewing, aroma filling the cottage. Some bread and eggs were in the refrigerator. Mary had been kind. She had stocked my cottage with a few essential groceries before we arrived. In return for caring for my place, I allowed David and Mary to use it when I was absent. It was an agreement between friends. Still, it was nice of Mary to supply groceries on short notice.

Butter slowly melted in a pan on the stove as I watched. Eggs were on the counter, ready to be scrambled. Bread waited in the toaster. Raspberry jam, plates and silverware had been placed on the dining table by the window.

'Want some breakfast?' I called from the kitchen.

'Sure, be there in a minute.'

Hearing a shower, I was tempted to join her lovely body, but discipline prevailed. Instead, I poured a cup of coffee and mentally prepared for my meeting with Phillip.

My hope was to get some information from him, anything, some clue which would help solve the mysteries surrounding my company. But at the same time, I had to admit that I had no valid reason to think he was involved. It was highly possible this was a fool's errand with me being the fool. I had to be prepared for this outcome. However, it was also possible he was involved. But if he was involved, he wouldn't tell me directly, especially since this information was incriminating. No, he was too smart for that. He wouldn't do something stupid. I also knew he had a big weakness: his ego. If he was involved, his ego would have difficulty keeping his secret. He would want me to know he was the one who was doing this to me, making my life miserable. In a face-to-face meeting, he would find a way, say something seemingly innocent, some sign or gesture, an offhand remark, something I would recognize, something which would tell me he was the source of my problems. He would love it, being able to let me know he was causing my pain. Point is, I knew he would find a way. Not directly, not something incriminating, just some word or gesture which implied involvement without actually saying it. And this was all I wanted. It was the reason I had come. I wanted something, anything which would help me begin to discover who was responsible.

I only hoped I would be smart enough to recognize it when it happened.

M arrived in the kitchen. No makeup, dressed only in jeans and a sweatshirt, her hair still wet from a shower,

'Want some coffee?' I asked.

'Oh, look at those waves.' She was immediately drawn to the windows in the living room. The sky had brightened. The lake was alive in all its magnificent glory. I handed her a cup of hot coffee.

I like eggs scrambled, not too dry and not too soft. And toast not overdone, bacon crisp, not soft; timing is everything when it comes to cooking breakfast. Occasionally, I stopped to watch her. She seemed momentarily content, her coffee cup steaming in between sips. Two sets of sliding glass doors framed a stone fireplace overlooking the lake where she stood. The room was large, divided into two distinct areas, one for dining and one for sitting. The kitchen, by comparison, was small but well-equipped with the latest appliances.

'This is a very nice house.' M returned.

'Thanks, breakfast is almost ready. Why don't you have a seat at the table? It will be my pleasure to serve you this morning.'

She looked at me with a smile, but didn't object, sat down at the table as instructed. I followed with a plate of scrambled eggs, toast and bacon.

'Would you like some orange juice?' I asked.

'John, I'm not sure I can eat all this food.'

I understood. The lady was normally a fruit and yogurt, breakfast girl. 'Just eat what you want. Leave the rest.' I smiled.

As we ate in comfortable silence, my mind quickly returned to preparation for Phillip, trying to predict how my meeting would go, formulating responses to any number of possible scenarios. Phillip could be unpredictable. The variables were many. He had surprised me too many times in the past. He was particularly adept at changing an agenda midstream.

In the background, the wind howled through barren tree branches, exhibiting no sign of slowing.

'You okay?' I asked.

'Sure. Why?'

'You're not eating. Don't you like your breakfast?'

'It's fine.'

'Just fine... That's it? I slaved like a dog, cooking this breakfast,' I imitated something Arny might say.

'John, we need to talk,' she said, ignoring my attempt at humor.

'Okay.' I tried not to sound as alarmed as I suddenly felt. It wasn't what she said. It was the way she said it. It didn't sound like the beginning of a pleasant conversation.

'This is not working,' she began.

'What's not working?'

She paused. 'I don't feel like I'm a part of your life lately. We hardly talk. It's as if you're far away even when I'm with you.'

'Look...' I started to apologize.

'No. Let me finish. I know what you're going to say. You're going to blame Arthur and all the problems of your company. It has been a difficult time for you. I understand, John. I'm not blaming you. Believe me.'

'Okay, then what's the...?'

'John, please try to understand. I told you I wanted to be involved. If you're not going to let me help, then...'

'But you are helping, M,' I interrupted. 'Look at what you did the other night. I can't thank you enough for working the phones.'

'Case in point, John.' she argued, now using her professional lawyer voice. 'You didn't even have the presence of mind to ask me to help. I just did it... I did it so I could feel like I was a participant. You didn't ask me. You didn't consult with me. And you pretty much ignored me the whole time you were preparing for the phone calls.'

'Look, I'm sorry. I've been so...'

'No need to be sorry. I told you I understand. I'm not looking for an apology.'

'Then what do you want?' I asked stupidly.

'I'm trying to tell you I don't want to be your secretary. I want to be more, but lately, it feels like you're treating me like just another one of your employees... I thought...or maybe I hoped ...'

'What?'

'Oh, come on, John.' She looked down at her hands.

I sat, looking dumb like the idiot I obviously was. Truth was, she was right. I hadn't been paying attention. I had not taken her into consideration. I was guilty as charged by her honor.

'M, stop, please,' I begged, looking for any way out. 'I'm meeting with Phillip this morning... and well...I can't do this right now.' I was obviously not prepared for her, especially not this morning. My head was in a different place. And she was smart. I couldn't just wing it with her.

'But that's the problem, isn't it?' she continued. 'You always have something else to do. Do you know this is the first time we have talked since the meeting with your partners? You know... like a real conversation between adults.'

'That's not fair. I have been extremely busy. '

'I know. I told you I understand.'

'Then why, M?'

'Because you don't need me anymore.'

'Of course I do.'

'No, you don't. I have been demoted.'

'No.'

'Yes, John. I have been demoted to being one of your secretaries.'

'M, we are way beyond that.'

'No, we're not. I'm nothing more to you than just another employee.'

'Please, M,' I said in exasperation. 'Can this wait until I return from seeing Phillip?'

'No.'

'Why.'

'Because we won't talk then. Your phone will ring, you'll take the call and...'

At this particular moment, as if to make her point for her, my telephone rang on cue. If I wasn't in enough trouble before it rang; I was now. I assumed it was probably David on the line and I had to talk to him. He was tracking Phillip for me. I couldn't put him off. But taking his call would validate M's argument. Either way, I was doomed. I looked at the phone. I didn't want to answer it.

'You need to answer,' M said smugly as if to say: see, this is what happens.

When I hesitated, she picked up the phone. 'Hello... Good morning, David. Yes, we're fine. Yes, he's here.' She handed me the phone and walked away.

'Hi,' I tried to sound more cheerful than I felt.

'Phillip just entered his office building,' David replied. 'I had my secretary stake out his place. I thought it would be better than calling Martha. He's there now. If you want to see him, this would be a good time.'

'Okay, thanks. I owe you. Any advice?'

'Keep your head low,' he laughed.

'Thanks.' I hung up.

M was busy cleaning breakfast dishes at the kitchen sink when I went to find her.

'Look, M, we've both been under a lot of pressure lately. Please, let me see Phillip. Then, I promise, we'll talk.'

'I don't want to talk, John.'

'Please, M. Give me a chance,'

'Go.'

'Can we talk afterwards?'

'Maybe,' she replied as steam from the sink rose into her lovely red curls.

10:15 A.M. JOHN

Thoughts of M and Phillip rattled alternately through my helpless brain like two runaway freight trains as I drove into town.

Several times, I almost turned around, wanting to take Monica in my arms and beg for forgiveness. But I had come a long way to see Phillip. I needed to know if he was involved.

The truth was, I was mad at M., Wondering why she picked this morning to dump on me. Okay, maybe I was to blame. Even so, why this morning? Didn't she know I needed every bit of my meagre mental capacity to deal with Phillip? Slowly, I calmed down and refocused on Phillip. Phillip, Phillip, Phillip, I silently repeated his name, trying to concentrate.

Arriving in Grand Haven, I drove down its main street, Washington Street. I was home again.

Old wood and brick buildings erected around the turn of the century stood solidly connected, built side by side in the usual fashion on both sides of the main street. The town fathers had tried to spruce up the commercial district by widening the street and replacing the great old elms and oaks which had previously lined the street with new young maples. Didn't work. The town looked barren, especially in winter when the trees were leafless. Even with strings of Christmas tree lights still glowing through their barren branches, the immature trees contributed nothing to boost dismal post-Christmas sales. Nothing like the past when great old trees covered in snow had shaded the street. That is not to say the town was not well-maintained. The storefronts presented a clean, attractive face to the public while their owners scratched out a meager business during winter months when sun-loving tourists were absent and the frozen streets were mostly deserted.

In the summer, this coastal town came alive with activity. Its sandy beaches were covered with sun-starved Midwesterners and retired snowbirds returning to their native lands after a winter refuge in warmer Southern climes. This was when the street pulsated with hotrods, and motorcycles, their male owners vainly attempting to attract the attention of lovely young girls in short shorts and halter tops walking the sidewalks. I knew. I had participated in this ritual. But that was summer. Today, it was winter. A cold wind rushed up the mostly deserted main street when I stepped out of my car.

Phillip worked in a relatively new, architecturally ambiguous, brown brick building down the street from the older retail area. I say new. It wasn't really new. Probably built in the fifties or sixties during a time when architecture had reached a functional low, it had no charm. It was simply a square brown brick building out of place in this attractive tourist town. At the time of its construction, the town's politicians must not have cared about maintaining its architectural integrity.

Phillip's office was upstairs on the second floor above an insurance office. In one respect the building fit him perfectly, fit his normal desire for anonymity. No sign announcing his presence was on the outside of the building, just his name on a small directory in the lobby.

I had visited his office before. I knew the layout. His place of business was a three-room office. One room served as a reception area where Martha, his secretary, worked. A second, larger room was designated as his office and a third room was used for nothing except accumulating junk, old files and other useless material. Phillip was a habitual hoarder.

I paused several times as I climbed two flights of stairs to his office. Now that I was finally here, I wasn't sure I wanted to stay. I had a sudden and uncontrollable urge to walk away. Something didn't feel right. I began to wonder if my paranoia was a warning sign. Was I in danger?

Nothing made any sense. It had all seemed so logical to me when I was in Charlottesville. Find Phillip and make sure he isn't involved. Eliminate a possibility. But now... now I questioned why I had come. Was Lin right after all? Was this nothing but a fool's errand? The more I thought about it, the more I wanted to leave. But for some unknown reason, I continued up the stairs, deciding it was better to confront my fears than to wonder what I may have discovered if I had followed through.

Taking several deep breaths, I opened the door to his office.

A look of surprise instantly covered his secretary's face before she quickly reverted to her usual professional deportment, acting cordial, even though it was clear she was slightly annoyed to see me.

'Hi Martha,' I tried not to smile.

We knew each other from high school when she was a senior and I was a fuzzy-faced freshman. We used to stare at her. She had been a beauty in her time, hourglass figure, big boobs. Unfortunately, time had not been kind to her since those days. Years of smoking had etched deep lines around her eyes and across her upper lip. Too much makeup and an out-of-style hairdo teased to the heights of 1960s fashion gave her an almost comical appearance. I wondered how I had ever found her attractive.

'Hi, John,' she replied. 'What brings you here?' Martha was direct, if nothing else. In a way, she was the perfect complement to Phillip's ambiguous behavior. He was never direct about anything. The two of them together were almost a complete package.

'I thought I might talk to Phillip. Is he in?'

'Yes, but he's on the phone. Would you like to wait?' she said with a hint of disdain in her voice.

'Yes.'

'Do you have an appointment?' she asked, trying to sound nonchalantly professional.

'No. I thought I would surprise him,' I honestly answered, knowing it was no good being coy with Martha.

'I see,' she nodded as if she was beginning to understand the purpose of my visit. I never could get anything past Martha.

Down a hall, it was possible to see into Phillip's office from where I was standing. A quick glimpse of his tall profile confirmed he was in fact holding court in his office sitting behind a desk covered with papers, phone in his hand, leaning back in his chair.

I took a seat in his small lobby while Martha eyed me uncomfortably.

'So, what really brings you here?' she asked as I listened to Phillip drone on in the other room.

'Nothing, really. I was in town. I thought I would drop in to see my old buddy, Phillip.'

'You have been back to Grand Haven before,' she retorted. 'You never stopped in before. Why now?' Her gaze was overtly cold.

I didn't bother to answer. It was none of her business.

'I never thought you'd show up here, John,' she added. 'In fact, I didn't think you had the guts.'

There was no putting this woman off. 'Well, I guess I just proved you wrong.'

I often wondered why she continued to work for Phillip. Rumor around town was it had something to do with her drinking. He had helped out of a couple of jams in the past.

Martha promptly stood up from behind her desk and without looking at me, walked down the hall in the direction of Phillip's office. After a minute or two, she returned with a cup of coffee in her hand.

'I'm not sure Phillip will see you,' she said flatly.

'It's okay, Martha. Just tell him I won't take much of his time.'

'He's still on the phone.'

'I can hear him.'

After this brief exchange, she returned to casually pecking at her computer, ignoring me and sipping coffee. Minutes passed. Martha's monotonous pecking began to annoy me as I waited, trying to calm my nerves. I could still hear Phillip on his phone. I sighed and flipped through a mindless tabloid until I realized nothing, but the silence was coming from his office.

'Sounds like he's off his phone, Martha. Could you please tell him I'm here and would like to talk to him?' I politely asked, stifling an urge to barge into his office, but thought it would be better to observe a minimum of protocol.

'Oh,' she looked up from her computer as if she was surprised to see me still waiting. 'I'll check.' After walking slowly down the hall, she returned with look of smug satisfaction on her face. 'I'm sorry. He seems to have left the building.'

Looking out an office window confirmed her statement. I saw him walking through the parking lot. As I watched, he got into a car and disappeared down the street.

'Sorry,' Martha said. 'I guess I should have told him you were here.'

'Oh, I think you told him.' I was angry. I made no effort of hiding my frustration it as I put on my coat and scarf.

'Oh, John, how could you accuse me of such a thing?' she replied with a smile.

11:40 A.M. JOHN

Head down in dejection against a cold, brisk, winter wind; I pulled up my collar and headed for my car while staring at the dark pavement.

To say I was discouraged would have been putting it mildly. More than discouraged, I was angry, outraged at fate's unruly twists and turns. Phillip was a dead end. And then there was Monica. What to do about Monica. I assumed it would not be wise to talk to her, not now. I might say something stupid in my current state of mental anguish. And that could and would be used against me by a good lawyer, which is exactly what she was. Making my situation worse rather than better.

No, I needed to clear my head first, sweep away the septic memories of Phillip to the far recesses of my brain where they belonged. A slow drive along the channel seemed to be the proper solution. I needed time to calm down.

The channel in Grand Haven is a ribbon of water emptying the Grand River into Lake Michigan. High walls of thick cement restrain both sides of its deep waters. Large storm waves rolled up the channel from the lake as I drove the street parallel to the channel. Filled with great chunks of floating ice, massive dark green swells constantly merging together as they crisscrossed the channel, occasionally washing up and over its concrete retaining walls. I turned into a viewing area, content for the moment to simply observe the flowing waters as I rested in the warm cocoon of my car's interior.

A cement boardwalk runs the length of the channel, extending into the lake on a pier which supports a red lighthouse. At the end of the pier sits a red building made of steel and cement. On foggy days, a low resonating moaning emanates from its foghorn, heard for miles up and down the shoreline.

It is my habit to walk to the end of the pier whenever I'm in town, except when this is not possible, like today when strong winds send cold streams of water rushing over the pier. When this happens, it's not safe to be on the pier. But taking a walk on the boardwalk paralleling the channel didn't appear to be a big problem.

I decided to get some exercise.

A shockingly, bitter cold wind penetrating my clothing greeted me when I opened the door of my car. Zipping my jacket and wrapping my arms around my body to preserve heat, I navigated some stairs to the boardwalk and headed towards the pier at a brisk pace, facing the wind.

Rolling mounds of dark water dotted with chunks of ice persistently washed up and over the cement sidewalk, forcing me to occasionally stop and dodge the rushing water. When I got close to the shoreline, I was able to observe massive waves crashing over the end of the pier where the cement building was located, hurtling relentlessly against its hard cement structure, sending great plumes of wind-driven white water up and over the brilliant red house. It was as if the lake was rebelling against this artificially created protrusion; this was a concrete pier and house which violated its natural space.

The closer I got to the pier, the stronger the wind blew. Arriving at a wide expanse of sandy beaches near the shore only increased my misery. Unconstrained gusts of wind blowing across the beach were filled with sand, stinging the exposed skin on my face.

Shivering from the cold wind, I was forced to look away to avoid the sand.

1:15 P.M. JOHN

'Monica?' I called after entering the back door of my cottage.
'M?' I repeated.
Nothing... no reply.
Throwing my coat on a chair, I went into the living room, hoping, expecting to see her curled up on a couch with a book or watching TV.
She was not there.
I called her name again.
No answer.
The house was strangely quiet.
I suddenly felt very alone.
She was gone.
Fate had turned against me again, my run of bad luck continuing. I didn't blame her. I couldn't. It was me. I was the problem. I had completely ignored her over the last few weeks. Sure, I had excuses, but none of which counted in her mind.

An aroma of hot coffee drew my attention. I poured a cup, thinking I would go out back. I couldn't remember seeing the rental car when I drove in, but I wasn't looking at the time. My mind had been on her. If the car was gone, she was gone. Gone to the airport to fly home.

I took a sip of coffee, taking small comfort in its warmth despite an overpowering sense of gloom. Before going outside to look for the car, I spotted someone on the front deck sheltering behind a sand dune, all bundled in a winter jacket and covered with a blanket. She was sitting on an old deck chair I had left outside with a cup of hot coffee in her hand, steaming in the cold, brisk air.

Putting on my coat, I quietly opened a sliding glass door to the deck. Rolling waves on the lake crashed monotonously against ice dunes, masking the sound of my footsteps in the snow. Softly touching her shoulder so as not to startle her, I knelt down next to her chair. The broad expanse of the lake stretched before us across the horizon. It was bitterly cold, but the wind had begun to die down and the sun made a few brief appearances between flying clouds, casting pools of light on shining on the agitated water. The sound of the constantly crashing waves, splashing up and over the ice dunes, creating an unnerving racket, overpowering any sense of tranquility this scene may have otherwise brought me.

She lowered her head to her chest when she saw me. I touched her chin to pull her face gently up to kiss. She resisted at first, then sullenly looked up at me with streams of wet tears sliding down her cheeks. I was stunned. Taking her coffee cup from her, I placed it on the deck. Gently helping her up from the chair, I covered her shoulders with the blanket, and without saying a word, I led her back into the cottage, closing the sliding glass door once we were inside.

'I'm sorry,' I said. Touching her lips to stop her from responding, holding her in my arms until she rested her head on my shoulder.

Taking her hands, I leaned over to kiss her and repeated, 'I'm sorry.'

'Don't talk, John.'

Dropping the blanket and her coat on the floor, she folded her hand in mine and guided me to the bedroom, where she smiled before lifting her heavy sweater over her head and unbuttoning her denim shirt. I cracked a window to allow some cool fresh air to enter the room before shutting the door to the problems which existed outside the room in another world, another place, somewhere I did not want to be at this moment. They were no longer important. My only desire was to replace her tears with happiness. My day had been a disaster. I was determined to make it better.

Her jeans slid easily down her legs; wool socks came off next while she sat on the edge of the bed, and panties last. Then, when she was finally naked and warm under the flannel sheets with a fluffy white comforter shielding her vulnerable body from the cool air entering an open window, it was my turn to undress and slide under the sheets next to her warm, sensuous body. We lay together, resting in silence, listening to the waves rhythmically colliding against the ice dunes through the open window.

In time, I touched her long, beautiful body, if only to be sure she was real. Slowly massaging her back, her taunt muscles began to relax in my hands. The soft flannel sheets caressed our naked bodies and insulated our warmth beneath the down comforter. Kissing her breasts, I reached between her legs, gently touching her, feeling her become wet, rising against my hand, slowly at first and then more urgently in pleasure, moaning into release. And then we melted together for a slow eternity until my pleasure came in waves of exultation.

She slept as I lay peacefully, resting with my eyes closed for a long time.

Memories from the last few days ran through my mind: a night of phone calls without sleep, a plane ride to my hometown, an evening with friends who were not her friends. Then remembering the anxious unfulfilled tensions, we experienced in this morning along with my disappointment in not meeting Phillip, and finally the joy I received from being with her.

Exhaustion finally took over my body, and I slept.

Sometime later in the afternoon, I woke to the sound of waves. My bedroom was cold. I slipped out of bed and shut the window, opening the bedroom door to allow heat from the cottage to enter the room. After dressing I went to find my cell phone. Checking voicemail, a few calls had come in. Nothing which demanded immediate attention. Sitting in a chair in the bedroom, I rested while occasionally opening my eyes to observe the slow rise and fall of her breathing under covers. In time, she opened her eyes and smiled.

We spent what remained of our day eating and reading. The subject of our relationship did not come up.

It was potentially too painful and problematic.

53

FEBRUARY 2, SUNDAY, 4:40 P.M. JOHN

A midwinter thaw descended on our lakeshore hideaway over the weekend with the arrival of a warm front.

Floating ice near the shore floated far out into the lake, driven by a persistent southeast wind, creating a stretch of open lake water, calm as glass beyond the ice dunes. It actually felt hot inside the cottage in the afternoon, with the sun shining through the sliders.

David had been checking on Phillip for me. Apparently, my antagonist had disappeared. No one had seen him lately. I tried to put Phillip out of my mind and concentrate on M instead. Dinner at a restaurant in town Saturday night was enjoyable. Other than this, we did nothing special but simply hung around my cottage, becoming familiar again, touching, smiling conversations while looking into her eyes, falling in love again, wishing for nothing more than to live in the light of her smile.

Sometime late Sunday afternoon I asked M if she would like to take a walk on the beach. Said exercise might be good for both of us.

The bitter cold winds of winter were absent that afternoon. A hint of spring was in the air. Still, we dressed warmly for our beach walk with boots, hats, scarves, and jackets before heading to the stairs that led down to the shore, half stepping, half sliding down through snow-covered steps up to our knees.

Thankfully, the shoreline was easier to navigate. Winter winds had blown clean patches of damp, frozen sand along the water's edge. I love walking the beach in the winter. Doesn't happen often. Normally it is too cold and windy. But when Mother Nature offers the opportunity, my vulnerability caves in. It is one of the few times during the year when the beach is free of human harassment, and the panoramic scenery can be absorbed in peace without interference. In those lonesome, beautiful moments I create pictures in my mind, mental images, to be preserved for those times when I am away from this lovely place.

We walked in silence as the calm and quiet sun slowly sank towards the water spreading an iridescent glow across the horizon. Radiant purples, blues and pinks reflected off the gently rolling surface of the water beyond the ice dunes. M was quiet, self-absorbed. The setting sun tinted her red hair and cast a warm pink glow over her cheeks.

In time, the continuously igniting yellow orb of energy in the sky slipped below the horizon, retreating in the aftermath of glowing rays rising out of the water, intensifying in color. Rich azure blues and soft ruby reds slowly transformed into deepening grays. Dark purples and faded pinks highlighted a few windblown misty clouds near the horizon in an ethereal visage of shifting colors. It was hard to look away.

The sky eventually darkened and stars began to appear in a gray moonless night. M paused occasionally to simply gaze at the night sky. Away from city lights, an infinite number of stars could be seen glittering against a dull black canvas sky.

With the disappearance of the sun, the temperature began to drop quickly. Soon, we found ourselves wandering a deserted beach, cold and alone. It was time to return. Pulling down my hat, I put my hands in my coat pockets for warmth, stopping momentarily to observe a solitary light that had curiously appeared in the distance over the lake. When I looked for it again, wondering if it was real, it was long gone, disappeared in the dead of the night.

We continued to retrace our journey back to the cottage at a leisurely pace in no hurry.

In the absence of wind and waves, sound travels easily over water. A low exhaust rumble from a boat's engine soon became impossible to ignore, even though it was several miles away. As it came closer, I scanned the horizon looking for a light, knowing marine regulations call for running lights on all boats at night. I saw nothing.

'Do you hear a boat engine?' I asked M.

'What?' she asked.

'The sound of a boat engine on the water, do you hear it?'

'Yes. Why?'

'I was beginning to wonder if I was imagining it.'

'I hear it,' she replied dismissively.

I couldn't imagine why anyone would want to be out on the lake at night in the winter. But then, human behavior is often difficult to predict. Some hard-core boaters will use any excuse to be on the water.

Assuming the boat would soon disappear, it was time to get back inside the cottage where it was warm. Not far now, the stairs to the deck of my cottage were only a few hundred yards up the beach. The faint outline of the windows in my cottage appeared above the dunes, calling me home. I had turned on some lights before we left in case we returned after dark. It is not always easy to distinguish one cottage from another in the dark. Most cottages are unoccupied in the winter. Their structures were little more than cold and gray, lifeless shadows in the dunes. But with the lights on in my cottage, it was easy to distinguish it from the others.

The boat's engine unexpectedly slowed.

Thinking that was odd, I stopped to listen as the low resonating rumble of the boat's motor came closer. It didn't seem to be in any hurry. The engine was idling, drifting somewhere out on the water near the shore not far from us, hidden behind tall ice dunes, impossible to see from where we stood on the beach. As I pondered the oddity of the boat, a red flash rose up out of an ice dune, lighting the sky, followed by a brilliant trail of white light streaking across the sky, half blinding my dilated eyes. The streaking light quickly erupted in an intense white explosion, which lit trees surrounding my cottage, followed by a loud shock wave riding the air over our heads, resonating in our ears.

I grabbed M, instinctively bending down in a defensive posture.

'Oh!' M exhaled.

'Stay down.'

A small red glow coming from the direction of my cottage quickly intensified, lighting the sky above the sand dune. Out of the corner of my eye, a second flash leaped out of the ice dunes, followed again by a white streak of light in the black sky, which exploded in a fireball. M flinched and covered her ears as a shockwave pulsed over the sand dune. Fire immediately began to burn my cottage, red flames rising high into the night sky.

The idling boat engine roared back to life, accelerating out into the lake.

M began to shiver.

'Come on,' I said. 'The boat is gone.'

M stood very still, momentarily paralyzed.

I grabbed her arm. 'We need to get out of here!'

'But... your cottage?'

'There's nothing we can do.'

'Shouldn't we call someone... the police, the fire department?'

'It's too late.'

'John.'

'We need to go.' I said forcefully.

The sounds of explosions still echoing in my brain made it difficult to think clearly. I pulled M towards the nearest stairs up the sand dune leading to a deserted cottage next to my place. It was a long, hard climb through deep, crusted snow. We went as fast as we could, stumbling up the steps through snow drifts in the dark, driven by fear-induced adrenalin. We did not stop until we got to the top of the stairs, winded, boots full of cold snow.

After a couple of deep breaths, 'You okay?' I asked.

'Yes,' M replied, head down, trying to catch her breath.

Through trees growing between our location and my cottage, the fire could be seen glowing into the sky, offering enough light to see where we were going, around the neighbor's dark cottage into a wooded area in the back. The distance from there to the main road was about a quarter mile. I could hear traffic, but an old-growth forest blocked my view of the road. Even so, I assumed someone would eventually see the flames through the trees and call the fire department. Didn't matter. From what I could observe, my cottage was already a total loss. We needed to go. I was worried someone might be watching, waiting to see if victims inside the burning cottage managed to escape the explosions. Killers, intent on finishing their murderous work, shoot anyone caught running, screaming from a burning cottage.

The rental car was parked behind my garage. Keys were somewhere under the seat. If we could get to the car without being seen, it might allow us to escape this nightmare without being killed.

A hundred yards of deep snow separated us from the car. Walking was difficult in a dark forest, tripping over hidden branches and grabbing at shadows of tree limbs to keep from falling. Low-hanging branches appeared out of nowhere in the semi-darkness, banging against our arms and legs. We went as fast as conditions allowed. We had to slow to avoid being hit. Not an easy task in daylight, almost impossible in the half-light of night. It was difficult to avoid the scratching, tearing branches until it was too late, cursing silently when they cut across my body, small twigs snapping constantly under our feet, making noise, too much noise. We were trying to be quiet to avoid being seen, but it was an inane hope.

'Stay low,' I whispered to M.

She silently followed behind me, her hands in front of her face.

A clearing appeared in the forest, the neighbor's driveway. If someone was outside my cottage, I hoped they were watching it burn, not searching for victims in the forest, not listening to the branches crack under our boots. As we got closer, the red glow of the fire made it easier to see, but it also exposed us. I remained patient when we arrived at my driveway, searching for signs of trouble, men with guns. The rental car appeared among trees not far from where we waited, partially sheltered by leafless maples and oaks.

I saw no one, no cars, no men with guns, only the roar of a cottage burning to the ground, a place filled with memories slowly destroyed.

'Wait here. I'm going get the rental car,' I instructed M in a harsh whisper.

'John...' she reached for me.

'I'll be right back.' I squeezed her trembling hands. 'If anything happens to me... run, just run.'

Taking a deep breath and crouching, I moved from tree to tree until I was behind the rental car. Nothing moved, nothing except a dancing red glow excitedly burning what remained of a cottage. Opening the car door quickly, the interior lights came on. I was exposed to the semi-darkness. I ducked down and quickly shut the door, fumbling around the interior of the car, searching beneath the seat, not remembering exactly where I had put the key, fearing bullets in the darkness. I jabbed my fingers a couple of painful times before finally, thankfully, finding the key under the mat. The engine started. I slammed it into gear, hit the gas hard, braking on the driveway where M was hiding. We were moving before she shut the door, determined not to stop for anything. A quick look down Lakeshore Drive at the end of the driveway before turning right, hitting the gas, speeding away from Grand Haven, away from Phillip, away from my burning cottage and faceless men who had tried to kill me.

'Do you have your cell phone with you?' I asked M.

Sirens sounded in the distance. I wasn't sure they were headed for my cottage. Didn't matter. It was already gone, destroyed.

'My phone is in the cottage,' I explained, with the image of my burning cottage searing the ragged edges of my mind. Angry tears blurred my vision. I quickly wiped my eyes to see the road, driving faster than I should. I needed to slow down.

'Yes, do you want me to call 911?' she asked.

'No, call directory assistance and ask for the number of the Airport Hilton in Grand Rapids. Then, call the desk and ask if Al Stapleton is staying there. If you get him on the phone, give the phone to me.'

Al was a pilot who worked for the air charter company I normally used. He was the guy I usually requested when I needed to go someplace fast. He had flown us into Muskegon. I had personally called him a couple of days ago. Asked him if he was available. Said I wanted to leave early Monday morning. Work was piling up at the office. It was time to go back. He said he would fly into Grand Rapids early Sunday and pick us up in Muskegon Monday morning. He had relatives in West Michigan. It was an opportunity for him to combine family and business. Said he would be staying at the Airport Hilton in GR. So, if he was there now, I hoped we could get out of town fast, maybe even tonight.

'But shouldn't we call the police?' M asked.

'I'll call David later and let him handle the police. Right now, I only want to get out of here.'

Thankfully, she didn't argue, although I wasn't sure she fully agreed. I hoped she didn't hear the panic in my voice. I was trying to be calm and concentrate on driving, but inside I was a mess.

Thankfully, Al was in GR at the Airport Hilton when she called. I explained our problem to him in simple terms. Said it was an emergency. Could we please leave tonight? He said he would call his copilot and go directly to the airport from his motel. The plane had already been prepped for early morning take off. It should be ready to roll shortly after we arrive.

Turning near Holland, we headed east toward the expressway to the Kent County Airport. It was a forty-five-minute drive.

Our weekend had been a mixture of disappointment, failure, joy, and now great violence.

BANGKOK, THAILAND, FEBRUARY 3, MONDAY, 9:40 P.M. LUANG

His hand trembled as he read the memo.

A courier had delivered it to his residence. The message was important. Nue wanted the information immediately distributed to all important family members.

The old patriarch reread the memo one more time to be sure he fully understood. However, he didn't really need to read it again. The words were precise with plain intent. A brief description of an operation was given: time, place, method of execution, death without remorse, black ink on white paper; no mercy, no regret expressed. The American had been killed, his home destroyed, and his girlfriend dead. Both were killed in an explosion.

Why? Luang asked quietly to no one.

Why had his nephew not waited? Why had he not allowed his new strategy to work? Had he learned nothing? Crumbling the communiqué in disgust, Luang threw it in a wastebasket. Nothing could be accomplished now, nothing to stop the needless carnage. The deed was done. Slowly, he turned down the covers of his bed and lay down. Curling under a blanket, he tried to sleep.

But sleep would not come. His mind whirled with possibilities but no solutions. And then he cried. Something he had not done since he was a child. It was not a cry of regret for a dead American. It was more than that. It was a cry of frustration, crying for himself. Because he was powerless, he knew what should have been done. He also knew he was helpless to make it happen.

Like driftwood washed up on an uninhabited shore to erode slowly into the sand, he was a useless old man.

CHARLOTTESVILLE, VIRGINIA, FEBRUARY 4, TUESDAY, 6:40 A.M. JOHN

When I'm extremely tired, it is almost impossible for me to sleep.

Monday night was no exception. Monica and I arrived at my Charlottesville apartment early, sometime before dawn. I had not been able to sleep on the plane. I was too keyed up, too much to do. M didn't sleep either. Said she saw flashbacks of the bombing every time she closed her eyes. We tried talking about it during our flight, hoping to relieve the tension. But the fire was still vivid in our minds, fear too real.

Fortunately, our plane was fueled and ready to fly when we arrived at the airport in Grand Rapids. It didn't take long to get off the ground. The pilots were great. We shared a snippet of our situation to justify the urgency. Figured we owed them this at a minimum. After all, we were asking them to fly us to Charlottesville in the middle of the night.

They said no problem. They were accustomed to flying unusual schedules.

I asked them to keep our story confidential. They agreed.

Trying to nap on my office couch Monday afternoon didn't work either. Every time I closed my eyes, my mind either raced over the events of the weekend or became embroiled in dreams permeated with red flashes and dark shadows over rolling water. Panic would greet me again and again, and I would feel more tired than when I lay down. Finally, I got up and worked with my eyes half open.

The joy that our restful weekend at the lake had given us was now replaced by fear and regret. It was all too obvious I had once again foolishly placed M in an extremely dangerous situation. By all rights, we should both have been dead, nothing more than charred remains in a burned-out cottage. My reluctance to face reality had put us both in serious danger. It was clear I was struggling to adjust to my new reality. I had not taken the necessary precautions the situation demanded, and it had nearly cost us our lives.

I tossed and turned Monday night, afraid to sleep, scared to dream, but badly needed rest. It rained intermittently during the night, with low, rumbling thunder providing an ominous background to my tortured existence. Time passed slowly, mostly awake in a dark bedroom. Finally, mercifully, dawn crept over the hills and into my window. Quietly, I got out of bed and dressed. M was still asleep, her eyes closed, her head casually lying on her pillow, beautiful in the faint light of a new morning. I was grateful she was alive and happy she was with me. But mostly, I was consumed with an overwhelming sense of guilt for having almost got her killed.

After leaving her a note saying I was going for a walk, I went out the back door of my apartment to stretch before heading for a wooded trail behind my office. It was something I often did in the morning for exercise. And even though I knew I should not be outside alone, I went anyway. I was too frustrated to care. I needed to be outside. I hoped the cool, fresh air would cleanse my mind from a restless night of no sleep.

Fortunately, the storm had passed. The sun rose brightly through the trees. It was a difficult climb, constantly weaving steeply uphill along uneven terrain. The view at the top of the hill could be spectacular and well worth the effort. Ground was still wet from last night's rain, my boots constantly slipped as I continued. Concentration was required. I knew it might take longer this morning, but that was okay because it gave me time to think.

One question in particular was bugging me. I wondered how the attack on my cottage had been organized so quickly. Sure, Phillip had seen me in his office, but he couldn't have anticipated my visit. And even if he was responsible, how did he do it so fast? I couldn't imagine he had the resources to mount an attack in less than three days. Did he keep a rocket launcher in his basement just in case I showed it one day? That seemed completely absurd. Besides, violence wasn't his style, not the Phillip I knew. He could be nasty, but in far more subtle ways, like spreading rumors and lies to destroy a person's reputation. I concluded I was being paranoid. Blaming him was illogical. I mentally crossed Phillip off my list. It had to be someone with more resources, someone impatient, someone desperate.

Ok then, who did this? And how did they know where I was? No one outside of a few people in my office had been told I was flying to my cottage in Grand Haven. I had been careful. The situation made no sense to me. Unless... and this was something I did not want to consider, but I had to question if I had a leak inside my office.

The trail became more difficult as I continued, steeper and covered with loose rocks. I needed to slow down now. My attention was torn between two things, and a slip could result in a bad fall. I picked my way up the hillside carefully, taking care to place my boots on solid ground, testing each foothold before continuing. After some strenuous climbing, I took a break. A flat rock embedded in the hillside about halfway up the trail was a good resting place. I wiped the sweat from my forehead as an array of catastrophes passed through my mind.

Number one was the London Distribution House. It was continuing to lose shipments at an alarming rate. Second was our Hong Kong Distribution House, its vaults cleaned out. Almost all its inventory was gone. And although these two situations were bad, they were nothing compared to the disaster in Cambodia. Scores of miners had been killed. Then there was the lab in Australia. Wiped out in a fire. Clarence and M almost killed. And finally, the smiling face of my dead friend Vidu slipped into the forefront of my mind.

One catastrophe after another. Awful when considered separately. Absolutely incomprehensible when considered together... Nothing I could have predicted or imagined possible: death, massacre, robbery.

Despite all this inconceivable mayhem, my company was not dead, not yet, anyway. Hurt, wounded, yes, but still kicking. If there was a common denominator in all this chaos, it was my company. And if this was about my company, if all these tragedies were not isolated events, if they were a concerted effort to destroy my company, then it was highly possible, if not probable, that another attack was imminent. And this joined the mountain of my concerns. Who or what might be the next target? It was a question I needed to ask and answer. And to answer it, I tried to determine where the next attack would cause the most damage.

The cutting factories in Sri Lanka were a possibility. Crippling these factories could be very damaging, and our supply delayed. But we could move our gems to other cutting facilities.

The New York Distribution House was a possible target. Stealing its inventory like Hong Kong would be very harmful. If we lost our inventory in New York, we would have almost nothing to sell.

The muscles in my legs ached as I rested, momentarily distracting my focus. I wondered briefly why this morning's walk seemed so much harder than normal. I guessed it was because I was already worn out. Ignoring my complaining body, I began to climb again, determined to reach the top regardless of my body's objections.

The trail rose sharply. After some hard climbing, a small level, grassy meadow appeared below the final climb to the crest of the hill. I took a break to catch my breath while mentally working through a list of our American operations, wondering which was the most vulnerable. The main office building containing the 'R and D' lab in Charlottesville was a possibility, but I didn't think it would be hit. If my adversary's intelligence was as good as I assumed, as good as it had been up to this point, they probably knew security had been doubled.

The New York Distribution House was a completely different problem. But again, security had been radically increased. Bob ran the operation like a military camp. Even I couldn't get in without going through rigorous security checks. Any attempt to hit New York could get messy.

Next was our mining operation in Montana. From a security point of view, Montana was vulnerable, especially in the winter when it was unoccupied. The High Valley Mine, which is what we called the operation, produced a reasonable quantity of gem-quality sapphires despite the fact it was operational only five months a year.

Putting thoughts of the mine aside for a moment, I concentrated on the last climb to the top of the hill. My destination was a rocky plateau, a great place to sit on the edge of a cliff and view mountains in the distance. It was accessible up a steep slope through a stand of trees. Slowly, carefully, each foothold carefully chosen, I worked my way up, feeling an ache in my legs as I neared the top, breathing deeply... finally, breaking out of the trees and into the warmth of the morning sun. A series of stepped flat rocks led to the edge of the cliff. This last section of the climb presented the biggest challenge. A fall here could result in death. My breathing quickened, and my thighs burned with the exertion. One step at a time, one foot in front of the other. Feel the burn, be careful, and don't slip on the damp rocks.

I had crawled out onto the edge of this cliff a hundred times, but that didn't change the fact I needed to use caution. A fall down hundreds of feet of vertical rocks would result in death, the penalty for being foolhardy. However, it was worth the risk. The view from the edge of the cliff was breathtaking. Bending my knees into the slope and literally crawling on my hands, I took my time over the last few feet. Finally reaching the edge, after sitting down, my feet were swinging in the air. The surface of the rocks was damp, moisture penetrating the seat of my jeans. However, the slight discomfort was worth it. The beauty of the Blue Ridge Mountains in the distance was breathtaking. A wispy fog lingered in the lower valleys as I rested, content for the moment with my achievement. Absorbing the splendor of this grand vista offered a welcome release from my problems. Unfortunately, it didn't last long. Worrying about what might happen next was too great.

Montana became my biggest concern.

In the last few years, our increasing control of sapphire purchased from all over the world made our High Valley Mine in Montana unimportant from a production point of view. It produced only a small quantity of the gemstones we sold. But this didn't change the mine's essential contribution. Its value lies more in perception than reality. Our advertising material was filled with Montana scenery. Pictures from the area visually represented my company to the outside world. The mine was a symbol of our stability. Damaging it would seriously injure our image. In addition, a portion of the gems produced from this mine were especially treasured by our clients. They were beautiful in color and rare in natural clarity.

The mine was vulnerable mostly due to its isolated location, especially at this time of year when it was largely unattended. Deep mountain snow made it impossible to work the mine in the winter. It was abandoned each fall, but not before essential equipment was hauled down the mountain. Everything except a couple of pieces of custom-fabricated machinery. They were called wash plants and jig plants. They lay dormant under a blanket of snow until spring because they were heavy and large. It was possible to move them, but it would be very expensive, requiring the machines to be completely disassembled and trucked down in pieces. Then, they would need to be returned in the spring and reassembled a costly and time-consuming operation. Instead, the machines remained in the mountains during the winter. Damaging them would cost us a year's production and costly repairs.

Fortunately, the machines were not defenseless. The snow and cold in the high mountain valley provided natural protection. Traveling to the mine in the winter was difficult, but it was not impossible. If someone wanted to hurt my company, they might attempt to cripple the machines.

I took a deep breath.

It was time to start down the hill, time to return to work. My morning deliberations led me to conclude that I needed to become more proactive. I couldn't simply stand aside and wait for the next catastrophe to hit. I had to try to stem the series of disasters plaguing my company. If I was wrong, I was wrong, but I had to try.

I only hoped I wasn't too late.

9:31 A.M. JOHN

By the time I showered, shaved, ate breakfast, and slipped into my office, the computer on my desk was already alive and blinking vigorously.

One screen showed charts detailing sold and shipped stones from the three Distribution Houses. An email from Clarence indicated some progress in rebuilding the lab in Australia. A third computer screen specified the daily count in carats of gemstones produced at our active mines. A fourth screen showed the hourly production of our R&D lab in town. It had been transformed into a working color enhancement laboratory producing as many stones as possible. No research at this time, only production until Australia was returned to operation.

The screens clearly indicated my company was rebounding, like a prize fighter showing signs of life after almost being knocked out in a previous round. Carefully formulated quotas for each client were being met or exceeded. So far, none of our big clients have bolted, at least not to our knowledge. We knew they were unhappy, but they weren't buying from someone else, not yet, anyway. In addition, they were cooperating with ongoing criminal investigations, attempting to locate the stolen gemstones. To date, none of our lost gems have reappeared on the market. And this was odd. They had to be somewhere. If they came on the market, they could be identified. All gemstones contain certain internal elements, which are markers that indicate the mine of their origin.

Charlie, Monica's friend and our connection at the CIA had been told this. He was also waiting for the gems to show. He said they were too valuable to hold. Eventually, they would be sold. It was only a matter of time. Then, it might be possible to trace them back to the thieves.

He was right. Their market value was several hundred million dollars. Most thieves wouldn't hold the gems for long first because they were evidence that could be used against them. And second, because the thieves would want to convert their ill-gotten booty into cash as fast as possible. It made no sense for the gems to be held... That is, unless they were not taken by ordinary thieves. And the longer the stolen gems stayed off the market, the more convinced I became that it was possible they were being held by people who were only interested in destroying my company. Perhaps my enemy had a plan, something bigger than stealing millions of dollars of gemstones. The problem was that I seemed to be the only person holding this theory. When M talked to Charlie about it, he sounded like he was becoming more and more convinced the whole mess was somehow tied to drugs or terrorists. He suggested to her, not directly, but kind of insinuated that my idea was the product of an inflated ego.

The problem was, he could be right, and I had nothing, nothing in the way of concrete evidence that could prove him wrong. But one thing I did know. His choice of words did nothing to endear him to me.

I looked at my clock. Tim, the manager of the High Valley Mine in Montana, had to be awake by now. It was 7:40 a.m. mountain time. I called his house, hoping to catch him before he was out his door.

'Hello,' he answered.

'Tim, it's John. How are you?'

'Good to hear your voice again, John. I thought you had forgotten about us poor Montana folks.'

'Hardly the case, Tim. Just thought it was time to wake you from your long winter's nap.'

'You know better. We have been hard at work preparing for next summer's mining.'

Tim always spoke very slowly and precisely. He was well-educated for a Montana miner, a college graduate in engineering. His father was a California lawyer who decided to leave LA before its culture corrupted his family. His dad's strategy had worked because his son Tim was a hard worker and a great guy. He loved the mountains, lived in Granite, a small town by a stream, maybe four hundred folks in the whole place. Its gas station served as a grocery store, bar and restaurant.

On one occasion, Tim had suggested we get away from it all and take a trip up the mountain to visit his dad's cabin. I laughed. 'Get away from what?' I asked him. 'Do you realize ninety-nine percent of the world's population thinks this town where you live is about as far as anyone can get away from civilization?'

He had smiled serenely.

'Okay, you can cut the crap now, Tim,' I said into my phone, 'and tell me how snowmobiling has been this winter.'

Tim loved to snowmobile in the mountains. He didn't have much work to do in the colder months. By contrast, he worked exceptionally hard in the summer, twelve-hour days, six or seven days a week. His mining season was short. Between melting snows of spring and the heavy snows that blanketed his valley in the fall, the mine ran two shifts in the summer, sometimes three. I think Tim worked a good part of every shift. I never gave him any grief about what he did in the winter, figuring it was a healthy balance to his overachieving summer activity. At the end of the year, I always gave him a bonus. It was a month's vacation in Hawaii so he and his family could escape winter's cold. He had earned it.

'Pretty good so far, lots of snow and bitter cold lately, but a warm up is predicted.'

'Have you been up to the mine recently?'

'No, but I was thinking about taking a snowmobile up there as soon as the weather breaks.'

'Good. Here's the situation, Tim.'

I discussed with him in general terms my concern for the safety of the mine. I told him I wanted to visit Montana and inspect the mine in person.

'If someone wanted to damage the mining equipment, how would they do it?'

'Simple, get some dynamite and blow up the machinery. Dynamite is pretty available in these parts. Lots of folks use it for various reasons. Don't really need an excuse to buy the stuff.'

'Okay, would it be difficult to hire someone to do it?'

'No, lots of guys are out of work in winter. Just need to find some discontented local, give him a few bucks, and it's a done deal.'

'So, you wouldn't need to bring in an outsider to do the job.'

'Not really.'

I understood. A stranger stood out like a sore thumb in rural Montana. It would be better to use a native.

I remember one of the first times I visited him. Tim had been showing me around, driving the back roads. He was helping me get a sense of his world. I think we had driven maybe thirty miles in Tim's pickup truck down two-lane dirt roads. Each time we passed another vehicle, which wasn't often, Tim would wave and tell me the name of the driver or family in the truck coming from the other direction. Usually, it was another pickup truck. There were only a few cars. One time, an old pickup truck passed, and Tim prepared to wave. Then he lowered his hand as the other driver passed. Mystified, he turned and explained he didn't know who this guy was. He said this was very unusual. Everyone knew everyone else in his valley.

I just laughed and commented I didn't know any of the people who drive past me on the roads in my world.

'I'm coming,' I said to him. 'I'll arrive on Thursday. In the meantime, get someone to the mine. I know this may be difficult, but we need to protect the equipment. I'll pay for the troubles.'

'Old Jones is up there now, John. He's been living at our cabin for most of the winter.'

'Okay, can you give him a call? Find out if everything is all right.'

'Sorry, can't really do that. No landline to the cabin.'

'Okay. Have the company apartment ready for me. My secretary will be joining me,' I added, remembering a conversation with M when we were in Michigan. I didn't want to leave her behind again. I knew the risks, but I wasn't willing to lose her.

'Do you want the two-bedroom unit?' he questioned.

I hesitated. 'No, the one-bedroom will do,' I replied, knowing instantly I had made a mistake.

'One bedroom for a party of two. Say, is this serious?' he laughed amicably. 'Is my favorite bachelor finally falling in love?'

'None of your business,' I smiled. 'And I'll see you on Thursday.'

'Can't wait,' he laughed again.

'And Tim, tell no one we're coming. I'm serious.'

'Right.'

HONG KONG, 8:47 P.M. LIN

Lin compulsively arranged the papers on his desk into neatly stacked piles.

Although he had fastidiously arranged his desk earlier, Lin reorganized it again because this was his habit when faced with a complex dilemma, a problem he could not solve.

His problem today was that John had called and asked him to monitor Arthur's activities.

Lin sighed, knowing he couldn't change what he could not control. Some situations were meant to be, regardless of how difficult they made one's life. He turned in his chair and stared at the clouds outside the windows in his office, perhaps hoping the answer to his problem might appear out of thin air.

This other habit of his, this staring out a window into the sky looking for answers to questions he instinctively knew had no answers. This was also a habit he shared with John. On more than one visit to Charlottesville, Lin had observed John staring out his office windows in Virginia.

Lin smiled as he considered how odd it was, this shared habit of theirs. It was as if John was his blood brother. Even though he and John were separated by thousands of miles and hundreds of years of history, their responses to most situations were almost identical. It was as if Lin could predict what John would do and say even before he did it. Because Lin knew he would do the same thing in a similar circumstance.

Perhaps, he wondered, perhaps intelligence and perception were far more important than time and place. Perhaps it was possible that some men shared a common bond that had nothing to do with their geography or culture.

This, however, did not make Lin's job any easier. Time and place were the reason for his existence. Nothing else mattered in his world.

He had to remain true to who he was.

COPPER, MONTANA, FEBRUARY 10, MONDAY, 1:35 P.M. JOHN

Out the window of our chartered plane, I observed a few stray clouds washing off the tips of tall mountain peaks in the distance, accompanied by singular spires of wispy smoke rising from the chimneys of isolated mountain cabins in the valleys.

These rustic retreats from the pains of cramped society were serviced by meandering two-track roads and long winding blemishes that marred the otherwise smooth, snow-covered landscape. At that moment, I would have given anything to occupy one of these lonely cabins, to become a solitary cabin dweller resting by a crackling fire with a book to keep me company.

With a sigh, I turned away from the window. My fate was in some other place, far from this fairyland.

At the time, Monica looked lost in thought, resting comfortably in a leather-cushioned seat next to me on the plane. We had not talked in depth since returning from Grand Haven. We simply existed, it seemed, in parallel worlds. It was as if we were afraid to discuss our situation, afraid we might be forced to recognize our situation was hopeless. Instead, we quietly went about the tasks of the day, wishing our life to be as it had been before.

Our destination that day was the Copper City Municipal Airport. Located in a valley not far from the Continental Divide. Wind currents sweeping off the mountains bordering its airport often created dangerous downdrafts that could make landing treacherous. As a result, pilots powered into the runway because attempting to land at low speeds could be dangerous. Maneuverability was required because these dive-bomb landings could be unusually rough. Winter was especially problematic when the Jet Stream was rushing down from the Canadian plains into Montana at great speed, sweeping over the mountain ranges and creating unpredictable wind shifts.

I warned M about the landing after the pilot alerted us. He said we were nearing the airport; time to buckle up firmly. She reached over and took hold of my hand as our Lear jet circled the runway once before plunging into the valley. We dropped into several unseen pockets of rushing air as it headed towards the ground, hitting the runway hard, engines screaming in reverse. The plane slowed abruptly before taxiing to a terminal.

'That was fun.' M exhaled after she had unglued her clenched fingers from my hand.

'You get used to it after you've done it a few times. It's pretty much the same every time,' I reassured her.

'I'm not sure I want to,' she chuckled.

Betsy, the mining company's secretary, met us in the airport lobby with the keys to my company car. Almost everyone in Copper drives either an SUV or a pickup truck. After several visits, I couldn't tolerate these overgrown, lumbering land rollers. I didn't feel like I was controlling these high center-of-gravity cabooses. Felt more like they were driving me than the other way around. I purchased an Allroad Audi Quattro and had it delivered to Copper. It had a four-wheel drive for the muddy, snowy conditions in the area, and it could really handle dry roads at speed. I thanked Betsy for bringing my car and told her we would see her at her office after settling into our apartment.

Our drive into the city of Copper was a visual treat for M. Most of the architecture dates back a hundred years, when copper mining was in its prime. Visiting the town was like traveling back into history. After copper mining slowed in the area, so did the town, and nothing has changed since. It looked just as it did in its heyday—maybe a bit more worn for wear, but essentially the same. Only a few small mines were still operating in the area.

After unpacking our suitcases in the apartment, we drove to the High Valley Sapphire Mine office, located at the end of a road that traveled through the center of town before going steeply uphill. Fortunately, the mid-February sun was bright and the road dry when we arrived. M stared out the car's window at the houses along the road. Built at odd angles, similar to what you might see in San Francisco, one house was on top of the other. Some were in good repair, some not. None were new. Many badly needed repairs.

'Not much to admire,' I commented.

'No, nothing like your commercials.'

'It doesn't all look like this,' I acknowledged her reference to Gemstones International's advertising campaign, which featured small picturesque villages in glorious mountain scenes. 'Tomorrow, you'll see another side of Montana.'

The office building was originally an old copper mine shop. It was a two-story, tin-walled building that had been completely refurbished inside. Freshly painted walls complemented with new office furniture contrasted sharply with its bleak outward appearance. Summer pictures of the High Valley Mine lined the interior walls of the lobby.

Tim greeted us at the entrance door.

'It's good to see you, my friend,' I said.

His handshake was firm, and his smile spontaneous. He was a tall man with curly auburn hair and the green eyes of his Irish ancestors, handsome with almost Hollywood good looks.

'John, a pleasure as always,' he replied to me, but his eyes had already strayed, captured by the site of the lovely woman at my side.

'Tim, may I introduce Monica to you,' I acknowledged his obvious interest.

'So, this is the little lady?' he smiled

M gave me a curious glance.

'Yes, this is my friend Monica,' I attempted to set the record straight.

'It's a pleasure to meet you, Monica,' Tim said.

'It's nice to meet you, Tim,' she replied.

M had seen the Australian mine office. She probably expected this office to be similar. It was not as modern. Still, it was very serviceable. After climbing the stairs to Tim's office on the second floor, I noticed something new. A big blue marlin was mounted on the wall behind his desk.

'What's this?' I asked.

'Fish I caught in Hawaii earlier this winter.'

'It's a beauty.'

Out of the corner of my eye, I noticed the frown line between M's eyes was in full crease. She was obviously not happy and didn't like seeing animals mounted on walls.

Tim also saw the same expression and immediately guessed the reason. The man could be very perceptive. 'It isn't real,' he apologized. 'It's just a fake. I had it made from a picture I took. The real fish is swimming in the ocean.'

To demonstrate his sincerity, he searched around his desk and produced a picture of the fish hooked to a line swimming next to a boat. He was standing in the boat holding the fishing rod with a big Irish smile covering his face.

'You just went from being a chump to a hero,' I said to him. 'This lady doesn't think fish belong on walls.'

'I agree with her,' Tim said with a disarming smile. He was one of those people who never make much noise, just always do what is right. A natural charmer, the man could sweet talk any lady within shouting distance without saying a word. His smile was his weapon. He was already working his charm on M.

'Can I get you some coffee, Monica?' he asked.

'That would be nice,' she replied. 'And please call me M. Everyone else does.'

'Cream and sugar, M?'

'Yes, please.'

'I'd like some too, Tim,' I said as he poured her a cup. By this time, he had completely forgotten I was in the room.

'Oh sure, John, black is it?' he replied, promptly leaving the room to get cream for M without waiting for my answer.

'He seems very nice,' M noted.

'Oh, he's nice, alright. He's Irish and he's a charmer,' I winked and poured myself a cup of coffee, thinking some things never change. Tim's natural attraction to women was constant. My presence was nothing more than a minor distraction as long as M was in the room. She came first, and I came—well... it didn't matter.

She smiled.

When he returned, I asked Tim if he had talked to Jones at the mine. He said he had not, but he assumed everything was good. Otherwise, Jones would have come into town and told him. When he turned his attention to M again, I took the opportunity to walk over to a window. From where his office stood on a hill, a vast range of snow-covered mountains could be seen in the distance. In the afternoon sunshine, it was a beautiful sight.

'So, how bad is it?' Tim asked when I returned. 'Do we have a potential problem at the mine, or are you just being precautionary?'

'At this point, I'm being precautionary.'

'I see.' Tim pondered my statement. 'Can I ask you something?'

'Sure.'

'Does this have anything to do with Phillip?'

'Why do you ask?' I replied, surprised by his question.

'Because I have heard rumors that he's in town.'

5:10 P.M. JOHN

The sun sets early behind the tall mountains of western Montana, and the air cools quickly in the valleys.

I pulled up the zipper of my jacket against the cold as M and I stepped outside Tim's office. Snow crunched beneath our boots as we hurried to the awaiting warmth of our car.

The apartment where we were headed was owned by the High Valley Mine. Located in the center of town, it was below the elevation of the office. Our drive down the hill was disheartening. Descending darkness made the houses look even older and dirtier than before, as though the town was slowly dying.

Before we left, Tim asked if we would like to visit him at his house in the morning and have lunch. He promised it would be a pleasant through the mountains. Tim assured us sunny, warm weather was forecast. He suggested we could discuss some ideas for making the mine more secure when we met.

A traffic light in the center of town momentarily delayed our progress that evening. I was daydreaming at the time, not paying attention. Being in the mountains always seemed to do this to me. I only caught a brief glimpse of a dark blue Ford Explorer turning left into the intersection while we waited, but it was enough to send an electric shock of recognition pulsing through my body. Phillip, I couldn't be sure it was him, but the driver's profile looked familiar. The man had a large, pointed nose, and his hair was pulled back in a ponytail, similar to the way Phillip did his hair.

'Did you see that guy in the SUV?' I asked M.

'Who?' M turned to me in puzzlement.

'The driver in a blue SUV,' I replied, sounding more agitated than intended. 'Did you get a good look at his face? I think it was Phillip.'

'Not really, and I don't know if I would recognize him even if I did. I only saw him once in London,' she apologized.

'Right, sorry. I just thought...'

The light turned green. I hit my left-turn blinker and waited impatiently for a couple of cars to cross the intersection. Then I made a hard left, accelerating, searching up the street for any sign of a blue Explorer.

'Do you see it?' I asked.

'See what?' M replied, confused.

'A blue SUV!' I said louder than I intended.

'No.'

The vehicle was nowhere in sight. I began to wonder if I had imagined the whole thing.

'Look down the side streets to your right.'

'Sure, a blue SUV?' she responded

I looked left but saw no blue vehicles of any kind.

'There,' she pointed.

We had already passed through the intersection before I could react. I hit the brakes and made a quick U-turn in front of a startled driver, then had to wait for oncoming traffic to clear before I could turn through the intersection. Unfortunately, the blue SUV had disappeared by this time, but Copper is not a big town. I kept driving around, hoping to find it eventually.

'Do you think it was him?' M asked as we cruised the streets in silent frustration, my mood getting darker by the moment.

'I don't know. Maybe he was just a figment of my imagination,' I replied, beginning to feel more discouraged than ever. Maybe it was just being in this town again. I never really liked it here, and the old, unkempt buildings always soured my mood.

M was quiet. She had seldom seen me this frustrated. Unfortunately, I was showing her a different dimension of my personality, which was not very attractive. I like to think I can control my emotions, but I'm not always successful, especially when stressed. I sometimes say or do things out of frustration I regret later. A kind of dark dread takes over my mood. It's hard to stop, and it is difficult not to show it.

I didn't like having M see me this way.

9:05 P.M. JOHN

'Come here, big boy,' she said with a grin, her words sounding more like a command than a request.

At the time, I was getting ready for bed, looking forward to a good night's sleep.

The one-bedroom apartment we occupied was one of two residences owned by Tim's company. These apartments were primarily used by clients, geologists, and consultants visiting the mine. They were warm and cozy, rooms small but clean, decorated with local Native American artwork. Although they didn't get much use in the winter, they were busy in the summer mining season. They had been purchased because visitor accommodations in the town of Copper were mediocre and expensive in summer when tourists roamed the town. Tim decided purchasing the apartments was better than paying the high cost of renting motel rooms in high season. He convinced me it would be cheaper in the long run.

Apart from the dismal nature of the town, I always enjoyed my visits to the mountains in Montana. It was a great area to get away from the pressures of daily life. However, this trip had taken on a distinctively different flavor almost from the beginning. Dinner with M at my favorite restaurant that night was okay. The food was good, but the conversation was lacking. The dark funk that had hijacked my composure when we were searching for a blue SUV had not completely evaporated. M and I ate mostly in silence. I was still encased in my dreaded funk while she was being respectfully quiet, leaving me alone to brood.

Crawling up behind me as I sat on the edge of the bed, she applied her fingers to the sore muscles in my back and shoulders. I took a deep breath to release the tension. Her touch brought both pain and pleasure as she worked the stress out of my back.

Eventually, I suggested it was her turn.

'I'm not done,' she objected.

'You're done,' I commanded emphatically. 'Lie down, please.'

Without further complaint, she lay face down on the bed, dressed in warm, flannel pajamas bought for this trip. Under the flannel, her back felt strong like an athlete, her muscles tight and hard. I moved my fingers from her shoulders down her lower back, finding tight tendons and massaging them slowly to relaxation. Her lovely bottom next gained my unwarranted attention before finally reaching down to softly massage the warm area between her legs.

Without comment, she rolled over on her back and stood up, slowly unbuttoning her pajama top in the process. Touching my lips softly with a finger kiss, she lifted my t-shirt over my head before reaching down to unbutton my pajama bottoms, allowing them to fall to the floor as she massaged an already erect appendage. I took her face in my hands and kissed her hard on the lips, neck, and bare breasts.

We made love slowly that night, like we never wanted it to end. Later, while lying under heavy down-filled covers sealing our warm bodies away from a cold Montana night, I quietly asked her if she was sleeping.

'No, just resting.'

'May I apologize for my behavior today?' I asked sincerely. 'I haven't been a very good host.'

'It's understandable, John. You're under a lot of pressure.'

'That's no excuse. I'll try to do better tomorrow.'

'You're doing fine. I just hope my being here is helping you.'

'You know it is.'

She didn't respond before asking. 'Does seeing Phillip today change anything?'

'I'm not really sure it was him,' I replied before adding, 'But Tim heard some rumors that he's here, and if Phillip is, he's up to no good.'

'Are we still going to see Tim and Sarah's home tomorrow like we planned?'

'Yes, why do you ask?'

'Could it be dangerous?'

'No. Why do you think that?'

'Maybe Phillip is here because he knows you are. You know what happened the last time he knew where you were.'

'Maybe, but that's all the more reason to go. Tim and I need to make plans to ensure the mine is protected.'

M did not respond.

'Don't worry,' I tried to reassure her. 'Tim lives out in the middle of nowhere.

Not much danger out there except from bears and moose.'

TUESDAY, FEBRUARY 11, 8:05 A.M. JOHN

The road was snow-dusted as we drove out of the town of Copper towards Tim's house in the mountains.

An overnight snowfall had cleansed the land except where hard rocks pushed up out of the snow, their jagged gray granite art forms distorting the smooth layers of frozen ice. Road crews had been busy overnight, plowing and sanding. Our drive wasn't difficult. Years of navigating Michigan's winters had taught me to make no quick moves on slippery roads, just a light touch on the accelerator and brakes, steady progress, and not be in a hurry.

We passed through the mining town of Golden before entering the high mountains, where the road became steep and twisty. M seemed content, looking out the window, viewing valley vistas over miles of open space. Guard rails protected the road where sheer drop-offs fell to oblivion.

As we approached the highest mountain elevation, I pulled off the road into a plowed viewing area. Tim and I had stopped here once during one of my first visits to the mine. It had been years ago. It was a great place to experience the mountain scenery. One side of the road fell several thousand feet straight down a rocky-faced cliff. I motioned for M to take a look, but she was reluctant to get near the edge of the cliff. Snowplows had pushed large banks of frozen snow up and over metal guard rails, creating a natural barrier. I climbed up on top of one of these snow piles for a better view.

'Come up here,' I beckoned. 'The view is wonderful.'

She shook her head 'no' while standing several feet below me on solid ground.

From where I stood, the mountain dropped so steeply it was almost impossible to look straight down the face. To view the rocks below, I would have had to lean over the snow, almost to the point of falling, something I did not try.

'The view is glorious,' I encouraged her again.

'No, this is close enough,' she held her ground, unwilling to budge.

I didn't push. Some people have a healthy fear of heights.

The mountain had been dynamited to create a level area for the road and parking lot. A vertical gray-brown wall of solid rock was transected with snow infested cracks. It was cold where I was standing, the wind bitter. Intermittent snowflakes flew horizontally through the air. After a few minutes, I returned with M to our warm car.

Soon, we were over the mountain and going down the other side. Great stands of green pines lined the road which twisted and turned, following a free-flowing rocky mountain stream which alternately cut through and dived under snow and ice. Eventually, the land became more level. The turns were not so tight. Accelerating through the straight sections and braking for turns, we smoothly rounded each corner at effortless speed while being careful to avoid patches of black ice. The Audi reacted well in the conditions, making the drive a delight with almost no traffic to spoil the experience. The scenery was breathtaking, filled with windswept snow fields and tall green pine stands.

'You're quiet this morning,' I said to M after we had traveled for miles without speaking.

'Just enjoying the views.'

Eventually, the road headed into Granite, Montana. This was Tim's hometown, located at the junction of two roads in an open valley. A white-wood church with a tall steeple stood on a snow-covered hillside overlooking the town. I turned at the intersection marked by the church and drove up the snow-crusted main street past several old wood buildings housing small businesses. A few new homes were included with the older, historical buildings. The town had perhaps only fifteen to twenty structures in total. Tim lived in one of the relatively new houses he had built on the outskirts.

Unlike most of the inhabitants of Granite, Tim did not work for a business supported by cattle ranches. Tim told me one of the largest ranches in the valley was owned by his father-in-law, a ranch that spread over miles throughout the valley.

When I pulled into his driveway, Tim immediately opened the front door to invite us inside. His house was warm and decorated in what I called early-American, traditional Aunt Mary style furnishings, patterned wallpaper, and new antique furniture. It was clean and comfortable.

'Coffee, folks?' he asked, directing us to his kitchen.

'Sure,' M replied.

We sat at a wood table in the small dining room adjacent to the kitchen with a sliding glass window overlooking a snow-covered backyard. A nearby mountain stream cut through the snow. It looked crystal clear and, according to Tim, was filled with fish.

Tim brought in a tray of chocolate chip cookies along with hot coffee, cream, and sugar for M.

'Got an idea,' Tim said as soon as he had poured our coffee. 'I know we talked about having lunch with Sarah.'

'Oh no, not one of your ideas,' I smiled, knowing Tim was always full of ideas, most of them nothing but trouble.

'Hey, this will be fun, and we can inspect the mine at the same time.'

'And how are we going to do that?' I asked, remembering I had seen two snowmobiles on a trailer attached to Tim's pickup truck in his driveway.

'Well,' he began before pausing and disappearing into an adjacent room without saying another word. When he returned, he was holding two snowmobile suits with a broad grin on his handsome Irish face.

'He thinks we should snowmobile to the mine,' I said to M, who was staring at the suits, wondering what they were. 'It takes about an hour and a half from the end of a mining road.'

'It'll be great.' Tim remarked, smiling from ear to ear. 'Sun is shining, and the snow is fresh.'

This was true. The sky outside had cleared after last night's storm. It was a sunny day, and the new snow made everything outside look bright, fresh, and clean. I had accompanied Tim a few times on snowmobiles into the mountains. The ride was a joy of wind, snow, and speed, but it was also physically exhausting and sometimes dangerous. I looked at M, expecting to see apprehension. Unfortunately, she was smiling. I knew instantly we were going snowmobiling, whether I wanted to or not.

'We don't have to go,' I told her, still hoping for a negative reaction. But Tim's natural Irish charm had taken over. I didn't stand a chance.

'I think it would be great fun,' she replied, smiling at Tim. 'That is if it's okay with you, John.'

'That settles it,' Tim replied without waiting for my answer. 'M can ride with me. Here, try on Sarah's suit. I think it'll fit you.'

'Oh no,' I quickly countered. 'If we go, she rides with me. Remember, I've seen you on a snowmobile.'

'No problem,' Tim replied with a grin. 'We can visit the mine, bring some supplies to Jonesy and work out the plans for security all at the same time. If we leave now, we'll be home in time for dinner. Sarah can see you then. I have a lunch packed and...'

'Didn't think I would say no?'

'No reason to say no, John.'

12:10 P.M., HIGH IN THE MOUNTAINS NEAR THE MINE, JOHN

A blast of dry white powder snow flowed over our machine in the crisp mountain air, accompanied by the high-pitched scream of the snowmobile's engine corrupting a previously silent and deserted forest.

Gleaming in the sunshine, the snow lay like a smooth blanket over the ground, clinging to barren tree branches intersecting a clear blue sky. M sat behind me, her arms firmly around my waist, holding on tightly with all her strength as I leaned into turns. She had not yet mastered the art of going with the flow of the machine. Instead, she pulled on me with every turn and bump, making my task harder, straining and maneuvering my snowmobile through rolling terrain. Ahead of us, Tim expertly broke trail with ease. He and his machine were one. We were following an old trail through a forest, careful to avoid large objects like fallen tree branches or rocks buried under the surface of the snow. According to Tim, this trail was a shortcut. I wasn't so sure. He just enjoyed getting off the beaten path and into the woods for fun.

The trail, if you could call it a trail, was nothing more than a narrow gap in the forest that ran parallel to a frozen creek bed, twisting and turning through a valley in the mountains. I would have been happier on the road, even if it took longer. A road would have been safer and a lot easier. But Tim's Irish charm had been very persuasive. He convinced us to follow him into the forest.

Thankfully, after an hour or more of struggling to keep up with Tim, the trees ahead began to thin. From past experience, I knew this meant we were almost to the open valley where our mine was located. This was great because I was beginning to feel a deep ache in my back and arms from constant exertion. Even though it was terrific to be outside in the clear, cool mountain air, I knew I would be sore tomorrow.

Behind me, M was doing better. She wasn't holding onto me as much. She had learned to lean with me, anticipating turns, looking over my shoulder as we rode several yards behind Tim. He was doing the hard work of breaking trail through newly fallen snow. A sled filled with supplies was attached to the rear of his snowmobile.

Tim headed up a rise and slowed at the top. I followed, turning up the throttle on the handlebars. Leaning forward, my snowmobile shot up to where he waited, perched on a small plateau. We pulled alongside, stopping to rest for a moment. The view of the valley was great. It had been months since I last visited the High Valley Mine.

It is an alluvial deposit, meaning sapphires mined on the site were formed millions of years ago deep in the heat of the earth before rising to the surface with the formation of the Rocky Mountains. The gems remained embedded in solid rock until the mountains began to erode naturally. Finally breaking free, they were washed down mountain slopes in rushing streams before eventually settling in calm ponds where the streams broadened through valleys such as this one.

From where we sat, the only objects that looked out of place in this natural valley scenery were a couple of large mechanical machines made of fabricated metal. The top of one of these contraptions was barely visible, buried under layers of snow in the valley. Still some distance from where we rested at the crest of a hill, stood a bright green machine was called a wash-plant. Its job was to clean mud off rocks scooped from the valley by mechanized shovels. On a hillside to our right was the other large metal machine. Most of it was clearly visible. Snow had been blown off it by wind, exposing its green, metal frame. It was called a jig plant. Its job was to separate heavy sapphire gemstones from ordinary rocks, which weighed less.

These were the two large machines that had been prepared for winter and remained in the valley when the first snows of autumn fell. All the other mining equipment had been taken down the mountain for maintenance and stored in warehouses near Tim's house. It was the vulnerability of these two machines that worried me the most. They were custom-built, very expensive, and difficult to replace. If destroyed, it could take months to fabricate new parts and deliver them to the mining site. A year of mining could be lost in the process.

I rubbed my heavy leather gloves together, hoping to restore circulation to my frozen fingers. Gripping the handlebars tightly had made my fingers grow numb in the cold. I was about to say something to M when a sound closely resembling a rifle shot echoed through the valley.

'What's that?' I asked, scanning the valley for signs of activity.

'Yeah, I heard it too,' Tim replied, frowning. 'Could be Jonesy out hunting.' He paused before saying, 'He shouldn't be. This really isn't hunting season.'

'That never stopped him before, did it?'

'No,' Tim smiled.

Just as Tim finished speaking, several more shots rang out in quick succession. It was difficult to determine where the shots were coming from. The mining equipment was some distance from us, down a hill and across a mostly treeless, open valley. Our current position was a crown between two hills, which formed the valley. Directly across from us, at the other end of the valley, was a stand of pine trees that protected an old log cabin built beside a frozen trout pond. The cabin dated back to the early eighteen hundreds. The story was this cabin had first been built by a pioneer family who died in this valley trying to live off the land. A long, bitterly cold winter had taken their lives. Gray smoke rose lazily from the cabin's stone chimney, curling in the calm mountain air, evidence that old Jones was living in the cabin. During the winter, he was a security guard for the mine. He loved the life of a hermit. Despite long, solitary winters, the job suited him fine.

Tim pointed towards the large green machine in the valley. 'I think I see someone moving around down there.' Opening a small storage compartment in his snowmobile, Tim took out a pair of binoculars. After peering into the valley, 'Yes, I see him. It's Jones alright, by the wash-plant.'

Shots rang out again, echoing through the valley. Although it was difficult to determine their origin, they seemed to be coming from a stand of trees on the hill to our left. Tim trained his binoculars in that direction. Shots sounded again, this time from a different position, closer to a rocky area farther up the same hill.

'I see someone behind those rocks,' Tim said incredulously.

He handed me his binoculars. I strained to find the area while focusing on the binoculars. Finally, I saw them, two heads darting out from behind some rocks, rifles in hand, taking random shots in the direction where Jones was hiding behind the wash plant.

'What's going on?' asked M.

'Damnedest thing I have ever seen,' said Tim. 'Looks like some guys are using old Jones for target practice.

'Either that, or they are trying to scare him off so they can get to the machines.' I immediately thought worst-case scenario.

'Could be. Problem is, I don't think they planned on dealing with a guy as stubborn as Jones,' Tim commented. 'He's not likely to give up without a fight.'

'He doesn't stand much of a chance without some help,' I grimaced.

Tim nodded. 'There are guns in the cabin. Look, I'll make a run for it. You two stay here.'

'No. we'll both go.' I was adamant. I didn't want to let Tim take all the risk.

He raised his eyebrows, 'You sure?'

'Come on, Tim, let's do this.'

M looked at us. 'You have got to be kidding. I feel like I just walked into a Wild West show. What about calling the police?' she asked.

'Look, Monica,' Tim explained as I put on my helmet. 'Police won't get here for hours. We need to give Jones a hand now. He's not going to give up until he gets shot.'

Tim unhooked the supply sled from the back of his snowmobile while Monica reluctantly got off the back of my machine. She gave me one of those looks females make when they think men are idiots.

I said nothing.

'Follow me,' Tim shouted, revving the engine of his snowmobile. Slipping his machine into gear, he headed down the hill, parting snow in waves of white dust while instantly shooting down and across the hillside.

I had the feeling this was the kind of moment Tim lived for. I, on the other hand, gripped my handlebars in utter fear. Turning up full throttle, leaning into the seat, I let out the clutch and took off after him, with a faint hope I wouldn't be dying today. Tim was already a good distance in front of me. I was having trouble keeping up with him. Weaving in and around trees and between rocks, we maintained cover for as long as possible. The snow was deep in places. Our snowmobiles got bogged down occasionally, slowing, burying the front runners in a snowdrift before shooting up and over the snow in bursts of speed like a boat riding on the top of the water. I held on to the handlebars, fighting to see the trail ahead through spraying white powder coming from Tim's snowmobile. Leaning into the side of the hill, turning to avoid rocks, and ducking between trees, I was able to hold onto my powerful machine, which felt like a bucking bronco at this speed. Snow blew off the front runners, brushing against my face like cold sandpaper, rubbing my skin raw. In the excitement, I had forgotten to pull down my visor. I didn't dare take a hand off the handlebars to adjust the visor for fear of losing control.

Initially, we were able to stay out of rifle range. The shooters on the other side of the valley were too far away. But when we passed through the last section of open ground between us and the cover of the trees near the cabin, we were definitely within their sights. We had no choice. There was only one way leading to the cabin. Hills on either side were too steep to traverse. We had to go through the valley at full throttle. A low thud hit my engine housing. I had no time to react. Ahead, Tim was already off his machine and running for the safety of the cabin. As soon as I got close, I slowed, jumped off the seat, and bolted for the open door.

A smoldering fire warmed the cabin and a half-eaten plate of eggs and toast on a small wood table was still warm, indicating Jones had not been gone long. He must have heard or seen something and went outside to investigate.

Tim found the keys to a gun case and unlocked it. Handing me a semiautomatic Winchester used to scare coyotes and bears from the cabin, he took a bigger rifle, one used to kill moose.

'I'm not any good at this,' I explained. 'Just so you know.'

Tim gave me a quick lesson on how to fire the gun while shoving some extra ammunition in my pocket. 'Just point it in their direction. We're not trying to kill anyone. Just scare them off.'

'Okay.'

He took a look out a window.

'So, what's our plan?'

'If we can get to the trees at the edge of the forest, we should be able to get off a few shots,' he suggested. 'Let them know Jones is not alone. Hopefully, that will make they leave.'

Opening the cabin door, he motioned for me to follow. We ran through deep snow to an area protected by tall pine trees at the edge of the forest. Tim stopped and braced his moose rifle on a tree limb, firing a few shots across the valley in the direction where we last saw the men who were shooting at Jones.

A dull knock sent splinters of wood flying through the air not far from where I stood. Another bullet brushed a hole in the snow, much closer. Tim dropped down and crawled back to my position. Jones could be heard firing wildly at some movement in the rocks across from him to my right.

'I need to get to the jig plant up the hill,' Tim said. 'That will give me a better vantage point. You cover me.'

'Okay,' I replied.

It all seemed unreal. I was just reacting without thinking.

Tim ran for his snowmobile, jumped on, started it, and drove through a cover of trees toward the jig plant, which was located halfway up a hill to my left. Leaning against a tree trunk, I fired a volley of shots across the valley to cover his progress. When a few bullets hit near me, I ducked down. From where I crouched in the snow, I could see Tim. He had made it to the jig plant unharmed. Parking his snowmobile behind the large machine, he quickly climbed the stairs to a top platform. After brushing snow off a railing, he placed the big old moose rifle on the railing and began to fire in rapid succession. I trained my rifle in the direction of the nearest target away from Jones and began to fire steadily. Jones followed our lead, moving around the wash plant, shooting in the direction of his assailants.

After reloading and firing several more times, I stopped when I heard the sound of engines across the valley. Two snowmobiles emerged from behind some rocks, speeding up and over a hill. Three others soon followed their cowardly buddies, disappearing over the hill.

Seems they weren't interested in a fair fight.

1:40 P.M. JOHN

The old man placed some fresh logs in the hearth.

Soon, the dark interior of the log cabin began to warm, the fire crackling a friendly greeting as I warmed my hands. Fresh coffee was brewing, its aroma filling the room.

My mood, however, was bleak. The happy exhilaration of riding a snowmobile through virgin forests under blue skies had been lost, replaced by fear, as the sounds of echoing shots reverberated through my head. No end to disastrous nonsense seemed in sight—just one more torturous affair after another.

Tim was gone. He had offered to retrieve Monica and the supply sled from where she had been hiding. Jones was busy cleaning soiled breakfast dishes, trying to make his place look presentable for guests.

I rested, lost in thought, wondering what would have happened if Tim and I hadn't decided to come to the mine today. Nothing good, I assumed. Jones probably would have been killed or wounded and the equipment destroyed, but this had not happened. Perhaps for the first time, we had prevented another disaster. This was a good sign. The tide is probably turning in our favor. Still, I couldn't stop my dread funk from burrowing deeper into my gut.

A good day had been spoiled.

When I heard Tim's snowmobile, I put on my coat and went outside to help unload the sled. Jonesy followed. M looked up and smiled as I walked towards her, like she wanted to give me a hug. I wasn't in the mood. I ignored her while giving Tim a hand with the supplies.

She was sipping a cup of coffee when I went inside. Once we had everything unloaded, I got a cup.

'Jones, I want you to meet Monica,' I said as Tim put the last package on a counter by the kitchen.

'Mighty nice to meet you, ma'am,' Jones said, taking off his old furry hat and thick gloves, offering her a big, calloused old hand.

He was a large man, probably in his seventies. If he had been born a hundred years before, he probably would have wandered the frontier as a fur trapper. Some people aren't comfortable in society. They feel more at home in the woods. Jones was one of those people. Tim knew his affection for isolation and had made Jones the winter caretaker for the mine. The job included room and board at the cabin and all the wild game he could shoot, plus a weekly stipend to keep Jones in essentials. Once a month, Jones trekked into town for supplies. Otherwise, he kept to himself. Tim gave him a cell phone for emergencies. To call, he had to walk to the top of a hill, where he got a weak signal if he was lucky. He didn't mind. To my knowledge, he had never used the cell phone. Tim wasn't sure he even knew how.

Jones' curly brown hair was streaked with gray, long and unkempt. He brushed it back with his hand and smiled at M. A big grin lacked a few teeth. You couldn't help but like the old guy. He was a big, friendly grizzly bear of a man. Long, bushy eyebrows and a shaggy beard helped him look the part.

'It's nice to meet you, Mr. Jones,' she replied with a smile.

'Ah, just call me Jonesy. Everyone else does.' He smiled again.

'Okay, Jonesy.'

'Mighty glad you folks came along when you did,' he turned to us. 'Otherwise, I'm not sure old Jonesy would a been around to see another sunrise.'

'Oh, nothing to it, Jonesy,' Tim smiled. 'We generally make a habit of rescuing hapless old men like you.'

'Old man, huh? Maybe ya didn't notice I was holding 'em off by myself before ya got here.'

'Yeah, sure, Jonesy. Odds were about right, you against four or five other guys.' Tim slapped him on his back.

'Did ya see me back down?' he challenged.

'Okay, okay. Just tell us what happened?' Tim asked.

Jones began by explaining how he heard some engine noises in the direction of the equipment and went out to investigate. He was glad he took his gun, just in case, he said.

Monica turned to me and asked quietly if I was alright.

'Sure, a little shook up, that's all,' I whispered back. She put her arm around my waist and held on firmly. I reached across and touched her hand, caressing her fingers, thinking moments like this can draw people together, cement a relationship. That is if we don't let them tear us apart first.

'Those buggers were determined to drive me off,' Jones continued. 'But I yelled at 'em. Told them this was private property and to keep moving. But they didn't seem like they were goin' away. They started yelling at me to get out, but I wasn't in the mood. We were sort of in a stand-off... 'cept just before you arrived, they started to move around my flank. I don't think they had anything good in mind for old Jonesy. At first, I thought they were just trying to scare me, but when they figured out I wasn't gonna leave, their shots got a lot closer. Seems like they were circling around the other side of the wash plant so they could get a better shot. I gotta admit... I was getting nervous.' He hung his head and wiped at his brow. 'I guess thanks are in order.'

'No, thank you, Jonesy,' I corrected him. 'If you hadn't done what you did, I don't think the mining equipment would still be intact.'

'It's my job, Mr. Van Laan. You don't have-ta thank me. You've been kind to me. This was my chance to repay you.'

'You did, and I thank you. But the next time something like this happens, you back off. Those machines are not worth your life.'

'Sorry, can't do no different,' he replied sincerely. 'Old Jonesy doesn't know how to do nothing but fight. Sorry, sir, but I won't back off.'

'Okay, then maybe we'd better get you some help.'

Tim nodded. 'I'll ride up to the top of the hill and call some of the guys. Maybe I can find someone to stay with Jonesy tonight. We can rotate guys in and out so Jonesy won't be alone.'

'I don't want nobody here,' Jonesy said indignantly, looking like he was about to spit before he remembered M was in the room.

'Look, Jonesy,' I said. 'I can't take a chance on something happening either to you or the machinery. I know you don't like having people around, but hopefully, it won't be for long.'

'Well, if you have to, I guess I can put up with those bums for a few days,' he conceded.

'Thanks,' I said, knowing it would probably be for more than just a few days.

I wondered how long it would be before Jonesy disappeared like he usually did in the spring when the crew returned into the valley. They never saw him again until the first snows of autumn. Then he would simply reappear and settle in for the winter. Nobody really knew where he went in the summer. Someplace, I suppose, where he could live in the solitude he desired.

Vast areas of unexplored wilderness lay in these mountains, perfect for a solitary existence.

3:40 P.M. JOHN

Fresh snow fell lightly as I backed out of Tim's driveway.

Behind gathering clouds, the bright sun reflected off a blanket of new snow, casting a mystical glow over the frosty landscape. Tim's hometown looked like a fairytale, but in reality, the snow was made of ice crystals, evidence of a deep freeze that had invaded the land, dusting dormant plants with tentacles of deadly frost. Beneath the snow, the ground was stone cold hard. Above ground, the air smelled like oiled metal.

Stopping at the main road junction in Tim's hometown, I waited for a pickup truck to drive through the intersection. The driver slowed and waved me through with a friendly gesture. Acknowledging his courtesy, I turned toward the mountains while dreaming of the soft sheets and warm covers on the bed in the apartment in Copper. I was dead tired. My arms ached from guiding a snowmobile through miles of snowy trails. An adrenalin-packed day had left me depleted and weak. I was looking forward to a good night's sleep.

Tim decided to stay with Jonesy. He couldn't get anyone to come to the cabin on short notice. In the next few days, teams of two guys plus Jonesy would live at the cabin and patrol the mine site. I told Tim I could find my way back down the snowmobile trail to where his truck was parked without his help. The road to his house was familiar. I had driven it many times. I said not to worry. We would be fine. But he insisted on accompanying us on his snowmobile to where his pickup truck was parked, just to be certain no one was waiting along the trail to harm us.

After loading our snowmobile on his trailer, we said our 'goodbyes' to Tim and drove to his house, where we parked his truck in the driveway. Sarah had not yet returned from work. We left a note explaining why Tim stayed at the mine. I added an apology for missing dinner plans. Said I hoped she'd understand. I looked forward to seeing her the next time I was in Montana.

Truth was I wanted to get on the road as fast as possible and make it through the mountain pass before night fell. It was beginning to snow and we'd had enough excitement for one day. Driving through a snowstorm at night on a mountain road can be treacherous. Snow reflecting in headlights severely limits night vision. And if the snow begins to come down hard, it can be like driving into a white wall.

To my relief, it wasn't snowing much as we drove out of town, only a light dusting. I hoped it wouldn't get any worse, but this didn't stop me from worrying. The back of my neck tightened as we headed for the high mountain pass. The dread funk that had taken hold of my mind at the cabin had dug deep into my uneasy thoughts. I couldn't dodge the sensation that my future wasn't going to get any better before it got a lot worse. I like to think I control my destiny, but as the sun set, I sensed this was an illusion. It was becoming increasingly apparent I had almost no control. The sad series of disturbing events that were currently defining my life was continuing at a steady pace. At any moment, I feared some new incident could change everything... And as if to verify my foreboding, snow began to come down harder. So far, my Audi was performing well in four-wheel drive. The pickup truck that had followed us out of town was slowly disappearing in my mirrors. When the road began to curve steeply up through the mountains, I had to slow down as snow swirled in clouds of white dust in my rearview mirror.

'You doing okay?' M asked tenderly.

'I'm fine, but I'll feel a lot better when we get through the pass. Why don't you put on some music? Look in the glove box. I think you'll find some CDs.'

M found an old Cat Stevens CD. The music helped unwind my taut nerves as my Audi weaved its way up the road.

Shadows form early in the mountains, long before the sun sets behind the high peaks. As snow began to accumulate on the road, driving became more difficult. Fortunately, the new snow was cold and dry. It wasn't too slippery. We were able to make steady progress. High rock walls defined the road on one side of the mountain with guard rails on the other side as mountain views dissolved into endless shades of muted grey.

Safety has become my main concern now. I told myself to slow down. I was driving faster than I should have because I wanted to get through the pass before daylight completely disappeared. Fortunately, traffic was sparse, and few locals were on the road. They knew better than to drive this road in bad weather.

Just make steady progress, I told myself. Once we are through the pass, the road would go downhill, leveling out in a valley. Driving the remaining miles to Copper should be easy. Even in bad weather we could to get through the valley. I just needed be patient now, make it through the pass safely and then down of the mountain.

M was quiet, kind of unusual for her. But then, I wasn't contributing to a conversation, concentrating on the road instead.

Snow started to come down heavier the higher we drove. I knew this might happen as we approached the pass. I had mentally prepared for the possibility. Westerly winds force humid air up the mountainside to where it is colder. The water vapor in the air condenses and turns into snow. In the half-light of evening, I was having trouble seeing the road ahead. Fortunately, traffic was almost nonexistent and I used an old method of driving mountain roads I had learned in the European Alps. I cut every corner using both lanes, flashing my lights and honking my horn around the corners blinded by high rock walls. Hopefully, oncoming cars would hear my horn and honk back, letting me know they were coming in time for me to get out of their way. It was a gamble, but better than sliding off a curving road. If we continued at this pace for maybe a half hour, I estimated we could still get through the pass before night fell.

Light and fluffy, the snow began to accumulate, only about three inches so far. Traction was not yet a problem, but seeing the road was. I had to slow, I didn't have a choice, even though I knew this would decrease our chances of getting through the pass before dark. Resigning myself to this new reality, I slowed even more.

It was better to be safe.

M rubbed my neck as the day faded into night. At times, the road briefly disappeared in a shower of white flakes reflecting in my headlights. No horizon, no sky, no road, only a vast white space where the road was defined by dimly seen guardrails or rock walls on the edges in my headlights. I plowed blindly on at a slow pace for what seemed like forever, with the road alternately appearing and disappearing in intermittent snow squalls. I estimated that the pass must be closed now. And true to form, the road leveled, indicating we had arrived at the pass.

I breathed a sigh of relief.

A pair of bright red taillights appeared out of the dark on the side of the road, looking like a two-eyed ghost evolving out of a dusty gloom of white snow. The vehicle appeared to be stationary, not moving, with brake lights on as we approached. I assumed someone had stopped by the side of the road, stuck in the cold with a mechanical issue. I slowed to help as the taillights began to move onto the road. It was a pickup truck, and I was relieved it was mobile. I really didn't want to stop. Wanted to keep moving. I progressed slowly, hoping the driver saw my headlights in his rearview mirror and would wait for us to pass before completely pulling onto the road. As anticipated, the truck slowed and stopped, half on the road and half on the shoulder. I moved left to pass him when two headlights materialized out of the dark on the other side of the road, darting onto the road directly into my path.

'Look out!' M screamed.

Braking hard, the car began to slide. Gripping the steering wheel in anticipation of a collision, I took a chance, accelerating blindly into an empty, dark opening right of the oncoming headlights past the stationary pickup on my left, hoping I could get through the gap before being hit. It was possible a guardrail was blocking my path, but I kept going, hoping to avoid a collision. The headlights continued coming, cutting off my escape route. M screamed again. It was too late to stop. I was committed and had to keep going.

I don't think the other driver expected me to accelerate. Probably thought I would break. Instead of a direct collision, his miscalculation caused the front bumper of his truck to hit the rear quarter panel of my Audi, throwing it into a spin on the slippery surface. Out of the corner of my eye, I caught the sight of M's brilliant red hair flying in the lights of the truck as her head jerked sideways. Instinctively turning into the spin, fearing a guardrail might be close, hoping it could prevent us from falling down a cliff. No guardrail appeared, to my relief. The road was wide. We were at the turnoff area where we had stopped earlier in the day to view the valley. I had room to maneuver. I slowed, regained traction, and accelerated past another pair of bright headlights, which suddenly covered us in their glare. A shot sounded. The window behind my seat exploded in a million splinters of glass.

'Get down!' I yelled at M, jamming my foot on the accelerator.

Go hard now, my mind screamed. Got to get out of here! Go! GO!

Fighting for a four-wheel grip in the snow, I accelerated as the second truck hit us with a jarring, glancing side blow that didn't stop us. Another back window shattered from a bullet burrowing deep into the cloth ceiling.

Lights shining through the broken rear windows illumined a mask of frozen terror covering M's face. Survival instinct took over. Snow blinded my headlights. Grey shadowed rock walls slid past on one side of the road, glimpses of guardrails on the other side, using both lanes, hitting my horn repeatedly, bright lights flashing; I continued, hoping no cars were rounding the blind turns ahead. Taking chances, we flew like the wind down the mountain, caught in a frigid nightmare with a cold death waiting for us if I failed.

Go.

Got to go now.

Cold air rushed through broken windows, my hands shaking in terror. Keep going, have to keep going, seeing lights behind, too close, hearing shots. The lights occasionally disappeared behind mountain walls as we rounded a curve. Getting ahead of the shooters slowly, the thug's trucks couldn't stay up with us. My car was faster, but I couldn't lose control. Going off the road could lead to a crashing death.

Minutes, seconds, and time passed suspended in a nightmare that had no end. Each curve in the road was a potential disaster: endless twisting, sliding, and drifting across the roads. The next corner was another accident waiting to happen. Eventually, thankfully, it stopped snowing as we rushed down the eastern side of the mountain in a blinding panic. The road gradually became visible in my headlights, the pavement free of snow. Faster now, I could see clearly, and the curves were less severe. Finally, as we drove into the valley, the headlights behind us fell farther behind until they were finally gone. Only a black hole existed in my mirror where once bright lights of terror had blinded me.

I shivered in the cold mountain air as a vice-like grip on the steering wheel turned my hands white-knuckle blue. I glanced at M, hoping she was alive, not sitting beside me, dead in a pool of blood from a stray bullet.

'You okay?' I whispered, hearing my voice quiver in the cold.

'Yes, I'm fine,' she replied weakly.

'Do you see anything behind us?'

'No, it's dark.'

Eventually the snow stopped completely and the road flattened in the valley. It was simply cold and dark now. Going as fast as I dared, I slowed when we reached the comparative safety of the city of Golden, looking for a police station.

A sergeant at the desk took our report and helped me patch the broken windows of my Audi with duct tape and cardboard. He offered to escort us to Copper. I accepted gratefully. The Copper City Police were called. They agreed to put our apartment under surveillance for the night.

I thanked a sergeant when we arrived at our apartment and promised to have Tim call him in the morning with a detailed report on the shooting at the mine.

COPPER, MONTANA, FEBRUARY 12, WEDNESDAY, 9:10 A.M. JOHN

Our silver-sheathed, twin-engine jet gleamed brightly under a clear blue sky.

Lifting gracefully off a concrete runway, the ultra-expensive means of personal travel gained speed, quickly arching upwards to avoid an unpredictable mountain downdraft from causing it to crash.

I settled into a comfortable leather seat, enjoying the thrill of acceleration and grateful to be going home. But underneath my casual outward composure, an uneasy sense of doom still troubled my soul. I was safe for the moment, but the recent, repeated doses of sheer terror had taken their toll. The unwelcome dread funk that had entered my soul when driving through Copper had by now burrowed so deep into my gut that I could do nothing to dislodge the nasty critter from my brain, no matter how hard I tried.

Just how long would it be... I wondered before my enemies tracked me again and, next time, finished their deadly work. It was painfully obvious, even to me, an eternal optimist, that they were intent on doing me bodily harm. It didn't really matter where: in the mountains of Montana, at my apartment in Virginia, at my cottage in Michigan. The only thing that counted was that the odds were highly stacked against my survival. It was just a matter of time before they succeeded, and I was a dead dog.

I touched her hand, just touched it, softly held her hand. I did not press hard, did not hold it tightly. My grip was not confining. I didn't want her to feel confined, imprisoned by my cruel fate. I wanted her to feel free to withdraw her hand any time she wished and walk away from me at will. She did not need to stay.

But she did not pull away. She wove her warm fingers into my hand. And the truth was that she alone was making my life bearable. Her smile, her eyes, and simply having her by my side were more than I could comprehend.

But in an odd twist of fate, the events that had brought us closer, those moments of sheer terror that had bonded us, seemed equally determined to drive us apart. And even though we had visited the consequences of our relationship before, talked about it, discussed it, and dismissed any solutions... I felt we needed to talk again. Because circumstances were different now... Worse... Escalated to a level that could not be ignored. Bullets meant for me last night could have had her number on them instead.

Why now, God? I asked, wearily rubbing my eyes, trying to make sense of it all. Why had I found her at this time in my life? Why not at another time, a time when my life was good, when we could have been free to smile together without constant fear of dying?

I wondered if she sensed my gloom, my dread funk. Did she know what I was thinking?

A strained expression covered her face at a silent breakfast before our flight. She was trying to act cheerful, upbeat. She smiled when I looked at her. But when she didn't think I was paying attention, her face changed, her eyelids dropped, and her lips tightened like she was summoning some internal strength from deep inside, some power to help her press on.

I saw the look, and it scared me.

Last night, during our daring drive down the mountain in reckless abandon, too scared to be careful; every curve, every guard rail, every minute wondering if we were going to die, fall down a mountain; fear had been in her eyes. Sure, we made it and she had braved it all. She was a remarkable woman. But it could have gone differently. She had to know this. Her current existence was nothing like the lighthearted reprieve from the tedium of government work she had envisioned when she took a job at my office.

The Rocky Mountains gradually disappeared in the distance as I looked out the window of the plane, and the Great Plains began to stretch out below in a thousand squares of land divided by man-made lines broken only by naturally flowing rivers. Soon, we would be in Charlottesville. What then?

By all odds, I should be dead. And what had I really accomplished on my trip besides miraculously managing to stay alive? Sure, I saved a couple of pieces of precious equipment. But it was not really a great victory compared to the devastation it had caused to what remained of my mental health. I felt complexly helpless as dour thoughts continued to reel slowly through my weakened brain like a lumbering, rumbling freight train.

Silently, mindfully, I visited my mantra to think about something else. It was a Psalm of David I had memorized.

> *'My heart is not proud.*
> *My eyes are not haughty.*
> *I have not concerned myself with matters too great for me.*
> *I have stilled and quieted my soul.*
> *I have stilled and quieted my soul.*
> *I have stilled and quieted my soul.'*

My phone rang.

M picked it up. 'Yes, he's here... yes.'

I waved no, vigorously shaking my head.

'It's Jason,' she apologized. 'He says it's important.'

'Nothing is that important. Tell him I'll talk to him when I'm in the office.'

'Sorry, Jason. No, he'll see you when... Yes, we're en route to Charlottesville. Yes... yes.' She put the phone down.

The whine of the jet's engines hummed uncomfortably in the background.

I saw no way out. It had to be done. 'We need to talk,' I started.

'Don't say it,' she replied sharply, eyeing me with suspicion.

'Say what?' I asked, surprised at her reaction.

'Say what I think you are going to say.'

'How do you know what I'm going to say?'

'I can see the look in your eyes.'

I was dumbstruck.

'How does it go?' she continued with an edge of sarcasm. 'You say my contract is up. Thanks, and have a good life. Something like that, right?'

This was not how I had anticipated our conversation would go, but I should have known better. Nothing was ever easy with her. She was always way ahead of me.

'I'm sorry,' I replied. 'Apparently, you already know what I'm going to say, so I'll just say it.'

'Don't.'

'I have to. I can't continue to put your life in danger, so I...'

'Nobody is asking you to. I'm doing this because I want to do it because I chose to.'

She was digging in her heels, and I couldn't help but admire her. But I also couldn't risk having something bad happen to her. Our relationship had to end. What happened last night was not the first incident, nor would it be the last. And the next time, she could be killed or badly injured.

'M, this isn't about you anymore,' I said as calmly as I could muster under the circumstances. 'It is not about me either. It is about what needs to be done. Not because I want to, but because it is right.'

'But, John, I can help!'

'M, don't you think I want your help? Don't you know I like having you with me? And you have helped more than you know... But think about what happened last night in the mountains. We almost died, and I saw the look of fear on your face. I know how scared you were. Because I was scared too... I simply can't continue to put you through experiences like that again.'

'No, John,' she pleaded as if she had not heard a word I said. 'You can't, you can't because I won't let you. Don't you know why?'

'Why?' I asked dumbly, knowing immediately I should not have asked. 'No, don't answer that question,' I whispered quickly, trying to cover my mistake.

'It doesn't matter whether I say it or not... because you already know the reason you can't do this.'

She was right. I didn't have to say another word. I knew where I stood. I had nowhere to hide. Our relationship had moved beyond that of a boss and his employee. It didn't matter if we used the 'love' word. We both knew it was true. But this additional bit of reality, love, only made matters worse in my mind. Made what I had to do more necessary. If I cared for this woman at all, I had to let her go. I had no choice.

'Okay, we don't need to say it. And I don't deny it's true,' I responded slowly, carefully.

'Then why, John? Why now?' Her eyes glistened.

'You know why.' I pressed her hands between mine. 'You anticipate everything. You know the reason.'

'To protect me, I suppose... But I don't want protection. I want to be with you. Don't you understand?'

'M, please try to understand. That just isn't possible now. I have a job to do, and it can't include you. I simply don't have the energy to worry about you and do my job at the same time.'

'Your company always comes first. Is that it?' she became angry.

I couldn't believe she was arguing with me about something which seemed so painfully obvious.

'Isn't that the way it always works with you, John?' she argued. 'Someone gets too close, and you run for your office, your safe harbor, your job.'

When I didn't reply, she continued now on a roll. 'So... My contract is up, right?'

'Yes.'

'I'm a lawyer. I know how this works. This is where I negotiate my severance, right?'

'Okay,' I replied warily, wondering if she was really giving in. 'How about I ....' I had prepared to offer her a generous settlement, but she quickly cut me off.

'Let's see. Is there extra pay for hazardous duty?' she argued.

'I guess.'

'And legal fees for my legal services?'

'Of course.'

'And a fee for lobbying my Washington CIA connection, right?'

'Okay, sure.'

'And let's not forget the sex. Sex certainly deserves extra pay, right?'

'M, please, let's not make this any worse...'

'No, on the contrary, let's call it what it is. I'm the whore, and you are the john!'

Heat was rising in her cheeks. I had to admit that she was gorgeous in her fury. Her statement shook the cabin of the jet plane. I wondered if the pilots were enjoying our conversation.

'Now we have everything straight. Right, JOHN?' she exclaimed.

'No, that's not the way it is, and you know it.'

'No, I don't know anything of the kind. It's just business, right John? With you, it's always just business?'

'M.'

At this point in our conversation, or should I say negotiations, she stood and moved to the rear of the plane, settling herself into another seat.

I followed her.

She turned and stared up at me, 'No more, John. No more talk. Send the severance contract. I'll sign it. Just make sure everything is covered. And I mean everything, including the sex, or I'll see you in court.'

'M.'

'No, John... no more.'

3:55 P.M. CHALOTTESVILLE, JOHN

Helen followed me into my office, waving a long list of telephone calls which she unceremoniously put on my desk. Just the important ones she noted.

I assumed this meant calls that required an immediate call-back, now, if not sooner. Others could wait.

Following close behind her, Jason waltzed in uninvited with the latest inventory numbers in his hand and a frown on his face, indicating nothing good. While I was reviewing these dismal figures with Jason, David called from Grand Haven. He told me the local fire department had contacted him sometime Tuesday with disturbing news. Seemed evidence of arson was found at my burned-out cottage. An explosion, in fact, several explosions, had caused the house to burn to the ground. Evidence was not conclusive, but fragments of something that appeared to be a small rocket were found among the debris. They wondered if this could be possible. The investigation was continuing, and they promised to call again when they had completed a thorough analysis. David was told the police had been alerted. Said it was regulations. He assumed the cops would be calling him soon. As my attorney, he wanted to know what he should tell them.

I told him I didn't know. I would have to get back to him later.

I knew my answer did not satisfy him, but he calmly refrained from commenting like the good lawyer he was.

I dutifully worked through Helen's list for what remained of my work day. It was difficult. But in a way, it was a relief from what was really on my mind. *She* was on my mind. By the time I was out of my office and into my apartment in the evening, every trace of Monica Sorenson was gone. The lady had simply packed and walked away.

Arny was whistling in my kitchen, making dinner while I changed into jeans. Most nights, I sit with him at the counter in my kitchen, making small talk while he prepares our meal. But that night, I poured a glass of wine and went into the living room to sit by myself, letting my thoughts wander.

'Dinner's ready!' Arny called from the kitchen. 'Get your ass in here before it gets cold.'

Living with Arny was a little like having a mother. Only difference was he had the mouth of a sailor.

'Why'd you do it, boss?' Arny wanted to know before I sat down.

'I assume you are referring to Monica.'

'Yeah, of course, I'm talking about Monica, you jackass. She wasn't too happy when she left. She was crying. I tried to talk to her and asked her why she was leaving, but she didn't want to talk. So maybe you would like to enlighten me.'

'I let her go because I like you better,' I said, hoping humor would make this conversation go away. I should have known better. Arny was seldom deterred from having a conversation he desired.

Looking me straight in the eye, 'Cut the crap boss,' he demanded. 'She was great, and it's obvious she loves you, man. Are you blind?'

'Enough Arny, I'm not in the mood.'

'Why ya doin' this?' Arny was undeterred. 'Don't you know what life is? Life is a girl like Monica.'

'What, marriage and babies? Is that what you think I should do? It certainly wasn't the path you took,' I replied, my words immediately caught in my throat.

He stared at me with angry eyes. I had touched on a nerve I shouldn't have. His life held a painful wound. It was one he didn't show very often, but it was real. He covered it up most of the time with bandages made of humor. But his wounds were deep, and they still festered. Wounds inflicted by society against a good man who was born with an intelligent mind and highly athletic body; only to be weighed down by the dark color of his skin.

'John, I never had the chance to have what you can have. Don't you ever be confused about that? If I coulda, I woulda done it all differently,' he said without humor.

'Okay, okay, I get it.'

'No, you don't. Because if you did, she would still be here, not crying her eyes out in her apartment.'

'Arny, damn it! Let me put this to you in simple terms so even your pea brain gets it.' Now, it was my turn to be angry. 'Someone is trying to kill me, and as long as she is around me, she has a good chance of being killed. So now, do you understand? I don't want her dead because of me. I had to send her away to keep her safe. I didn't have a choice!'

I picked up the food he had placed on my plate while we argued and walked out of the kitchen and into the dining room. Somehow, I managed to force the food down my throat in a haze of anguished silence as the half shadows of the evening fell over the room and images of Monica danced through my head in a bizarre mental whirlwind.

By the time I finished eating, Arny had cleaned the kitchen and was gone to his apartment for the night. I picked up my dishes to return them to the kitchen... hesitating for a second... sensing M's perfume lingering in the empty room.

I smiled, but only for a second.

BANGKOK, THAILAND, FRIDAY, FEBRUARY 14, 11:05 A.M. LUANG

The old patriarch read the memo from his nephew one more time.

The American was still alive. The man must be very resourceful, he thought to himself. In a way, the old man admired the American. He wished he could have a chance to talk with him. Maybe together, they could find a solution to the problems his nephew was pursuing. But this was only an idle thought, nothing more than the product of a useless old mind seeking glory where it could not be had. The old man knew his time was over. He could daydream now, speculate about what he might do under the same circumstances, but nothing more.

Rereading the memo, he let his mind wander to times and places that existed somewhere between the past and the present. Not as it was now, but as he wished it to be. Times when he had power and prestige, when men came to him for advice. Now, he was only a useless old man sitting alone on a couch in the corner of his room.

Outside a window was a garden filled with beautiful flowers. He loved his garden. He worked in it often when he had energy. It was his joy now. But the wonder of his garden could not replace his longing to be useful.

He folded the memo and returned it to the envelope it came in.

Aimlessly, he went outside, seeking peace in his garden.

CHARLOTTESVILLE, FEBRUARY 20, THURSDAY, 9:40 A.M. JOHN

My bed was empty in the morning.

No red hair casually flowing over a lovely face lying on a pillow beside me. No sly smile to greet me when I opened my eyes. No warm, soft body to embrace. Nothing beautiful in my life to ease my rebirth into a new day. Only the shadows of uneasy dreams and a vacant space where she used to sleep.

I told myself it was no big deal. My life had simply returned to what it was before I met her. I could get used to that again—or so I thought. But my life wasn't the same as before, and I didn't like it. I didn't like being without her.

Get up and go to work, I told myself.

This was the same command I had been giving to myself every morning for the last few days. It was what I did to stop thinking about her. In order to accomplish my goal, I returned to the high-intensity work routine I had known in the past. I immersed myself in my job, all hours of the day, all days in the week. The phone would ring. I would answer it. E-mails needed to be written. I wrote them. Reports needed to be read. I read them, read them in detail. I did anything and everything with one goal in mind: trying to take my mind off her... her smile.

Jason daily presented his latest projections. Sales were beginning to increase, and inventories were slowly improving. Life once again began to assume its normal anxious existence. At the end of each day, I collapsed in bed, hopefully too exhausted to wonder why I was alone.

This Thursday was like every other day, like all the recent days that had preceded it. Except it was not the same. I had a problem I could not solve that day: her. I could not get her out of my mind. I had tried everything I could think of, but nothing was working, not today.

I began to wonder if focusing my thoughts on the man I still considered responsible for my problems. I wondered if perhaps this would help me stop thinking about her. Even though I had no evidence he was involved, I decided to focus on Phillip. Mostly because I desperately wanted to put a face on the problems of my company. And with no other face available, I decided to make his face the face of my enemy. Even though I knew this was irrational. I did it anyway. I guess because it made my unimaginable situation feel almost real.

'John,' my intercom loudly put an immediate end to my irrational thoughts, forcing me to return to reality. 'Lin is on the line,' Helen barked.

'Of course, Helen put him through.'

'I got a call from one of our board members,' Lin began. 'He told me Arthur came to see him. Said he is not the only board member Arthur has seen. Arthur has been traveling, meeting with board members.'

'He has?' I commented.

'Yes, I did some checking,' Lin continued in his usual unemotional manner. 'I called a few other board members, and they confirmed what he said. They admitted to meeting with Arthur. Then I called Arthur's office. He wasn't in. His secretary said he was out. I asked her where he was and when would he return. She said she didn't know. He was out of the country, traveling.'

'So, it's true?'

'Yes, I thought you would want to know.'

'Thanks. I guess. What exactly is he doing at these meetings?' I asked, even though I could easily guess what he was up to.

'He's shoring up support for the next board meeting, having face-to-face meetings with members who will talk to him.'

'What's he telling them?'

'You have lost control of the company.'

'So, I should step down.'

'Right. He's saying it's time for new leadership, and he's presenting himself as the man for the job. Claims he can put the company back on track.'

'What should I do?' I sighed, feeling defeated. 'Do I get on a plane?'

'You can if you want, John.'

'Would it do any good, Lin?'

Silence answered my question, accompanied by a sinking feeling in my gut. I knew the answer, just needed it confirmed.

'Lin?'

'Yes John?'

'Would it do any good?'

'No, I don't think so. I'm sorry.' Lin spoke quietly.

'Am I going to lose when the board is convened?'

'You are, John. I have talked to enough members to know. They agreed to put off the decision until the next meeting out of respect for you. Most didn't think it was fair to do it by teleconference. They want a chance to thank you in person for your accomplishments. But they will vote with Arthur and Bob.'

'I see.'

'I'm sorry, John.'

'Don't be, Lin. It's not your fault. I have obviously failed.'

'It's not you, John. It's the circumstances.'

'That's kind of you to say, but I know better.'

'John...'

'It's okay, Lin. These things happen. Let's move on. Have you uncovered any evidence that Arthur is involved with the people who are trying to destroy us?'

'I have no evidence.' Lin said without emotion. 'I think he simply wants your job.'

'But isn't his negativity undermining our company as much as anything else? Especially now when we should be working together.'

'I agree with you, John. You know I do. But his behavior can be interpreted two ways. One way, he is greedy for power. The other, he is concerned about you and the company.'

'Concerned about me?'

'It can be interpreted as your job is more than you are capable of handling. You take it too personally. You need relief. You have done enough for the company. Arthur is the right person to take control now.'

'That's ridiculous.'

FEBRUARY 24, MONDAY, 3:45 P.M. JOHN

I was trying. I really was.

I called and talked to clients, heads of mining companies, board members, and anyone and everyone who would talk to me. But the conversations felt fake like I was talking to a voice behind a dusty window. I could hear the person on the other end of the phone line, but something stilted seemed to be standing between us, something that held us back, something that wouldn't allow our conversations to cross a line that made real communication possible.

I seldom saw Arny.

Mostly because I never returned to my apartment until late at night, which was okay with me. I didn't want to talk to him. A repeat of our last conversation, the one about Monica. I didn't need to hear that again, not from him. And the only way to avoid the subject was to avoid him. Because I knew Arny, and I knew he wouldn't stop beating me up about her whenever he was given the opportunity.

Arny put cold dinners in my fridge for me. He had seen the pattern before. He knew the drill. I worked, I slept. I almost never left my office. I did it because I had work to do. Or so I rationalized. But it was a lie. I knew there was another reason. The late hours helped me avoid a lonely apartment and an empty bed. I only went to my apartment to eat and sleep. Hoping to be too exhausted to think about anything else.

But as hard as I tried, it wasn't working. She was always on my mind. In the middle of the day, I would visualize her looking at me with a question on her beautiful lips as she sat at the conference table across from me in my office with papers piled high. Or I would see her smile in my mind... see a mental picture of her red hair blowing in the breeze when we took a walk. I could not stop thinking about her.

My other problem was my job.

Life as I knew it was about to change. Even though I had been avoiding any thought of the looming, unwelcome alteration in my lifestyle, the company board meeting was fast approaching. And it could change everything. Without something new to give to the board members, I was a dead duck, kicked out, forced to resign, cannon fodder for my old buddy Arthur and his henchman, Bob.

Regardless, I prepared for the meeting. Even though Lin told me I didn't stand a chance of retaining my job, I wasn't willing to simply give in, not just yet. I wasn't going down without a fight.

I decided to call Bob... just because he, more than anyone else, made me mad.

I didn't bother calling Arthur. I didn't trust him.

Bob was a different matter. I still thought of Bob as a friend, and I was having a hard time stomaching his betrayal. The idea of Arthur having Bob in his hip pocket pissed me off. I knew it was probably futile, but I decided to confront Bob, force him to tell me to my face he wouldn't help me, maybe even get him to change his mind.

From experience, I knew my former friend Bob was a man who lived by a rigid schedule, something he learned during his military service. He always arrived at work at the same time, early in the morning, and left work early midafternoon to beat rush hour traffic out of Manhattan. So, because he had made me mad, I decided to call him a few minutes before he normally left his office.

'Bob, how are sales?' I began, assuming a casual tone, hoping to string out our conversation, forcing him to delay his rigid military schedule.

'We are moving gemstones to customers as fast as we can,' he replied hurriedly, obviously in a rush. 'You know, as soon as the stones arrive in New York from Sri Lanka, they are out the door to our customers. It is all going according to schedule.'

I knew all this. I had established the strict distribution schedules he was using to deal with an artificially low inventory. Our gemstones never remained in one place for more than twenty-four hours. The first step was to run as many stones as possible through our research lab in Charlottesville. The furnaces were working on a twenty-four-hour schedule. As soon as the stones were color-enhanced in our lab, they were air-lifted to Sri Lanka, where the gems were cut and polished. After being sorted by computer to match the jewelry manufacturer's needs, most of the sapphires were sent directly to our clients. The remaining stones were shipped to the Distribution Houses to meet emergency demands.

'Are you hearing complaints from your clients?' I asked.

'Oh, they grumble a bit, but nothing out of the ordinary. Even when we had more gems than they could buy, they always found something to complain about.'

'Do you know if your customers have started buying from our competition?'

'No, not to my knowledge. They seem to be holding with us.'

'Good. By the way, the new furnaces are on a plane to Australia. They should be operational within a week... at least some of them.' I strung out our conversation.

'That's good news. Can I tell my clients?'

'You can, but perhaps you should say it will be a couple of weeks before the lab is completely operational. This will buy us time in case we run into unforeseen problems during installation.'

'Okay, good. Thanks. I have to go.' Bob attempted to close our conversation.

'Bob, can I ask you for a favor.' I pressed him, ignoring his growing need to get off his phone and into his car.

'Uh, sure, anything, John.'

'Can I count on your support at our board meeting?'

'John...'

'No, wait, let me finish before you answer,' I interrupted him. 'I know what you are going to say, but before you do, I want you to think about how long we have been friends. Then, I want you to consider what we've accomplished together. I know if you do...'

'John, stop. You know I can't...'

'Bob, I'm not asking for your answer now. I am only asking you to take some time to think about it.' I pressed him. 'Shouldn't friendship and loyalty count for something?'

'John, this is best for you too.'

'Why don't you let me decide what is best for me!' I replied, instantly hearing Monica's words echoing ironically in my mind.

'I don't think...' he began to say.

'John, call on line one.' Helen interrupted me on the intercom, her distinctively penetrating voice making it impossible to hear what Bob was saying.

'Bob, hold on a minute,' I said. 'Helen is talking to me on my intercom.'

In a way I was grateful for her interruption. I had made my point to Bob. Nothing more could be accomplished by extending our conversation. Besides, Helen never interrupted me when I was on my phone unless it was an emergency.

'What is it, Helen?' I asked.

'It's Monica, John. She says it's important.'

My pulse instantly jumped at the mention of her name.

'Bob, I have another call,' I apologized. 'I need to take it. Let's talk later.'

'Oh... all right, but ...' he started to say.

'We'll talk later.' I cut him off. 'In the meantime, please think about what I said.' clicking off before he could utter another word.

I stared at the blinking green light on my phone console... a call from Monica... The solitary light was temporarily paralyzing. I desperately needed to switch gears, but I was having difficulty knowing how to do that. And why was she calling, anyway? Why now? Why when I wasn't prepared?

The light continued to blink, and I had to...

'Hi Monica,' I instinctively answered after a deep breath.

'John, how are you?'

'I'm fine.'

'John, please listen to what I have to say before you reply. And please... don't try to read anything more into this other than what I tell you.' Her voice sounded sincere yet cautious, like a lawyer making a prepared statement to a judge.

'Okay,' I responded weakly, wondering where this conversation was headed.

'After you fired me, I went to Washington.'

'I didn't fire you, M. What I did was for your protection.'

'Whatever, John, just please listen to me and then... Well, just listen. I didn't call to argue with you.'

'Okay.'

'I've been working with Charlie,' she announced.

'You couldn't leave it alone, could you?' The mention of Charlie's name set me off.

'John, are you going to listen to me or ...'

'Okay, okay.' I was trying to maintain my composure, I really was, but I was angry at her. I had asked her to leave because I wanted her safe. I had directed my security company to keep an eye on her apartment in Charlottesville. They had reported back. Said she was gone. This didn't make me happy. It meant she was somewhere out there in the big bad world, unprotected. Adding to this unhappy circumstance was the fact her severance contract had been returned unopened, unsigned. The weekly checks mailed to her were not cashed and returned unendorsed. I had tried to ignore all this because there was nothing I could do about it. She was an intelligent, independent woman. I couldn't control her. But still, it bothered me. Okay, so now I knew she was safe, and I was glad. But I didn't like the fact she had been talking to Charlie.

'I have something to tell you,' she hesitated. 'Are you willing to listen to me, because if...'

'I'm listening.'

Silence.

'I said, I'm listening. What is it you want to tell me?'

After another moment of silence, she began, 'Charlie has been tracking Phillip. He did as a favor to me.'

'Does he know where Phillip is?'

'Yes, just listen, please?'

I said nothing.

She continued, 'Phillip has not returned to Michigan since you went to see him. Charlie thinks maybe someone told him the police were looking into his involvement in the bombing of your cottage. So he got out of town before they could bring him in.'

'Really?'

'Yes, and it's true. The CIA asked the local cops to check him out. I assume you can guess why.'

'Because Charlie asked them?'

'Yes. So far, the investigation has uncovered nothing. No charges have been filed,' she continued. 'But it appears he knows he's a suspect. Apparently, he has a buddy in the local police department. Anyway, as I said, we think he has been traveling to avoid being picked up and questioned. He has been able to move around undetected because he has more than one passport. The CIA discovered someone at the State Department gave him a diplomatic passport under an assumed name years ago and he's been using this passport to stay under the radar screen.'

'I remember him telling me he had connections. Some favors he did for the State Department when he was young. I never knew whether to believe him or not.'

'That makes sense. Anyway, once Charlie discovered how Phillip was moving around, it was easy to track him. Every time his bogus passport was checked, his location was entered into the system.'

'Where is Phillip now?'

'He's on a plane to New York from Thailand. He has been living in Bangkok.'

'Do you know what he was doing there?'

'Some conference involving gemstones,' she replied. 'Charlie doesn't know specifics. Only that it was in Bangkok, and Phillip attended.

'I see.'

'But here's the interesting part. CIA sources in Bangkok report a rumor is circulating in the city. People are claiming the sapphire business will soon return to Thailand.'

A cold chill invaded my spine. Everything I had hoped to avoid was becoming true. Even though it felt good to know Vidu's suspicions were confirmed. The prospect of a fight with the Thai was something I had hoped to avoid.

'What's behind the rumors?' I asked, fearing her answer.

'We don't know.'

My mind briefly took a moment to consider what M was telling me. New York... Phillip was en route to New York... And then something Lin mentioned occurred to me... something about Arthur. Wasn't he also en route to New York City, headed to the city ahead of our board meeting? Lin said he didn't know why Arthur was coming early.

I began to wonder if a connection between Phillip and Arthur was possible, like a reason for their both being in New York at the same time.

'John.'

'Yes, Monica.'

'The information I'm telling you is confidential,' she interrupted my thoughts. 'Charlie told me I could tell you, but only if you agreed to keep it to yourself.'

'Okay.'

'Don't make me look bad, John. You can't tell anyone.'

'I promise.'

'And John.'

'Yes.'

'I'm not asking for anything from you. It's just that...well, you remember I once told you I like to finish what I start.'

I didn't reply, and she was temporarily silent.

'M.'

'Yes?'

'Can we meet someplace?' the words escaped my mouth before my brain could restrain the impulse.

She didn't answer immediately.

'M, I think we need to ...'

'I'll call you again, John,' she interrupted. 'If Charlie discovers anything new, I will pass it on.'

'Okay... but,'

'Goodbye, John,' her words sounding coldly final.

My phone went dead in my hand. The caller on the other end of the line was gone. I held the impersonal instrument of communication for a moment, hoping perhaps for something more before finally giving in to its passive inhospitality.

Her call created so many unanswered questions I didn't know where to begin. The clock on my desk read after five in the afternoon. Work was piled high on my desk. I had planned to put in several more hours at my office before going to my apartment. The work seemed so unnecessary now, completely irrelevant. She had called, and everything was different. I now lived in an alternate universe.

Buzzing Helen, I asked her to hold my calls.

As I sat at my desk, my computer continued to blink fresh digital data regardless of its importance. Finally, I stood up and went over to the bar on my office wall and poured a whiskey, taking a deep sip, then another before returning to my desk.

Pressing my intercom, I called Jason.

'Get me a helicopter to New York. Today, I want to go today... Yes, I know it's late.' I said, going over details in my head as I talked to him. 'Then call the Club and reserve me a room for the next few nights. Tell them I will be arriving late today... No, make it for a week... or maybe two weeks.'

'Just get me a room.'

NEW YORK, FEBRUARY 25, TUESDAY, 7:15 A.M. JOHN

Breakfast at the Club is a ritual like everything else.

Suit coat and tie are required. Personally, I detest dressing formally just to eat, especially for breakfast. But rules are rules, and traditions are traditions. Besides, some comfort can be found in tradition. After all, how bad can it be? It had been like this for a long time.

After dressing in the required attire, I wandered done a hall to an elevator from my room.

The Club's dining was on the second floor. The place was nearly empty when I arrived. Apparently, the other guests of the Club were living a more leisurely lifestyle. An empty table next to a window had a view across Madison Avenue to Central Park. It seemed a good choice. Green trees had a calming effect, better than staring at cold, impersonal architecture.

To order at the Club, you don't ask for a waiter. Not because waiters aren't available; they are. Plenty of starched white-coated mannequins are always standing around. No, instead, you write your selections on a slip of paper. Then, place the paper on the corner of your table and wait patiently for a prompt waiter to take it to the kitchen.

While I waited for breakfast, I absentmindedly glanced through a complimentary copy of the New York Times, more or less forgetting everything I read. My mind was occupied with my problems, such as being out in the real world again, exposed to ugly possibilities such as a quick death. No bodyguards had accompanied me. In my haste to get to New York quickly, I had shoved prudence aside and decided it was more important to be free and go where I wished to go without bothering to wait for a bodyguard. But now, I wasn't so sure this was a very good decision. However, as apprehensive as I felt, I was still glad I came. I was tired of waiting. I sensed my problems would be resolved soon, one way or the other.

Food came: eggs, toast, and jam. I was in a hurry and ate my breakfast quickly, anxious to escape the stuffy atmosphere of the Club.

Most of my visits to New York in the past had been highly orchestrated affairs evidenced by frantic, tightly wound schedules, one meeting after another. Today was different. I had no agenda. Didn't have to meet with anyone, didn't have to go anywhere. Still, transportation is required in the Big Apple even when you aren't sure where you want to go; you just need to get out. To navigate the city, I normally use a private car with a driver. It's much cleaner and less stressful than a taxi.

I'm a good tipper. I assume that's why one of my regular drivers, name is Mike, gave me his card with his cell phone number and told me to call him whenever I was in town. I'm not sure the company he worked for embraced his suggestion, but this is New York, and entrepreneurship is a norm for the Big Apple.

The truth is, I like Mike. So, I didn't mind. Our arrangement suits me fine because I have times when I need a car in a hurry, like that morning. I dug Mike's card out of my billfold while returning to my room to retrieve my coat and called Mike. He was waiting at the curb outside the club a few minutes later when I walked past a wrought-iron gate to the sidewalk. How he accomplished this feat, arriving this fast, was anyone's guess. But then Mike had a talent for efficiency. He could navigate New York traffic, which stymied most other drivers. He drove a big, dark blue Buick Park Avenue, which he kept immaculately clean. It looked like the other chauffeured cars didn't attract anyone's attention, blending into city traffic.

'Where to, boss?' he asked in a heavy New York accent as soon as I sat down in the rear seat.

'Hey, Mike. Good to see you again. Thanks for coming on such short notice.'

Mike was a big, muscular Italian with a round face, black curly hair, and broad shoulders.

'It's nut'in boss,' he said sheepishly. 'I told you I would take care of you. Just got to call.'

'Can you drive around for a while, Mike? I need time to think,' I said. 'And keep an eye on your rear-view mirror, please. I don't want to be tailed.'

'Right,' he replied without batting an eye.

Gotta love New York, I thought. Nobody questions your motives.

Morning rush-hour traffic was the usual stop: go half a block, stop again, wait, horns honking, waiting. Cabbies screamed at each other, tires squealed, and cops yelled. I tried to shut it out. It wasn't too bad if you weren't in a hurry. But this was New York, and I was probably the only person on this island who was *not* in a hurry.

'Did ya see that guy?' Mike asked, pointing to a yellow taxi that had just banged into the side of another cab.

I didn't see the accident. I just heard a crunch of metal. The two cabbies involved in this minor fender-bender were quickly out of their cars, yelling at each other and pointing at the damage. Stalled cabs behind were honking and bellowing at them to move. The participants in the accident ignored their horns while shouting at each other as if they were the only people on the road. After they had worked off a required amount of New York steam, they returned to their cabs and left the scene.

'That's it?' I asked. 'No accident report?'

'Could take an hour,' Mike explained. 'Time is money. If the cabs aren't too badly damaged, they forget about it. If you're going to drive in New York, you need to drive a car which can hit and be hit.'

'Okay,' I replied, casually checking out a pretty woman striding the sidewalk with a runway flair, dressed to the hilt, with long legs, high heels, and flowing hair.

'You doin' okay?' Mike asked, peering at me in his rear-view mirror after we had driven for about a half hour. He had never driven me before when I wasn't in a hurry to go somewhere.

Usually, we talked, mostly because Mike liked to talk and wouldn't shut up if you gave him an opening. It could be annoying at times, listening to Mike. But I liked him, and the truth was, he had taught me a lot about New York. This morning was different. I needed silence to think.

'I'm okay, Mike. Thanks for asking, only a little preoccupied.'

'No problem, boss.'

'Why don't you find a good cafe? I could use some coffee,' I suggested.

'I know just the place.'

His big Buick immediately darted across two lanes of solid traffic like a Magic Johnson pass on a basketball court.

8:55 A.M.

Mike dropped me at a corner.

'Keep your cell phone handy. I'll call you when I need you again,' I instructed him.

He smiled when I handed him several hundred-dollar bills.

Chrome-bordered countertops and pink vinyl stools greeted me inside a 50's style diner. Black and white square tiles covered the floor. With harshly contrasting colors, mirrors, and bright lights, the restaurant was hard on my eyes, but the view outside was great. A table by a window offered a show of lovely ladies strolling the sidewalk in their high-heeled, fashion finery.

'Can I get you something?' asked a cute waitress dressed in one of those ridiculous-looking, doll-like uniforms waitresses wear in restaurants like this. It was pastel blue with a short skirt covered with a little white apron. Her long black hair had been pulled back in a ponytail. She had big bright eyes and thick red lipstick and when she smiled, I was in love again.

'Coffee and a pecan roll,' I answered after a quick glance at a menu.

I thought about Charlie as I sipped some coffee, wondering if I could convince him Thailand was the source of our problems. I assumed he would probably think my idea was ludicrous. I understood. I had no real evidence that would link the Thai to my company's problems except Lin's observations and a statement from a dead man. Not enough to make a case, not nearly enough to ask the CIA to investigate highly connected citizens of a foreign country.

The waitress brought my roll with a smile.

'Thanks,' I said and looked away.

New Yorkers hurried past my window in an anonymous stream as I sipped coffee, allowing my thoughts to wander to my other pressing problem, M. I knew that firing her was the right thing to do. I didn't want her in danger. Yet, it felt wrong somehow. And what had she done in return? She had not gone away as I asked, someplace safe. No, instead, she stayed involved even though I did not want her involved. But that was her decision, not mine. I couldn't control her. Still, her involvement didn't make it easier for me.

Even though I probably should have been grateful. She was trying to help me, wasn't she?

Questions, questions, nothing made sense.

A woman passed my window, a tall female with red hair blowing in the wind, walking upright with purpose, who looked like Monica. The woman turned as if she felt me staring. She was not Monica. I was disappointed and quickly looked away.

After finishing my coffee and a delicious pecan roll, I left money on the table to cover my bill, including a generous tip for my pretty waitress. Deciding to take a walk, I was immediately swept up in step with the Manhattan crowd as soon as I stepped outside the restaurant. I didn't mind, simply fell in line, just another anonymous face in a mass of ambivalent humanity. A kind of group psychology took over our existence, masking uncertainty, everyone walking in tandem, no one asking questions. I blended in. Everything seemed fine.

A small corner office located in our New York Distribution House had been previously set aside for my personal use. Whenever I was in New York, I could go there to work between meetings. It occurred to me I should go to this office now, make some phone calls, and check off a few items on my mental agenda. The office was only a few blocks away.

Perhaps when I was finished, if I was in the mood, I might continue the conversation I had begun with Bob on the phone yesterday, finish what I had started, this time face to face. I wondered how he would react.

My cell phone vibrated.

'Yes,' I answered, continuing to walk.

'John,' she said, and I knew it was her.

'Yes, Monica.'

'Look, Charlie and I are in New York. We want to talk to you.'

My first reaction was to be annoyed. No one was supposed to know where I was. I had given explicit instructions to Jason before I left the office to tell no one.

'How do you know I'm in New York?' I demanded.

She didn't answer immediately. 'Don't get upset,' she finally replied. 'Helen told me, but not until I convinced her I was who I said I was.'

'How did you convince her?'

'I told her things I know about you.'

'What did you tell her?' I asked in exasperation.

'John!!!'

'Okay, okay, I guess it doesn't matter... How about lunch at the Club? I'll make a reservation.'

At first, she was reluctant to take Charlie to the Club. The grand old establishment of upper-crust snobbery was not on her list of desired options. I couldn't blame her. The place could be a bit much, especially for a first-timer like Charlie. Not exactly his cup of tea. But it was convenient, and it was safe. She suggested some alternatives.

As we talked, I felt like I was listening to our conversation as an observer. Like it was too intense, too complex to experience in real life. An out of body experience, as if I was listening to myself enjoy hearing her voice. I found myself desperately wanting to hold her in my arms.

After a brief discussion, I decided lunch at the Club was the best option despite her objections. No other restaurant offered as much privacy or security. We set a time and said goodbye.

After my phone went dead in my hand, I stood stationary for a moment on a sidewalk as people walked around me. I ignored them. Talking to her again had been frustrating. It was bad enough thinking about her.

It was impossible to listen to her voice without being able to see and touch her.

9:40 A.M. JOHN

I breezed through the lobby of the New York distribution house and walked right past a cute blonde sitting at the receptionist's desk.

When she saw me, she opened her mouth to speak, then stopped. Her usual smile quickly disappeared, uncharacteristically absent. Did she, I wondered, along with everyone else in this place, already assume I was history, fired in their minds, no longer CEO of the parent company? So why smile at him? What is this deadbeat doing here? Was this what she was thinking, or was I just being paranoid? I didn't know, and I wasn't sure it mattered.

The shortest route to my corner office was down a hall past a door to Bob's office. I could have avoided him if I had gone around a long way, but I chose not to.

'Hey, Bob.' I waved when I passed his office. His head bobbed up, and a surprised look returned my brief greeting.

My corner office was as I had left it, cleaned but otherwise undisturbed. No one had moved in and taken over, not yet. I picked up a phone, deciding to call Helen in Charlottesville, I thought I might give her some grief for talking to Monica.

Bob arrived unannounced. 'John, I didn't think you...' he started to say. 'I mean, I didn't expect to see you here this morning.'

'You mean you didn't think I had the balls to come here.' I replied, putting an immediate end to his nonsense.

'No, I mean that....'

I cut him off. 'If you don't want me here, Bob, just say so. I'll leave. Otherwise, I have work to do.'

'Of course, you can use the office. This is your office until...'

'Until you throw me out next week at the board meeting,' I finished his sentence.

'John, that's not the way it is.'

'That's exactly how it is, Bob.'

He said nothing, temporarily out of words, which was a rarity for him. The man usually had something to say about everything, regardless of whether it was relevant or not.

I glared at him triumphantly. 'Bob, I have work to do,' I repeated. 'So, unless you are planning to listen in on my telephone conversations, please excuse yourself.'

'Oh.'

'And Bob, shut the door, please.'

He exited slowly, his expression blank. I smiled in satisfaction even though I knew our exchange had accomplished nothing except to let off a little steam. Obviously, I was carrying some animosity and it had felt good to get it out. Unfortunately for Bob, he just happened to be in the line of fire. For that one brief moment, an illogical notion came over me. Maybe I could discover a way out of this mess. Maybe it was possible.

I called Helen, forgetting to chastise her about talking to Monica. We discussed several issues related to the board meeting. I didn't want the meeting to begin like it was no different than all the other meetings. Of course, this would not be true. My job depended on the outcome. I knew this, but I wanted everyone to arrive at the meeting like it was just another board meeting.

It was my hope, as futile as it seemed, that Arthur's arguments, his negative knee-jerk response to the bleak situation at the company, and his excuse for seeking my resignation; I hoped all might miraculously disappear by the time the board met.

When I finished with Helen, she put Jason on the line. He and I spent time on delivery schedules. We did this twice daily when I was in my office. We also discussed the company's quarterly payment to the Miner's Foundation. Historically, this payment was a percentage of our gross revenues. I decided not to lower the amount from the previous payment despite a dramatic decrease in our current revenue. I didn't want the loyalty of our miners to waver, not now. Without the support of the miners, without sapphires from twenty-plus countries across the world, we had nothing to sell, no business. Jason was hesitant. He was my numbers guy. He said we would have to tap our investment funds. Not enough cash in our bank account.

I authorized the use of the funds partly because I needed the votes of the miners who sat on my board. But this wasn't the only reason. It was simply the right action to take. Our foundation paid for schools, medical facilities, and housing. It improved the lives of our miners. I didn't want this good work to stop.

I wondered what Arthur would have done given the same situation. I think I knew. He would have lowered the payment.

Once off my phone, I debated going to Bob's office and telling him my latest news. Perhaps if he knew what was happening in Thailand or how Phillip had been over there, perhaps he could be convinced to rethink his loyalty. I still liked Bob. He simply disappointed me.

Instead, I turned to stare out my office window at a jagged New York skyline, lost in thought. So much was still unknown.

Lunch with M was next on my agenda, M and her smile. How should I deal with her? I didn't know. In less than an hour, I would once again be forced to live in her presence. How long had it been, two weeks? It seemed like forever.

I was tempted to chuck it all. Ask her at lunch if she would like to run away with me. Stop fighting, travel instead to an island far away for the rest of our lives, lollygag in warm ocean waters, and take long walks on a beach.

A knock on my office door interrupted my daydreams. Bob poked his head inside.

'John,' he said gingerly. 'May I interrupt you?'

'Sure, Bob, come in. Let's talk,' I replied, thinking this might be as good a time as any to include him in my confidence and tell him about Thailand.

'Arthur is here. We wondered if we could talk to you,' he said.

Any vision of converting Bob to my side immediately evaporated. Just the mention of Arthur's name soured my mood.

'Sure, I didn't know Arthur was in town,' I lied.

'And I didn't know you were coming either,' Bob countered. 'But since you're both here, perhaps we should talk.'

'Okay.'

I followed Bob down a hall to his large conference room, the one reserved for important meetings. I had been in this room before, but only a few times. The curly-haired rat, Arthur, was already there, casually sitting at the long conference table in the leather armchair at the head of the table usually reserved for the person responsible for running the meeting. How appropriate, I thought, already assuming the position of CEO. I walked to the side of the table, which had a view of the intense skyline of New York City. Large windows graced the opposite wall. Objects of human imagination could be seen rising into the sky, vast mechanical structures defying gravity. The view was spectacular. I took a moment to take in the view, thinking if I had to put up with these two buffoons, I might as well have something pleasant to look at.

'Hello, Arthur,' I greeted him with half a smile, resisting an urge to turn and walk away. However, leaving could be viewed as an act of weakness, a sign I had given up. And weakness was the last emotion I wanted to show these two bozos this morning. No, they had asked for this meeting. I would be gracious and listen. There is strength in grace.

Arthur motioned towards one of the old-fashioned formal leather armchairs that circled the conference table, the one next to him. 'Please sit down,' he said.

I complied.

Bob sat opposite me next to Arthur; three men were sitting at the end of a long conference table reserved for large gatherings, surrounded by empty chairs in a big room. It felt distant and awkward from the beginning, too formal and uncomfortable. I waited for someone to speak.

A moment of silence followed.

'Okay, I'm here. What do you two want to talk about?' I asked, deciding it would be wise to take control of the meeting. 'I have a luncheon appointment at twelve, so perhaps we could move this along.'

Arthur grimaced, obviously annoyed.

Bob made a stab at light conversation. 'Oh, who are you meeting?'

'I'm having lunch with Monica,' I stated with some satisfaction.

'John,' Arthur interrupted as if he had not heard a word. 'Bob and I have discussed this matter at length, and we would like to suggest that requiring a vote on your resignation at our board meeting is both unnecessary and unwise.'

'Why wouldn't I want the board to decide?' I replied.

'You don't have the votes, John,' Arthur continued in his stately snobbish British accent. 'You're going to lose the old boy. Why force the board to go through this rather unseemly exercise? Haven't we all endured enough grief lately? Surely, you can see the logic. It would be in the best interest of the company if we spared ourselves the drama and potentially negative consequences, you know, outward appearances and all.'

I didn't immediately respond, allowing them to have their say first.

'You have had three serious attempts on your life to date,' Bob stepped in. 'Certainly, you understand the logic in your stepping aside, if for no other reason than your personal safety.'

'I think I should be the judge of what is necessary for my personal safety,' I replied, once again hearing Monica's words echo through my mind.

'Bob and I have reviewed your severance package,' Arthur continued. 'I would like to go over the new proposal. I think once you have heard what...'

'Stop, Arthur, don't waste your breath. I'm not going to make any decisions until after the board meeting. If the board asks me to resign, I will do as they wish, but not before.'

'This is all so unnecessary,' Arthur replied. 'Can't you understand that?'

'I don't understand anything except you want my job,' I said, feeling a vile, bitter acid begin to churn in my stomach.

'That's totally unfair,' Arthur replied, his voice rising like it always did when he became excited.

'What's unfair about it?' I countered.

'Please, John,' Bob interrupted; our meeting was not progressing as he had hoped.

'No, Bob,' I stated emphatically. 'You do know Arthur is using you, don't you? And Arthur, please... don't insult my intelligence. I know what you are up to. And it has nothing to do with being concerned about my well-being.'

'But certainly, you realize a fight at the board meeting is not in the best interest of the company,' Arthur countered.

'I realize that, Arthur. But I also don't think that having a sniveling idiot like you as the CEO is in the best interest of the company either.'

'Really?'

'Really! And I wonder to what lengths you've gone to get us to this point.'

'And what does that mean?' Arthur's lily-white English skin was turning red.

I was also getting excited despite my resolve. I had no intention of being this mad. But... Arthur got under my skin.

'Are you implying Arthur has something to do with what has been happening?' Bob asked.

'I'm not implying anything,' I replied, backtracking. I had gone too far, and I knew it. 'I simply don't like what's going on here. I thought we were friends. I never thought you two would use the problems of the company to take my job. Lately, you guys have been acting more like my worst enemies than my friends.'

'But we've explained. This is in your best interest,' Bob said.

'And I have told you I'm capable of deciding what's in my best interest,' I replied again, this time with more intensity.

Arthur remained silent. He knew it was useless to continue. He was probably calculating how he could use my tirade against me. See, he would say to Bob and the other board members, John has lost touch with reality. He is now insinuating I'm responsible for the company's problems... one more reason to get rid of him.

'Gentlemen, unless you have something else you wish to discuss, this meeting is over.' I didn't like the prospect of Arthur using my own words against me, but there was nothing I could do about it now. I had said what I had said. I couldn't take it back. I hesitated for one second and gave them an opportunity to respond.

When they said nothing, I left the room.

11:15 A.M. JOHN

I hailed the first taxi I saw, going directly to the Club from Bob's conference room.

It was early for lunch when I arrived. The table by the window where I had breakfast was empty. A waiter brought a cup of coffee while I waited in silent fury. Monica and Charlie were not scheduled to arrive until around noon. Good, because I needed some time to calm down. My mind was vacillating between being angry at Arthur and at myself. I knew I shouldn't have gotten into it with him, but the situation got out of control fast, too fast for me to react properly.

Lately, this was how it seemed to go in every situation. The same sequence of events was repeated over and over again. I was given no time to consider the consequences, just time to react, nothing more. React and regret what I did later. I wasn't in control. I felt like nothing more than an innocent bystander caught up in a fight I had been watching from the sidelines, drawn into a battle I never wanted.

I offered a small prayer to God, who existed in the middle of all this complexity. His will, not mine, I prayed; his wisdom, not mine.

A cup of hot coffee tasted good and helped settle my nerves as the dining room began to fill.

It had been weeks since I'd seen M. I was nervous, almost afraid to face her. I had tried to forget her. I thought I could. Now, I understood that was impossible. But what I didn't know was what to do about her. I wondered stupidly if she had begun a new relationship, maybe with Charlie. I always suspected they may have had a previous affair. It was the way they greeted each other when I first met Charlie, the smile on her face... and his, like they were happy to see each other. But I never asked her, and my suspicion was probably nothing more than a product of my overactive imagination. Besides, it was none of my business then. And it was certainly none of my business now.

Still, I wondered.

I picked up a menu; same old Club fare. It never changed much. Apparently, the members didn't like variety. I wrote a number for an omelet and a salad on an order form lying on the corner of my table, thinking it would be good to get this task done before the others arrived. A white-coated waiter came and tried to pick up my order. I told him to wait. I had guests coming. He nodded and went away after refilling my coffee.

Time passed slowly. Noise overcame serenity. It was almost twelve-thirty. They were late. I began to wonder if they were coming. Maybe something had happened. Or maybe Charlie decided he didn't want to grace the rooms of my snobbish club after all. I looked at the menu again, thinking I might change my order.

'Hi,' M said casually like we had lunch at this club every day.

Dressed in a light gray suit with a black scarf... man, the lady sure looked good. Her long red hair flowed easily over her shoulders. Her dark brown eyes were smiling at me. I quickly realized that my memories of her were clearly not nearly as wonderful as the real person. I was so absorbed in her at the time I didn't bother to notice Charlie.

'How are you, John?' she asked softly.

'I'm okay, I guess. It's great to see you again.'

'Thanks. You too.'

'Mr. Van Laan.' Charlie extended his hand from across our table.

I turned, noticing him for the first time. 'Charlie, hey, thanks for coming,'

We shook hands as I tried to regain my composure.

Charlie wore the obligatory uniform of the Agency: dark blue suit, starched white shirt, and the non-descript tie of a bureaucrat. I always felt sorry for government types. They all looked like automatons in lockstep.

Our waiter arrived with a coffee pot. I passed menus to Charlie and M. The noise level in the dining room increased, but it was still bearable due to the size of the room and the high ceiling. This was one of the reasons I liked this place. A conversation could be had without shouting.

I watched M look over my menu, wishing to be alone with her.

Charlie caught me staring.

'Decided yet?' I asked.

Charlie chose a fish plate, and M ordered a shrimp salad. I dutifully wrote their requests on the order form and placed them on the corner of the table for the waiter to pick up.

'Maybe we should get started,' M said. 'Charlie, why don't you tell John the latest information?'

'Right,' he began, 'But first, let me state for the record the information you are about to receive has been gathered in an official CIA investigation.' He said, sounding like he was reading from a prepared statement. 'As such, it is privileged. You may reveal the information to no one.'

Apparently, he had said the words so many times he had it memorized, word for word.

'Cut the crap, Charlie,' M intervened. 'You're wasting time.'

'Monica, I have regulations to follow.'

'Charlie.' She stared at him.

'Okay, but Mr. Van Laan needs to understand that the information I am about to tell him is confidential.' Charlie met her gaze evenly.

In my state of weakened insecurity, their conversation sounded like a lover's quarrel.

Charlie turned to me and continued, 'Okay, Mr. Van Laan, do you understand you can tell no one what I am about to tell you?'

'I understand,' I said, trying to see into Charlie's soul. Something hard and unwavering was buried deep behind his chiseled good looks and dark eyes. He was a strong and handsome man, a man who knew his place and purpose in life, comfortable in his work. I was envious of his strength and simple vision. It was easy to see the world through Charlie's eyes.

He began by talking about Phillip. But Phillip was not the real reason they had requested a meeting. Sure, the CIA had tracked Phillip halfway around the world. And it was true he was wanted for questioning in Michigan about the bombing of my cottage. But the case had suddenly become far more complicated.

Charlie explained that an informant in Thailand was the source of his information. Nothing was confirmed, just rumor at this time. It was believed a powerful and influential family in Bangkok might be involved in events related to my company. And recent information evidence had surfaced of a planned attack on the New York Distribution House.

'How can they hope to attack New York?' I asked, trying to process what he was telling me while, at the same time, thinking how ironic it was that I didn't have to convince Charlie that the Thai were involved. He had come to convince me. Good, but his news was bad. If the inventory of the New York Distribution House was taken, my company was as good as dead.

'Some Thai immigrants in New York form gangs,' Charlie explained, 'And these gangs can be recruited. It's simply a matter of money and drugs... like everything else. In this case, however, the Thai government may also be involved at some level. An important Thai official has recently entered the US under a diplomatic passport. He was accompanied by more than a normal assortment of bodyguards. It's possible some of these men came here to work with the local gangs in executing the robbery. Not with official Thai government approval, of course. The operation is totally undercover.'

I didn't know how to respond.

Charlie continued. 'However, let me caution you. Our information is sketchy; nothing has been confirmed. But if even a portion of it is true, then at a minimum, we have determined who has been trying to destroy your company.'

'How high up is the government official?' I asked.

'Very highly placed.'

I stopped Charlie at this point and asked how the CIA discovered this information.

'From an opposition party person in the government, a person who is not happy with what is going on.'

'Okay, that makes sense, but why now?' I asked. 'Why didn't they come forward before?'

'I think because we started snooping around asking questions. Perhaps they thought we knew more than we did. I'm guessing they assumed it would be better to come clean before anything more happened. Their mission was to convince us this was not an approved operation of the government. Or perhaps they hoped to discredit a political opponent. Or maybe they saw it as an opportunity to gain a favor from us which can be used in the future. These situations are complicated, John. It's politics, you know, active on many levels. You explain human behavior to me. I never understand why people do what they do. I don't question it. I just try to deal with it.'

'Yes, but none of this would have come out if you hadn't agreed to help us,' M stated directly to Charlie.

'I understand Monica. And thank you for adding to my already heavy caseload,' Charlie replied with a wry smile.

Monica simply stared at him.

Charlie continued. 'Monica is right, John. Phillip Palmer led us to Thailand. We started asking questions, and this was the result.'

'Are you in New York to stop the robbery?' I asked.

'Yes and no. Of course, we don't want it to happen. But more importantly, we want to determine who in the Thai government is involved. But first, we need to establish that the information we were given is not false and purposely misleading. It's complicated.'

'Is anyone in my company involved?' I had to ask.

'We don't know, but I'm guessing it would be difficult to rob one of your distribution houses without inside intel,' Charlie answered truthfully.

'This original thought came from me,' M smiled, looking at Charlie without emotion. 'The CIA doesn't indulge in creative thinking.'

Charlie didn't argue.

Mercifully, our lunch arrived at this time, and an unspoken truce was called so we could enjoy our meal in relative peace. Personally, I had lost my appetite. I was wound up trying to mentally digest everything Charlie told me, wondering what implications the information might have for me. M and Charlie chatted and enjoyed their meal as I sat stewing, isolated, my food getting cold.

It was all happening as I had envisioned. But living with something in reality is completely different from imagining it. An enemy as rich and powerful as a Thai family aided by their government would not be easy to beat. It would have been far better to have discovered that our problems were nothing more than a series of unrelated robberies and catastrophes. But apparently, this was not true. It now appeared I had been right all along. However, this was little consolation because it was the worst possible outcome for my company and me.

'May I ask a few questions?' I finally interjected.

Charlie nodded, his mouth full of food.

'How confident are you of your information?'

Charlie took a sip of water, swallowed and wiped his mouth with a napkin. 'We are cautiously confident, John. That's all I can tell you. But until confirmed, it's just speculation.'

'And Phillip's involvement?'

'Hard to say. It's true he was in Thailand when all this was being organized. But it's also possible he went there to buy and sell gems... pure coincidence, nothing more.'

Charlie continued to eat his lunch while I sipped coffee, ignoring my food.

'Since we're discussing Phillip and coincidence,' Charlie continued, taking a break from his lunch, 'Let's talk about what happened to you in Grand Haven. We believe you were being tracked. And while you were at your cottage, someone took the opportunity to eliminate you.'

'Does that mean Phillip may not have been involved?' I asked.

'Right, the fact that Phillip knew you were in Grand Haven at the time could be nothing more than a coincidence.'

'So, you have no concrete evidence implicating him?'

'Right, it's all circumstantial.'

'But Phillip traveled to Bangkok soon after it happened,' M intervened. 'And Bangkok is where the people responsible for trying to take down John's company live. Doesn't that seem to be more than circumstantial.'

'I don't disagree, Monica,' Charlie replied. 'But John asked if we could prove Phillip was involved. And the answer is: we can't... Do circumstances point to certain conclusions? Sure, but not nearly enough to even bring him in for questioning. Not that we would. Right now, we would rather wait and watch him.'

I sat back in my chair. The noise in the dining room, which had disappeared into the background as I concentrated on listening to Charlie, that noise now returned. People were casually talking and laughing. They didn't know I was going through a crisis. They didn't care.

M picked at her salad. Charlie finished his fish.

I wondered what M was thinking. I hadn't seen her for days. Seemed like months. Before, we had been together almost every day. And when she left, I didn't think I would ever see her again. Maybe that wasn't completely true, but I had tried to believe it. Now, I desperately wanted to be with her again, talk to her, hold her, and see her smile.

'So, what happens now?' I asked Charlie, trying to refocus on something besides her, anything but her.

'For now, we wait.'

'Can I tell my people about the danger?'

'Like who?'

'Like Bob Anderson, the man who runs our New York Distribution House?'

'No, I don't think that's necessary.'

'Why not? Shouldn't he be preparing for a robbery?'

'No,' Charlie said.

'I don't understand.' I frowned.

'Okay, let me explain,' he sighed. 'First, we don't know if he is involved. And second, even if he isn't, he might involuntarily leak the information to someone who is. As long as we suspect someone inside your company may be involved, we can't take a chance. Do you understand?'

I didn't respond.

He continued. 'For now, we have all the information we need to protect your place of business. Please let me assure you we will be prepared if a robbery is attempted. Don't be concerned, John. Let us handle this.'

I nodded. 'What do you want me to do?' I asked, dutifully humbled.

'Nothing. In fact, it would be better if you returned to Virginia. We have the situation under control. You'll only get in the way if you stay.'

'Then why did you tell me?'

Charlie paused to look at M as if to say I told you so. 'I did it as a courtesy to Monica. She insisted I tell you.'

M looked away.

'I see,' I responded.

'Ready to go?' he said to her.

'Okay,' she replied, glancing at her watch.

'Thanks for lunch, John,' Charlie stood up. 'Monica has already told me I can't pay in a place like this.'

'You're welcome. And thank you for your update. I appreciate it.' I stood to exchange a brief handshake.

'No problem. Remember, John, it's confidential. My bosses would not be too happy if they knew I was talking to you.'

Monica turned to leave.

'M,' I said.

She initially ignored me, placing her purse over her shoulder.

'I'd like to talk to you. Could we...'

'I don't think that's a good idea,' she finally replied in her lawyer voice.

'Look, it'll just take a minute.'

'No... Charlie, let's go.' She was adamant.

'Right.' Charlie smiled at M and started to walk away.

She turned to follow. I reached for her, touching her arm. She resisted.

'M, please, we need to talk.'

She hesitated. Then, gently but firmly pulled her arm away.

'Monica, please.'

Maybe it was using her full name. I didn't know why, but for whatever reason, she sighed, 'Okay, John, but just for a minute.'

'You coming, Monica?' Charlie asked.

'No, go ahead. I'll catch up with you later.'

Charlie looked disappointed.

I began to sit down.

'I only have a minute, John,' she said. 'I don't think we need to sit down.'

'Please.'

She sat reluctantly.

I didn't say anything immediately, trying desperately to formulate wildly random thoughts into something vaguely coherent.

'M... look. I know you're angry with me. I don't blame you.'

'John, you don't need to explain. I get it. My contract is over. You terminated me. Nothing more needs to be discussed.'

'That's true,' I agreed. 'I have no rights. But maybe...' I stopped, unsure of what to say next.

She turned towards a window. Then turned again to look at me.

I was afraid she was staring into my inner soul, seeing the sad, scared man I had become. For a moment, I thought she would walk away, but she didn't.

'John,' she said, reaching out to place her hand on mine. 'This is doing neither of us any good. Whatever we had is over.'

'M, I still care about you. Please, try to understand this from my point of view.'

'I do understand, and that's your problem, John,' she interrupted me. 'It's always from your point of view. It's always about you and what you want. What works for you? How does it fit into your plans... Look, I've tried to look at it from your point of view. That's all I've thought about lately. But for me, it always comes down to this. If two people choose, they stand together. They work together. No matter what happens, they deal with it together... Or they choose to stand alone... and John... you chose to stand alone. Am I right?'

She waited for me to answer.

I had none, no defense, no answer. I didn't know what to say. The problem was she was right. I tried to think, say something, anything more than simply plead for mercy, which was the only idea that came to mind.

'Can I order you something to drink?' I asked lamely.

'No.' She withdrew her hand.

'M, I was wrong and ...'

'No, John. You were right. It was the decision you needed to make. It was the decision you will always make.'

1:55 P.M. JOHN

Clouds shrouded the sun, dulling the vibrant colors of New York's grand vistas.

A heavy, chilling wind whipped around the tall buildings and darted through the restless streets like a scared alley cat looking for a way out. After the dismal meeting with my partners and an equally dismal lunch with M and Charlie, the cold air outside felt refreshing. I took a deep breath and decided a walk might help clear my head.

Central Park was probably the last place on earth I should have been that afternoon, alone without a bodyguard. But I wasn't thinking about my health and welfare at the time. All I could hear in my mind were M's words over and over. *It's the decision you will always make.*

She was right, of course... unnervingly right. I always did what was prudent. I never took a calculated risk where the downside outweighed the upside. But what did I lose in the process? The current answer to this conundrum was... I lost her. That's what I lost. No guts, no glory. That was me. She was right, and it hurt.

The cold wind penetrated my light sports coat. I turned up the collar and kept walking, picking up my pace to stay warm. Everything had become overly complicated: Monica and the Thais, Arthur and Phillip. The prospect of fighting all these battles simultaneously made me weary just thinking about them.

A few strangers walked the sidewalks of the park with me on this cold, windy day, strangers I did not know. I searched their faces, sometimes afraid. Fearing a callous look, a malevolent grin, a gun under a coat, a man sent to kill me. But the faces kept walking, taking no notice of me. My companions that day were not my enemy. Still, I looked and watched while wanting a woman who was gone because I was too bloody cautious.

The weather began to turn ugly. Looked like it could rain... or worse... snow at any moment. Suddenly, I felt very weak and exposed. I wondered what I would do if I was attacked.

Run...

Sure, I could run, but who can outrun a bullet? I was defenseless, and I knew it. Hunched over in resentment, I marched on, head down against a stiff wind. What now, I wondered. Wasn't it only a matter of time before my enemy killed me? Good, that would solve all my problems. So why worry? Why not just die here and now? What difference did it make?

The sky darkened. Gray clouds raced overhead. Wind whipped through the branches of the leafless trees, sounding like an oncoming freight train. The chaotic weather fit my mood, somehow comforting. I leaned against the hard, cold wind, folding my arms around my body to stay warm as I walked.

An empty park bench beckoned.

I sat down to rest, feeling defeated.

In my current state of irrationality, it occurred to me that everything was my fault. I should have been smarter. I would have seen all this coming. The Thai... weren't they simply reacting to what I did to them, taking back their business?

It all made sense.

But did it, really?

Life is full of changes.

That's the way it is.

People need to understand.

Life never stays the same.

We all need to learn to adjust to new realities. Adjust, not fight, not fall into violence, not try to kill and destroy to regain something that can never be again.

When I formed my company, I simply did what the situation dictated. But then, what had I achieved? Nothing really. All I saw was chaos, no order, no progress, only violence and fear.

I wondered how chaos could dominate a world so beautifully complex, so startlingly complicated. A world seemingly ruled by scientific laws, order, and symmetry. How could chaos exist in such a world; a world of ideas, strategic business plans, tactics for life, policies for a better world; everything I wished it to be?

But wishes are futile. And plans can be useless... too many variables exist to ever be certain of anything.

As I sat on the park bench in Central Park, momentarily paralyzed by the utter hopelessness of my situation with the wind swirling around me and storm clouds assembling overhead, my life seemed to have evolved into nothing more than a series of unrelated catastrophes... no order, no rules... only pain, mayhem and chaos. In my despair, I asked God to help me understand how heaven and hell can exist side by side. How a world ruled by complex scientific laws can exist embedded in such utter and complete turmoil?

Then I took a moment to consider complexity of it all: the intricate weaving of life as we know it, the existence of so many complicated life forms. When I thought about the vast reaches of empty space, stars, galaxies, the possibility of life in places beyond the possibility of time travel, a universe beyond imagination, beyond comprehension, it was incomprehensible to me that such a complex world could exist without the hand of God.

And this thought alone offered me a small measure of peace.

7:10 P.M. JOHN

The window next to my preferred table in the large dining room of the Club was dark at dinner.

Not bright and sunny like for breakfast in the morning. Not full of promise as at lunch... just dark and foreboding, nothing much to see outside; only a few street lights shining in an empty black void where earlier a view of the trees in Central Park had promised life.

A pastoral mural filled with childlike angels and wispy clouds graced the room's vaulted ceiling. It was pleasant enough; classical artwork gave the dining room the proper upper-crust artsy décor. But at the same time, it looked false, like the room belonged in another place and time... Medieval Italy, maybe, not New York City.

The events of my day sifted past my mind's eye as I picked at my food.

There are times when the full impact of an incident cannot be comprehended immediately. It is sometimes better to wait and let the details simmer for a while before deciding anything.

I began by going over my morning's meeting with Bob and Arthur. I knew Arthur could be a self-serving jerk at times. Still, the reality of his turning against me was hard to stomach. And Bob, I believed Bob was under the influence of Arthur. It wasn't completely Bob's fault. Even so, the impact of both of my former friends and partners turning against me was devastating.

Money and power, I decided it was nothing more than a play for money and power.

I remembered better times, times when we had struggled through the first few years of my company's existence, working together. We sacrificed and put in long hours. We were dedicated to building a company. And we had fun doing it. When money started to flow, we were happy. But it did not take long for petty jealousies to raise their ugly heads. Not the obvious kind of jealousy, not the screaming, fighting kind. More like the snippy variety, the trite under-your-breath comments, the holier-than-thou attitudes. It all made sense now. Situations I had previously dismissed as relatively unimportant, even humorous; they were symptoms of bigger problems to come. Problems that were in clear view now, evidence of a complete breakdown in trust. The terminal stages of the disease had taken over. The body of my company was convulsing in pain.

I wondered if this was inevitable, predictable; just the normal cycle every successful business follows? I didn't know. I didn't think it needed to be. But perhaps I was wrong in assuming it could happen to others, but wouldn't happen to me.

I sipped some wine.

A dinner of yellowtail snapper was delicious, but I had lost my appetite. I picked at the fish and looked around the big, dimly lit room. It was surprisingly quiet, with only a few members and guests. I abruptly wanted to be somewhere else, anywhere but here. My half-eaten dinner on the table was left behind.

A desk clerk smiled when I approached. She was friendly. At my request, she checked for messages. My box was empty.

It was too late in the evening to return to Charlottesville. With nowhere to go and nothing to do, I wandered aimlessly to the elevator to my room.

Normally, I don't spend much time in the guest rooms. I don't mind how they are decorated. But that night, it felt old and oppressive. I tried to read, got bored, and finally put my book down. I needed something to do, but what? I could have worked. I had work to do. But work seemed utterly unimportant now. After all, I was about to be fired. I decided to call Lin. His voicemail picked up, unusual for Lin. He normally answered his cell phone. I opened a book again, absentmindedly scanning the words, comprehending nothing. The lights of New York City flickered through the windows of my room, casting shadows across the furniture. My cell phone was on the table next to where I sat. I impulsively picked it up and clicked through the preset numbers until I came to her number... paused... and hit dial before I could consider the consequences.

'Hello,' she answered.

'Monica, it's John.'

Silence.

'Look, I called to give you a heads up. I've been thinking about your contract and did some checking. Seems you didn't sign your termination contract. I'm notifying you the termination agreement has been withdrawn and your original contract with my company is current.'

'That's bullshit, John.'

'It's all very legal. Your salary has continued to be paid. Just because you have chosen not to cash the checks is irrelevant; thus...'

'Well, here's news for you. If I wasn't fired, then I quit. You'll have my resignation faxed to your office in the morning. Anything else?'

'I won't accept...' I countered.

'You won't accept what?'

'Your resignation.'

'Well, accept this. I'm out of your life. And as soon as this is over, you won't ever see me again.'

I heard the hardness in her voice. My attempt at levity was failing badly.

'Okay, M, how about this approach... I made a mistake, a big one. I'm sorry. I know you're hurt, and I'm responsible. I'm sorry.'

'Too late for that, John.' Her voice caught in her throat, a heartbreaking sound.

'No, M... no, it's not. It can't be. Look, I need to see you.'

'I'll think about it.'

A slight crack in her armor surfaced. Did she say she would think about it? She didn't say no, did she? I pressed her. 'Tonight, M; can I see you tonight.'

'No, I don't think so,' she sounded resolute again.

'Look, M. I took a long walk in Central Park this afternoon. I've never felt more alone and confused. Seeing you again, well... I think you...'

I stopped in mid-sentence. I didn't know what else to say, so I said nothing. Some noise in the background came from her phone like someone else was in the room. I wondered if it was Charlie.

'I saw Bob and Arthur this morning,' I continued, not really knowing what to say, just wanting to hear her voice.

'What happened?'

'I don't want to talk about it over my phone.'

'Then why did you tell me?' Her temper flared.

'Because I need to tell someone. Someone I can trust.' I pleaded, thinking if it took sympathy to get her to see me again...well, that was fine with me. 'Can I see you?'

Silence.

'M, please.' Last resort, if not else works, beg.

'Okay, I guess.' She sighed wearily. 'There's a bar at the Hotel Ambassador where I'm staying. I'll be there in about twenty minutes. Do you know where the hotel is?'

'I'll find it. And... thank you.'

No response.

10:35 P.M. JOHN

The night air was clear and cold.

Rain had softened to a wet drizzle as I walked out from under the Club's sheltering canopy.

Glancing over my shoulder, searching for shadows in the murky darkness, a growing paranoia began to dominate my soul. Suddenly, I wanted to live. Just hearing her voice again gave me hope.

It felt good to be out of my room and into the cool night air. The lights of the city were bright. Horns, and constant sirens; it was all invigorating, far better than being cooped up in a small room. Besides, I was going to see Monica. It felt great, even though I knew it was foolish to hope. From our conversation at lunch, it was obvious she was still angry and probably regretting she had agreed to meet with me. Maybe she wouldn't show. But that was not like her. If she said she would come, she would. At least, I hoped she would.

I hailed the first cab I saw. The cabby seemed innocent enough. An Arab, I think. He spoke some English, enough to get by. Okay, fine with me. I wasn't interested in small talk. It occurred to me as I sat in the back of his cab I needed to prepare. Like any important business meeting. Goals and strategy were essential. Rehearse what you're will say. Consider alternative courses of actions if the meeting doesn't go your way. Be prepared.

But I was not preparing.

I was acting more like a schoolboy on a first date, knowing nothing, wanting everything, simply hoping not to make a big mistake.

Taxi jerked to the right and screeched to a stop at an intersection. My driver yelled something foreign to a fellow cabby in the next lane and punctuated it with a hand gesture. As soon as the light changed, he accelerated from the corner only to screech to a halt at the next intersection after one block. Mercifully, after only a few more similar incidents of incivility, we arrived at her hotel. I handed the cabby a twenty and hurried inside.

Elaborate brass fixtures, polished to perfection, sparkled in the dim lights when I entered the bar of the Ambassador Hotel. A mirror behind the bar reflected the light through bottles of hard liquor. A four-piece jazz band played softly in one corner of a dance floor. Several couples slowly swayed to the music.

I searched the room. Didn't see her. I guessed I was early.

A booth in the back corner looked like a good choice, as far from the band as possible. Although the improvised jazz was enjoyable, I wanted to be able to talk to her without shouting. An attractive middle-aged blond waitress came to my table. I mentioned something about waiting for a tall redhead and ordered a drink.

The beer tasted good. The first few sips are always the best.

As I waited, I searched the room for eyes looking in my direction. No one seemed to have followed me inside. Nothing hostile caught my attention. Everything appeared to be normal. Everything except for me wasn't normal. I was alone in a New York bar, and I was about to be fired from my job. And if this wasn't enough, some powerful foreigners wanted me dead. Nothing about my life was normal.

I told myself that no guarantees come with life, and difficult times are supposed to be good for the soul, build character, and all that nonsense. But I couldn't help but wonder, why me? I didn't need any more character. At least, I didn't think I did. I had it all together. Or did I? Apparently, M didn't think so. So… probably not.

It was as if God was laughing, laughing at me. Me, a male who didn't think he would ever need a woman. Yet here I was, sitting alone in a bar, desperately hoping a certain woman would show up.

My pretty blond waitress returned. 'Anything else I can get for you, sir?' she smiled.

'Another beer, please,' I answered, thinking how particularly pathetic I must look, sitting alone in the back corner of a bar, feeling sorry for myself.

The band took a break.

Elevator music played faintly in the background. TV screens blinked above the bar. A basketball game was being shown, the constantly flickering screen assaulting the senses of the customers sitting at the bar. I hate TVs in bars. They are distracting and hard to ignore. I slid into the back corner of the booth to avoid looking at the TV and waited, hoping a certain redhead would arrive soon.

Or not.

Probably not coming.

Why hang out with a deadbeat like me?

Good... because I didn't know what I would say to her if she did come.

Should I ask her if it would be okay if I just stared at her in silence and caressed her with my eyes? Should I tell her we didn't need to talk? If she would simply allow me the pleasure of observing the soft corners of her mouth, the line of her neck, the crinkle between her eyes, that's all I really needed. Or perhaps if she didn't mind, could I touch her arm or hold her hand? Would that be okay?

Probably not... probably pathetically not.

I had to think of something to say, anything.

Although... if she didn't come... I wouldn't need to think of anything.

I took another sip of beer, hoping to calm down.

The band returned and began with a rendition of Duke Ellington's 'A Train.'

A tall, dark silhouette appeared near the entrance to the bar; a woman came inside with a quick step. Just a shadow in the light from the hall behind her. I knew instantly it was her, the way she walked, confident, good posture.

She stopped and looked around.

My pretty waitress was standing at the end of the bar near the door. The two ladies exchanged words. The waitress pointed in the direction of a pathetic guy sitting in a back corner of the bar, probably after asking Monica if she was looking for some lonely guy hanging out in a back booth looking lost. Monica said yes, that would be him.

I stood so she could see me in the dim light.

My mood improved just seeing her. She was wearing dark slacks and a tight gray sweater. Her red hair fell gently over her shoulders.

'Hi John,' she said in a business-like tone. 'Sorry, I'm late. Got a call from home. My mother wouldn't let me off my phone.'

'No need to apologize. I'm just glad you're here.'

'I'm not sure I should have come,' she eyed me warily. 'But here I am. Now, what is going on with you? You mentioned something about a meeting with Arthur and Bob this morning.'

The waitress asked M if she wanted a drink.

'I'll have a glass of wine, red,' she answered.

'M, I don't really want to talk about them,' I began. 'And I don't know how to say this... so I'll just say it as simply as possible.'

'Whoa.' She held up her hand. 'You got me to come to this bar at ten o'clock at night because you said you wanted to talk about Arthur and Bob. Did something happen or...?'

'Well, yes, Arthur is in New York.'

'So, what happened?'

'Well, I went to my office in Bob's building. I thought I might get some work done. Maybe even try to talk to him alone. But Arthur was there, and they asked for a meeting. Said I should resign to save the company trouble. The meeting wasn't as friendly as the last time. Truth is, I got mad.'

'Why is Arthur in town?'

'I don't know.'

'He didn't come to see you, did he? He didn't know you were in town?'

'No, he didn't.'

'So why is he here?' she asked, the wheels in her mind turning.

'I don't know.'

'And come to think of it, why are you here?'

'You told me Phillip was coming. And I knew Arthur was flying to New York because Lin told me. Both of them in this town at the same time; seemed too much of a coincidence. I decided this was the place to be.'

I took a sip of beer. It was too late to be drinking beer. It dulled my mind but tasted good. The waitress delivered a glass of wine to M and asked if we wanted anything else. M said no. The band played softly on the other side of the room. I took a deep breath, simply enjoying the experience of being close to her again.

'You aren't thinking Arthur came here to talk to Phillip, are you?' she asked.

'Not really. But maybe. Why else would he be here? The board meeting isn't until next week.'

'Lots of reasons,' she responded. 'Like strategy sessions with Bob prior to the board meeting, for instance.'

'Okay, you're probably right.'

'I could ask Charlie to put a tail on Arthur? That's the only way we'll know for sure.'

'Would you?'

She dug into her purse for her cell phone. 'Are you worried about the board vote?'

'No, I'm going to lose.' I grimaced.

'Do you know that for sure? Or are you just being negative?'

'I know. Lin told me. He has been talking to the board members on my behalf. He said I'm going to lose.'

'And it bothers you.'

I didn't reply. Of course, it bothered me.

It reminded me of how angry I was while talking to Bob and Arthur. But I didn't want to think about them right now. I just wanted to be with her. Her face, her voice, the curve of her shoulders, the graceful way she moved, her long, slender hands. I loved being near her again. It was as if she had come to give me a present wrapped up in brightly colored paper. I wanted nothing more than to slowly unwrap the present with my eyes, enjoying the moment.

I guess I was smiling oddly because she stopped talking and looked at me pointedly.

'John.'

'Yes.'

'You don't seem to be concentrating. This could be important. But that's not what you're doing... are you?'

'No.'

'Why not?'

'M, I made a mistake. A big mistake...'

'John, don't go there.' She shook her head.

'M, I don't want you out of my life, not ever again.'

'John, could we talk about this later.'

'Nothing else is as important.'

'Please, not now. I need to call Charlie.' Her cell phone was in her hand, ready to dial.

'M, forget all that. What will happen, will happen. Right now, the only thing I want is you.'

She didn't answer. The frowny line between her eyes curled in consternation as she was thinking. And it was obvious she didn't like what she was concluding.

'What happens when this is over?' she asked. 'When you can return to your previous life, working full-time again. You know, when you don't need me anymore? What happens to me then, John? Out comes the severance contract, and I'm gone... right?'

It was difficult to see her in the dim light of the bar. 'M, you're not listening to me.'

'And you, John, how long has it been since you listened to me? Do you have any idea how badly you hurt me? And after everything we have gone through together. How could you?' Tears fell. Angry tears.

'I'm so sorry.'

'I don't know,' she retreated.

'M, I made a mistake. Please try to understand. It has been so crazy. I have just been reacting...'

'Yes, but when I needed you most, then you ...' her voice trailed off.

The band played a piano solo quietly in the background. The soft lights of the emptying bar reflected in the tears on M's cheeks. Our blond waitress headed in our direction as I reached across the table, hoping to touch M's hand. She didn't pull back. Her delicate fingers tightened, holding my soul in her hands.

Our waitress stopped and retreated back to the bar without saying a word.

11:55 P.M. JOHN

Lights from the city peeked through a narrow slit in the drapes of her hotel room, casting a dim glow over the bed where she lay waiting for me.

I slid under the sheets and curled against her back, relishing the familiar warmth of her body, caressing her full breasts, and kissing the back of her neck. She rested peacefully on her side, holding my hands to her naked body as if she were reluctant to let go. Eventually, I slid back and gently rubbed her back as I had done in the past, feeling her long, tight muscles melt under my hands. I ran my fingers through her hair while reveling in the fact I was near her again, feeling joy. It was like I was a young boy again, playing with a favorite toy he had found after it was lost. It was, at the same time, both comfortable and thrilling to be touching her again, smelling the familiar scent of her perfume.

When she was ready, she allowed me to once more be together with her, moving in unison to the restless rhythm of a New York night.

FEBRUARY 26, WEDNESDAY, 9:06 A.M. JOHN

A phone rang in the far corner of my dreams.

I opened my eyes in time to see M turn over and reach for the receiver.

Behind her hotel drapes, the sun was bright. A digital clock on a bedside table read nine-o-six a.m.

'Hello?' M answered.

'Okay,' she replied in a one-sided conversation. 'Yes, sorry, it seems I've overslept... Yes.'

I lay half awake, half listening to her, half wondering how anyone could look as good as she looked this morning. One beautiful bare breast had escaped from beneath the sheets as she talked, propped up on her elbow so she could hold the phone to her ear. Instantly, I wanted nothing from the outside world, only desiring to make love to her again.

'Maybe you can pick me up at my hotel,' she suggested, instantly destroying my erotic daydream. 'Yes. Give me about twenty minutes... Sure, that's more than enough time.'

I reached over to hold her around the waist as she tried to get out of bed. She turned over and kissed me.

'It seems they can't find you,' she said. 'They're concerned. According to the Club, you left last night and didn't return.'

'Charlie?' I asked.

'Yes.'

'He can wait. I think it would be a lot more fun to...'

'I can feel what you are thinking,' she chuckled. 'But I have to go, and so do you...' she turned, sweeping the hair out of her eyes.

'Why didn't you just tell him where I was?' I asked.

'Well, I...'

I laughed. 'It's okay, you don't have to explain. I'll call Charlie on my cell.'

'Would you?' she smiled.

'Sure, I'll tell him I'm in your hotel room, and we're going to make love. So, go away.' I grinned.

'John!' She gave me a playful shove.

'Okay, okay... Say, what were you talking to Charlie about anyway?'

'He has decided to tail Arthur himself. Said it's easier than trying to explain to his boss why he needs extra help. Charlie asked me to join him since he'd never met the man. He doesn't know what Arthur looks like.'

I had forgotten about M calling Charlie last night on the way to her hotel room. She suggested Charlie have someone track Arthur and see what my former friend was doing in town, specifically with whom he was meeting. Charlie agreed. I told M to tell Charlie he could probably find Arthur at the Plaza Hotel. Arthur always assumes it's his divine right as an Englishman to stay at the most expensive hotels whenever he's on company business.

'Charlie's picking me up in a few minutes,' she said indifferently. 'I guess I'm going on a stake-out this morning. Fun, huh?'

'I have some other fun in mind.'

'It can wait.'

'Spoken like a true lady.'

She looked at me pointedly. 'I assume you can find your own way out. And if anyone asks, let's play this like last night didn't happen.'

'Why?'

'I just think it would be easier, too many questions otherwise.'

'If that's the way you want it.' I was quickly becoming aware that I was no longer in control of this relationship.

'I do.'

'But something did happen,' I protested.

'Yes, it did, John. Any regrets?' she asked curtly as she slid out of bed in all her naked glory.

What could I say? 'M, the only regret I have is I ever let you go.'

She jumped back on the bed, pinned me down, and kissed me hard on the mouth.

'And don't you ever forget it, John Van Laan.'

With that, she rolled off the bed and got into her shower, leaving me a wreck of a man, happy but wanting.

It felt a bit awkward returning to the Club, walking into its ornate old halls still dressed in last night's wrinkled clothes, unshaved, hair uncombed. I wasn't wearing the Club's required sports jacket and tie. I couldn't advance beyond the elevator, Club rules. Had to go directly to my room.

M had kicked me out before Charlie arrived.

I would rather have stayed, met Charlie at her door, given him a big broad smile...

I let it go when she promised to keep me informed and meet me for dinner at seven tonight at my Club.

9:55 A.M. JOHN

Shower, shave and clean clothes helped revive my crumpled spirits.

I was headed out the door of my room for breakfast in the Club's dining room when my cell rang. It was M. She called to tell me that she was with Charlie, and they were staking out the Plaza, waiting for Arthur to appear.

Of course, I already knew this, but Charlie didn't know I knew. And apparently, she didn't want Charlie to know I knew. So, I guess this was her way of covering her sweet ass with a phone call. That was my interpretation, anyway.

Nothing else to report she said. I thanked her and asked her to keep me informed. She said, I had her cell phone number. I could call her anytime if I wanted something. I started to tell her what I wanted... but she guessed what was coming next and hung up before I could express my deeply seated physical needs.

Nothing is as vicious as a woman spurned. I had the feeling I would be paying for my past indiscretion for a long time. It was justice in her eyes.

Suddenly, I wasn't hungry anymore. I wanted to be where they were, discovering what Arthur was doing. I knew this wasn't possible. So I called Mike instead. He was waiting in his Buick outside the Club before I hit the sidewalk.

'Where to boss?' he asked.

'Don't know, just drive.'

He smiled and headed into traffic.

New York swirled around us in a meaningless mass of human confusion as he drove. I wasn't paying attention. My mind was in another place, a place where I could be in her arms.

'Hello. It's John, anything happening?' I called her cell phone number out of boredom.

'Oh, John,' she replied casually as if she had forgotten my name. 'No, nothing much going on. Arthur went to Bob's office. He's up there now, and we're sitting in Charlie's car across the street waiting. This is going nowhere, but Charlie says we need to be patient. I told him I'm not the patient type. I guess I'm not cut out for stakeout duty.'

'Okay, thanks. Just thought I would check in,' I said, trying to sound casual.

'I told you I would keep you informed. If anything happens, I'll call,' she scolded me.

'Thanks, M.'

'What are you doing?' she asked abruptly as if she could sense I was up to no good.

'Oh, going for coffee,' I replied, suddenly feeling silly for calling her.

'Okay... and John, stay out of trouble. Charlie says you are a marked man. Do you have a bodyguard with you?'

'Of course, do you think I'm stupid?' I smiled at Mike.

'Okay,' she hung up.

Mike drove a couple of blocks before abruptly pulling his Buick to a curb. 'Come on, Boss. Let's get some coffee.' He sensed I needed some cheering up.

Vito's Restaurant was Mike's kind of place, Italian with red patterned wallpaper, wood tables and chairs. A stained wood bar was in the back. It didn't look open for business, but the locals knew where coffee was brewed and donuts could be had. A ceramic bowl on the counter was for donations to cover the cost. It was self-serve. I poured a cup of coffee and reached for my wallet.

Mike tapped my arm. 'No, no, this is my joint, boss.' He threw a ten in the bowl.

'Thanks, Mike.'

I was introduced to the boys, Mike's buddies. They all looked like they could have been his relatives, with dark wavy hair, easy smiles, and bright, happy eyes. Their conversation flowed easily, dominated by a combination of Brooklyn-Italian accents, which at times was hard to understand for a Midwestern boy like me. Still, I listened, fascinated, as they talked about local politics and the inevitable Italian topic of first choice... women. Their jokes got a bit racy at times, all in good fun. It took my mind off my worries. Their animated faces were very expressive. I envied their easy-going ways, their love of life.

Eventually, I got bored and needed some air.

I went outside and leaned against the side of the restaurant, spending the time people-watching.

4:30 P.M. JOHN

Morning dragged into the lunch hour.

We returned to Mike's restaurant for a good Italian meal. Then back into Mike's Buick again with nowhere to go. Mike drove and talked. I did my part, listened, and made just enough conversation to keep Mike entertained. I called Monica one more time. She said Arthur had left Bob's office after lunch. He was now out shopping, acting like a regular tourist. Nothing was happening. Their stakeout was looking like a big waste of time.

'Hey, Mike. It's four-thirty. Let's stop for a drink somewhere,' I said.

'You're the boss.'

'You okay with that?' I asked, assuming his company had a strict policy about drinking on the job.

'One beer's going to hurt nothing.'

'Sorry about today,' I apologized. 'I know it's been pretty boring.'

'I've had worse days. Believe me. I know a bar I think you'll like.'

'Let's go.' I rested in the back seat in his car, finally relaxing. I had told Mike earlier to make sure we were not followed. Mike reported several times he was checking his rear-view mirror and no one was on our tail. Seemed reasonable, as much as he zigzagged through traffic. He would have noticed a tail if it existed.

My cell phone rang, startling me. 'Yes.'

'Something is happening,' M said. 'Arthur is on the move, moving quickly. Charlie has brought in a second car to help tail him. Right now, his limo out of sight, but we know where he is. The other car reported his location. Just thought I would let you know. Today may not be a total loss after all.'

'Thanks. You okay?' I asked, enjoying the sound of her voice.

'I'm fine, John.'

'Okay, stay in touch.'

I put my cell phone down. 'Forget the drink, Mike. Seems my friend Arthur is up to something.'

'Where you wanna go?'

'Don't know yet. Let's wait and see.'

We drove. Minutes dragged.

My cell phone rang. 'Yes.'

'He's heading for China Town,' she said.

'That's it?'

'That's all for now.'

'Okay, thanks.'

'What are you doing?' she asked, sounding suspicious.

'Nothing much, just thought I would go out for a drink.' I half lied, trying to sound nonchalant.

'That's all?' she asked as if she suspected more.

'Yeah, call me when you know more.'

'Sure,' she hesitated.

I hung up before she could ask another question, like, what was I really doing?

'Mike, find a bar quick and make it a noisy one. We need to be inside when she calls back. I think she suspects something.'

'You got it, Boss.'

The bar was loud. Wall Street tycoons are letting off steam at the end of the day. Mike ordered us a couple of beers from the bartender while I found a table away from the bar, hoping I would be able to hear her voice when she called.

We sipped beer while we waited. Mike watched for trouble and said all was okay. No one was looking at us. The beer in our glasses went stale as we waited. Mike ordered another couple of beers and some nuts.

I hate waiting, always do. When I couldn't stand it any longer, I called.

'Well, what's happening?' I asked.

'Sorry, I was just going to call you. Arthur stopped at a restaurant. It could be nothing. He's inside, probably having dinner.'

'I see. So, what are you doing?' I asked her first before she could ask me the same question again.

'What do you mean?' she replied.

'I don't know. Are you just waiting outside?'

'Yes, why are you asking?'

'Oh, I was just wondering if you were kissing Charlie.' I smiled.

'John,' she sighed.

'Sorry, just wanted to be sure you still love me.'

Silence...

'Look, John, I'll let you know if something happens,' she sounded annoyed. 'In the meantime,'

I cut her off, 'Okay, thanks.'

'John.'

'Yes.'

'Be careful. You know what Charlie said.'

'See you at dinner.'

5:37 P.M. JOHN

Traffic is murder in the late afternoon in the Big Apple.

Rush hour, everyone is either trying to get in or get out of the city. Mike knew all the back alleys, but this didn't help much. Traffic backed up. We got bogged down and couldn't move. Horns honked; pedestrians were making more progress than us. I fumed, wondering what Charlie was doing. Was he just sitting in the car, smiling at M, doing nothing, making small talk? I didn't like thinking about the two of them together in a car all day. I thought Charlie should be doing something, anything besides just sitting around outside waiting. Like maybe he should go inside the restaurant, see what Arthur was doing, who he was talking to. Information was valuable. But then, maybe he had gone in. I didn't know. And I didn't think it was my place to ask. Still, it would have been nice to know.

I got bored, frustrated, and bored.

'Let's go back to my Club,' I told Mike, assuming the day was a dead-end. Two beers had dulled my senses. I was sick of sitting in a car. Mike headed towards the Club.

When I got up to my room, I lay down on the bed in my clothes and closed my eyes.

6:10 P.M. JOHN

I woke up from my nap more tired than when I closed my eyes.

Dinner with M was scheduled for seven. I needed to be alert and alive and clear the beer fumes out of my head. A short walk seemed like a good idea. I ducked outside, collar up, hat on and head down, not concerned about my safety under a grey evening sky.

The wind was cold, spitting rain in my face, an instant wake-up call. I continued, breathing the cool air while blindly looking down, following squares of wet sidewalk. Ugly thoughts roamed my head. Nothing good had come from this day. Charlie and M had learned nothing, nothing I could take to my board meeting. The foul weather matched my mood, lost in thought. A quick glance at my watch to check the time, I didn't want to be late for dinner with

M. It was almost six-thirty. Time to return to the Club. M was once again in my life, making it tolerable somehow.

Phillip, I thought about Phillip, I didn't know why. He just popped into my head. Guess I couldn't let go of the idea he was involved.   Charlie had informed me he was in New York. I wondered why Phillip was here. Did he know something, anything that might help me, something I could take to the board?

Phillip often stayed at the Sherry Netherlands Hotel. I had passed it as I was headed back to the Club. On a whim I turned around and went inside the hotel lobby.

Marble floors greeted me, along with some highly fashionable furniture, warm and comforting away from the cold, damp, gray drizzle that existed outside.   The desk clerk looked familiar. I had stayed at this hotel in the past when I wanted a better room than the Club offered. It was close to the Club and convenient for meetings scheduled there.   Maybe the clerk would recognize me.

'Good afternoon,' I greeted him with a smile.

'Mr. Van Laan, it good to see you again, sir.'

'Yes, you too. Say, can you give me Phillip Palmer's room number?'

'I'm sorry sir, I can't give...'

'I know it isn't hotel policy, but I have a meeting with him. And well, I forgot his room number.' I replied, noticing the desk clerk's nameplate.

'Are you staying with us?' he asked.

'No, at the Club this trip, Tony.'

'I could ring him, sir?' Tony suggested, confirming that Phillip was staying at the hotel.

'That's not necessary. He knows I'm coming up.'

'He just came in, sir.'

'I know. We were in a meeting. You know, one meeting to another.' I lied easily, reaching for my wallet.

'Yes, yes, well, let's see. I guess it would be okay. The clerk searched his computer. 'Room 2019.'

'Thanks, Tony.' I slipped him a twenty.

Fear immediately began to eat a hole in my gut. I headed quickly towards the elevator anyway, putting aside any consideration for what I was doing. I was elated to have found Phillip. But I also knew if I thought about it for more than a few seconds, I knew I shouldn't try to see him. It was too risky, too many unknowns.

I hit an elevator button, putting my brain on hold. My cell phone began to vibrate in my pocket as I waited. It could be M. She wouldn't approve my seeing Phillip, especially not alone. Probably have Charlie tell me it was too dangerous, stay away, idiot. I ignored my cell phone and let it buzz in the pocket of my jacket. Thankfully, the elevator was empty as it rose in quiet technical efficiency; a low hum, a slight sensation of moving, was the only evidence I was rising high above an anxious, cold world outside. Floors clicked off repetitively, flashing white lights on the elevator panel until it slowed and the door opened. Down a deserted hallway, fear walked with me, talking to me, wouldn't shut up. Said I was making a mistake. Men who wanted to kill me could be with Phillip. I would make their task easy and walk into a trap of my own creation. Paranoia took hold. I hesitated and almost turned around.

Eerie silence lingered in an empty hotel hallway as I vacillated, dreading terror behind each closed door. But only my imagination assaulted me. Still, I knew I shouldn't be walking down this hall. I shouldn't be doing what I was doing. I should be turning around... Images of Monica passed through the dense matter behind my skull, screaming at me for being so dumb. I ignored her ranting. Phillip was in this hotel. I needed to talk to Phillip. It was a gamble, worth the risk.

A door marked 2019, I knocked and waited with my back to its peephole.

'Who is it?' I recognized Phillip's voice.

'I need to see you, old chap,' I said in my best rendition of Arthur's snooty British accent. Don't know why I used his accent. Just seemed the thing to do.

Phillip unlocked his door and opened it a crack. The latch rattled, still attached. I drove forward, ramming my shoulder into the door with as much force as I could gather. The latch snapped.

The swinging door caught Phillip square on the side of his face, sending him sprawling backward into his hotel room. A gun flew out of his hand when he hit the floor. He turned over, scrambling on his hands and knees towards the gun, which was sliding across the floor.

I closed the door, stepped into the room, and said as calmly as I could, 'It's me, Phillip. It's John Van Laan. Don't shoot. I don't have a weapon.' I placed my hands open at my side where he could see them.

He scrambled for his gun anyway, turned, and pointed it at me while on his knees.

I waited, standing over him.

'I just want to talk, Phillip,' I said. 'I'm alone. You have nothing to fear. Please put down your gun.'

For some reason, I felt quite calm.

When he had caught his breath, he touched his cheek where it had been bruised, and the swinging door hit him in the side of his face.

'Why shouldn't I shoot you, John?' he asked. 'You just broke into my room and assaulted me.'

'That would be pretty hard to explain, wouldn't it? Since it's me, someone you know, not a stranger. And I don't have a gun.'

'I guess.' He rubbed a red mark, which was beginning to swell on his forehead, and brushed his long gray hair back in a familiar habit.

I calmly walked past him and took a seat on a couch.

Phillip always traveled first class. His room at the Sherry Netherlands Hotel was no exception. Overstuffed chairs, expensive satin drapes and thickly sculptured rugs decorated his two-room suite. A dark wood desk stood in one corner of the room. Papers covered its surface. I sat on a couch, watching him get up off the floor. He came over toward me, pointing the gun at my head.

'Let's talk, Phillip,' I said calmly. 'It's been a long time since we talked. And we have some things to talk about, don't you think?'

He put his gun on a table and sat down in a chair opposite me. I knew he wouldn't shoot me. This wasn't Phillip's way. The Phillip I knew was not a violent man, conniving but not violent.

'So, how are you, John?' he asked, staring at me with unblinking, coal-black eyes.

'I've been better, Phillip.' I leaned forward. 'You see, someone is trying to kill me.'

'Life can be dangerous sometimes.'

'Wouldn't know anything about that, would you, Phillip?'

'No, why should I, John?' His voice was calm, laced with sarcasm.

'And I suppose you don't know anything about the people who sabotaged our lab in Australia?'

'No.'

'Or an armed robbery at our Hong Kong Distribution House?'

'No. I thought you came here to talk. Why ask me questions I can't possibly answer?'

'I think you can.'

'Ridiculous.'

'Let's just say I asked you these questions to establish a foundation for our conversation.'

He didn't respond.

'One more question. Been to Bangkok lately?'

'I haven't been to Bangkok for years,' he replied casually as if he half expected my question.

Phillip could lie as well as anyone without showing any outward emotion, not a clue to his deceitful behavior. He was remarkable in this ability. Lying had become an art form for him. He had been doing it for so many years he was an expert. Today was no exception.

'Oh, I think you have,' I replied. 'And I think you're working with the people who are trying to kill me.'

'That's preposterous, even for you, John. Where did you come up with this idea?'

The fact he chose to lie to me about Bangkok told me he was hiding something. The Thai were involved. I knew this for a fact. And he could be their inside man. That's the only thing that made sense. Still, I wanted him to confirm it.

'Let's just say I have my sources.'

'Well, your sources are telling you lies.'

'Okay Phillip, have it your way. I knew you would deny it. But I don't care because I know it's true.'

'I have not been ...'

'It's okay, Phillip. I understood you the first time. You don't need to lie again.'

Phillip sat very still, looking stoically arrogant like he was enjoying himself. The next move was mine.

'I'm here to ask you to stop all this insanity.'

I knew he had a big ego, and if I stroked it, he might tell me the truth. 'I'm asking you to stop before someone gets hurt, like me.'

'Why are you talking to me?' he replied. 'Why not talk to the people who are trying to kill you?'

'Because I believe you are the only person who can help me.'

'I have no idea what you're talking about.'

Phillip spent more time playing roles than he did living life. I sometimes wondered if he even had a real life. Or if he only lived in the fantasy world, he created in his mind. Now, as I watched him assume another role, I knew the answer.

'And furthermore...' he continued.

'Stop Phillip, remember who you're talking to. I know all about your ability to bullshit. For once, let's just deal with facts.'

'I'm talking about the facts,' he responded without hesitation, launching into a diatribe of half-truths and outright lies.

I sat back on the couch and let him rattle on, not really listening.

Life is hard. Facing life is difficult. And apparently this was especially true for Phillip. He had a difficult time dealing with real life, more than most people. He made retreating from reality an act of genius. But it often got him into trouble. His brilliant retreats from reality became his greatest impediment. His ability to create detailed, lifelike fantasies out of lies developed into his worst nightmare. Because in the end he began to believe his lies. And eventually it got so bad he couldn't distinguish between the truth and the fiction he created in his head.

I waited until finally, he stopped when he saw I wasn't paying attention.

'Why are you here?' he asked, his voice suddenly rising as he assumed a new character when he realized his old character was not convincing.

'Look, Phillip,' I responded calmly, 'I've come to the conclusion you're the inside person who has been working with some high government official in Thailand, orchestrating a reign of terror on me and my company.'

'That's absolute nonsense.'

When he began to say something else, I cut him off. 'Just shut up and listen for once.'

My cell phone vibrated again in my pocket as I spoke, probably M again, wondering about dinner. I ignored it and pushed the issue. 'Do you want me dead, Phillip? Is that what you really want?'

'You've lost your mind, John.'

'I don't think so.'

When he didn't respond, I continued to stroke his ego. 'Look, Phillip, I'm here because I need your help.'

I needed him to admit to working with the Thai. So, I did the only thing I thought might work, I appealed to his desire to be helpful. This was his only weakness. He was not a bad man, not deep inside. And I knew he would have trouble turning me down if I asked him for help. Because he liked helping people. That was the one anomaly in his unhinged personality.

He didn't respond immediately; he just looked temporarily lost. My request was bothering him. It had taken him by surprise. This was where his multiple personalities clashed. Deep down, somewhere inside his twisted brain, a kind man existed.

Finally, he responded. 'Why should I help you? You destroyed my company, my life.'

'Phillip, that's where you are so terribly wrong. I never took anything from you. Your company failed because of you and you alone. No matter how many times you tell everyone who will listen, your problems were caused by me. That's not true. *Phillip, you failed. You alone caused your company to fail.*'

This was too much for him to digest. I had gone too far. I watched almost in awe as he changed characters again, retreating into another one of his fantasies. I should have shut up then and walked out at that point. I should have known there was nothing more I could do, but I had come for the sole purpose of making him admit he was involved. I had to try.

'You had the same opportunities I had.' I pressed him. 'You failed and blamed me for your shortcomings.'

'That's simply not true,' he responded.

'Phillip, you can't make a lie true by simply repeating it twenty times.'

He was close to losing it. His face was getting red. His lips were twisted and tight.

I continued. 'This insanity has got to stop. I know you. And I don't believe this is what you want.' I paused and looked him straight in the eye. 'Tell me who is trying to kill me. If you don't help me, I'm going to die. Do you really want to be responsible for that happening?'

He looked at me like I was a hallucination, something that would disappear if he stared at it long enough.

Finally, I exploded, venting weeks of pent-up frustration. 'Well, are you willing to let me die, Phillip? Or will you help me? Because I need your help.'

He became uncharacteristically silent and didn't seem to have anything to say, which was out of character for him. I wondered if I had finally gotten through to him.

His hotel phone rang. Instinctively, he reached over to pick it up, hoping to move to another world. I jumped across the room, tore the phone from his hand, jerking the cord out of the wall, forcing him to stay in my world.

'I need your answer!' I demanded. 'It's just you and me. So, tell me. Do you want me dead?'

'No,' he finally answered. 'No, John.'

I believed him. It was the only time I thought he told the truth.

'Then tell me who is doing this.'

After a long pause, he replied softly as if he were sinking into a dream. 'I don't know what you are talking about.'

I had failed. No matter how hard I tried, it always ended this way. He always slipped away. I had made a mistake. I should not have come.

I stood to leave.

He sat on his couch, looking at his gun on a table. Then he said something that gave me chills.

'It's out of my hands, John.'

7:25 P.M. JOHN

Under stark streetlights, a gray mist floated in the air like tiny diamonds rising on occasional gusts of wind, riding the night air without a care in the world.

It occurred to me as I returned to the Club I should be thinking about my safety. I had just left Phillip's hotel room. He could have called someone while I was in the elevator and alerted them I was leaving his hotel. It was an opportunity to do me in.

Instead, my concerns drifted in the night air, floating on the mist with the wind as I sank into dejected misery. My meeting with Phillip had accomplished nothing. I should have known better. I had taken a big risk, and for what? Why did I think he would tell me anything? Did I really think the shock of confronting him face-to-face would jolt him into telling the truth?

It was only a short distance to the Club from his hotel. As I walked, Phillip's last comment kept running through my head, with the cold air chilling me to the bone.

It's out of my hands, John, he had said.

Could this be an admission of sorts, I wondered, especially coming from him? Normally, he was too smart to give anything away. However, just maybe this time I had broken through his defenses after all, if only for a brief time.

The doorman greeted me in the usual fashion as I entered the comfortable warmth and quiet solitude of the Club.

'Mr. Van Laan.'

I nodded and continued walking, deep in thought.

'Mr. Van Laan,' he said louder.

'Yes?' I turned to face him.

'Mr. Van Laan, I let a woman in. She said she is a friend of yours. She insisted on waiting for you. I couldn't stop her. I hope I did the right thing.'

'Tall redhead?'

'Yes, sir.'

'Very pretty?'

'Indeed, sir.'

'It's okay. Where is she?'

'I saw her go into the bar.'

'Thank you.'

My cell phone vibrated in my jacket pocket. Monica calling again? How many times had she called; two, maybe three times? I couldn't remember. Dinner with her was scheduled for seven! I had completely lost track of time. I looked at my watch. It was almost seven-thirty. I was in trouble, big time.

She was sitting at a table by the fireplace in the bar. A drink and a cell phone were on her table. A bartender smiled as I passed. I think he knew I was in trouble.

'Hi, M,' I said casually with a smile.

She looked up, obviously irritated. I could see it in her eyes. Her frowny line was in full tilt. She stood quickly and gave me a hug, a tear in her eye. Such displays of emotion are not commonly accepted practice at the Club. Stoic behavior is preferred in the common rooms. A few heads turned in annoyance. I kissed her cheek, ignoring my fellow club members, and held her close.

'Let's sit down,' I said quietly.

The waiter appeared immediately, probably wanting a ringside seat for what he assumed would be an interesting confrontation.

'Whiskey, straight up,' I told him as a fire burned in the background.

'I owe you an explanation,' I began.

The waiter lingered. I turned to him with a stare. 'That's all.'

'Very good sir.'

'You do...' she answered. 'Do you know how many ways I envisioned you dead?'

'I'm sorry.'

'That's it? You're sorry?' she fumed.

My drink came. I took a sip, allowing the liquid warmth to slide down my throat. Only the truth could get me out of this mess. That is if there was any possibility of getting out of it.

'I saw Phillip,' I began to defuse the situation.

'You saw Phillip?' She looked surprised.

I let this morsel of new information sink in before continuing. I knew she could understand immediately what I had done. And she would not like it as soon as she had time to think about it. I had only a brief window of opportunity to dispense as much information as possible before an explosion hit.

'I remembered Phillip sometimes stays at the Sherry Netherlands Hotel when he's in town,' I continued. 'I took a chance. He was there. I conned the desk clerk into giving me his room number. I met with him in his room. We had an interesting conversation. Would you like to know what he said?'

'Yes, of course. But John! Didn't you think it was dangerous?

'Yes, but I wanted...'

'Did you consider talking to Charlie and me first?'

'No, I...'

'Why?' She was pissed. Obviously, the relief of seeing me alive was fading fast. Before I could say another word, she interjected, 'No, let me answer for you, John. You didn't call because you knew what Charlie would say. He would have told you not to go. It was too dangerous... Instead, you did what you always do, didn't you? You did what you wanted to do, and to hell with everyone else.'

'No, that's not true. I went because I wanted to confront Phillip on my own terms.'

There was some truth in what I said. I hoped maybe it would slow her down, but it didn't.

'John, you could have been killed.'

'Didn't happen. See, I'm alive.'

I think she wanted to throw her drink in my face and leave. I waited... hoping she would calm down.

'Okay, what happened?' she finally asked.

'Well, nothing really, nothing serious, he stonewalled, lied as usual, admitting nothing. He wouldn't even admit to being in Bangkok, even when I told him I knew he had been there.'

She thought about this for a moment before asking, 'So you got nothing out of him?'

'No, except at the end of the conversation, he said something curious. He said it was out of his hands.'

'What did he mean?'

'I'm not sure.'

This gave her something to think about... but only for a second. 'Still, you took a big risk!' she stated emphatically.

'Not really... we had a short tussle when I rammed my shoulder into his room door. And he had a gun, but...'

'John!'

'He wasn't going to shoot me, not face to face. He isn't capable of murder.'

'Are you sure?'

I took another sip of whiskey. 'Well, he didn't do it, did he? So... yes, I'm sure. Anyway, let's change the subject... Have you eaten?'

That was the wrong subject!

'No, I've been waiting for you. And calling you and thinking you were dead. I lost my appetite a long time ago.'

'I truly am sorry.'

'All because you decided what you were doing was more important than answering my calls,' she stated, ignoring my apology.

What could I say?

She looked at me without pity. I was dead meat, and I knew it.

'I'm going to my hotel.' She stood to leave, mumbling to herself, 'Charlie needs to know you talked to Phillip.'

'M, let me buy you dinner. You don't need to leave. You can call Charlie from here.'

She hesitated.

I took her arm and felt her resist.

She sighed and relaxed. 'I need to clean up first.'

'Okay, let's go to my room.'

We never made it to dinner.

Instead, we made love until we were both exhausted, the kind of sex that makes every atom of your body come alive. And when it was over; when I was finally totally spent, contentment settled over me and I fell into a deep and dreamless sleep.

When I woke up in the morning, she was gone.

CHARLOTTESVILLE, VIRGINIA, FEBRUARY 27, THURSDAY, 4 45 P.M. JOHN

Listening to the sound of M's recorded voicemail message was pleasant enough the first few times, but after a while, it became distinctly distant.

It wasn't the same as talking to a real person. In fact, after countless attempts to reach her, hearing her same monotone message every time became slightly maddening. I wanted to talk to the real her, not some bloody machine.

After her tenth half-hearted recorded promise to call back, I began to seriously doubt she had any intention of making good on her mechanized pledge. Eventually, even I was smart enough to know it wasn't going to happen. I had screwed up. I had ignored her calls the night I met with Phillip and she was ignoring mine now. I got it. I would have to pay for my sin.

Charlie called instead. Apparently, he had become their newly designated director of communication, representing the two of them. He politely told me Arthur had returned to London. And then, with some sarcasm, he informed me Phillip had disappeared; mostly, he assumed, due to my indiscretion. After I met with him, Phillip must have assumed he was being followed and decided to use a different alias. Charlie let me know in no uncertain terms he was upset I had not called him before meeting Phillip. But he did say Monica had explained my reasoning, and he guessed it made some sense. He would let me off the hook this time. But if it ever happened again, well...he said if I wanted to remain in his confidence in the future, I had to promise to return the favor. No more excuses next time.

I accepted his terms of communication and thanked him. I didn't ask him about M. And he didn't volunteer anything more except to suggest I return to Charlottesville where it was safer. I agreed, returning that afternoon.

Work was piled high on my desk when I stepped into my office. I had no enthusiasm for the task. Why bother, I reasoned. I was going to be fired. The board meeting was in a few days. I dreaded this meeting more than any other time in the history of my company. Without a break, without some new information, anything to explain what was happening to us and why; without this I had nothing to say at the meeting which would help me retain my job.

Now, that was not exactly true. The truth was I did have the information I could tell the board, really important information. But the problem was I couldn't use it. I couldn't tell the board what I knew about the Thai because Charlie would not let me. When I called him to ask for his help, he courteously explained that any mention of him or the CIA at the board meeting would severely jeopardize his ability to build a case against the Thai official. He explained his reasons for not wanting anyone at the meeting to know what he was doing. He began by reminding me I had potentially blown his case when I talked to Phillip. Because it was possible some of my board members were involved. Therefore, bringing them into the loop was out of the question since they would immediately report the information to my enemy.

But my job was on the line, I pleaded.

Charlie said he was sorry. He understood, but his hands were tied. He had done more for me than he should have. Besides, his career was on the line too. He had gone out on a limb for me because of Monica. And oh, by the way, he reminded me again that I had returned his help by not informing him I was meeting Phillip. And this, according to Charlie, made his job far more difficult. He again reminded me he had accepted my reasons for not telling him. Now, it was my turn to accept his reasons for my staying out of his way.

I felt like a schoolboy who had just had my hands slapped by a smiling teacher. And to make matters worse, I had the distinct impression M was monitoring my punishment in Charlie's presence. And she was enjoying it.

I spent the next few days mostly ignoring my job when I should have been spending every minute calling board members, trying to gain their understanding and support. Instead, I daydreamed and agonized; I daydreamed about a certain lady who wouldn't return my calls and agonized about the board meeting, but

I talked to almost no one. I declined to answer most calls. And I didn't return many messages.

The exception was Lin. I listened to his counsel. But even his tightly wound oriental logic couldn't move me to take action. I simply could not bring myself to do what he suggested. He told me it was time to ask the board members to repay some long-forgotten IOUs. I had generously given to them in the past and supported their businesses with loans and orders when they needed help. Now, it was time for them to help me. I needed to get on the phone and talk to them, he said. Tell them you want their support.

I agreed with him, but I couldn't do it. Not because I didn't care. I cared deeply. I did not want to be booted out of my job.

But I couldn't bring myself to beg.

BANGKOK THAILAND, MARCH 3, MONDAY, 2:10 P.M. LUANG

The old patriarch decided to make one final attempt to influence his nephew.

A recent memo from his nephew to the family presented an opportunity.

The confidential internal communication detailed activities relating to a certain American executive who was alive and well despite several attempts to kill the man. The memo did not go so far as to blame anyone for failure and this seemed odd to the old man. He knew his nephew was fond of placing blame. But in this case, rather than blaming anyone, it seemed his nephew had simply accepted the fact the American CEO had simply been lucky.

Luang thought this was an omen, something he could use. He decided to suggest to his nephew that there might be a reason the CEO was still alive. Such as: negotiating with the American might be better than killing him?

Building a company from scratch could cost far more than simply taking control of the existing one. The difference was millions of dollars and years of time lost attempting to bring a new company up to the current state of organization, which the American company now enjoyed. And the task could prove to be difficult, perhaps even impossible to accomplish. The American CEO had built something very special. So why not consider another way to accomplish the family's goals, a better way that does not include violence? Why not consider buying the existing American company rather than destroying it?

Luang had been his nephew's mentor from an early age. He had spent years attempting to teach the boy about the importance of money. He now hoped his work was not in vain. Appealing to his nephew from a financial perspective might help him succeed where he had failed in the past.

He also knew the task would be difficult. Any attempt to openly convince his nephew to follow his direction would be rejected immediately if his nephew felt this new direction came from his uncle, and was, therefore, not his nephew's idea. If his nephew had a fault, it was arrogance. He never did anything which did not originate in his brain. In order to succeed, the old man had to convince his nephew that the idea was his nephew's idea, something his nephew had discovered, not an idea that had come from an old incompetent uncle. He would have to point his nephew in the right direction without telling him what to do.

Sitting at his desk, the old man took out a clean sheet of paper. Carefully, he began crafting a handwritten letter to his nephew. Every word needed to be considered. Every sentence was fashioned to say exactly what he intended. No blame for past failures would be included in the text. Nothing would be communicated except two simple facts: First, the American CEO was alive for a reason. Second, the cost of building a new company would be expensive, time-consuming, and difficult. The letter would contain only these two simple observations. It would be up to his nephew to discover the proper course of action.

After patiently editing his letter several times, rewriting the sentences until he finally decided his letter was perfect. Only then did he copy it slowly on a clean sheet of paper, sign the letter and place it in a sealed envelope addressed to his nephew, marked confidential. A man servant was directed to hand deliver the letter to his nephew with strict instructions to entrust it to no one else.

When his servant had closed the door to his room, the old man lay down on his couch and tried to rest. He was tired. He knew his letter was important, and he was happy he had taken the time to write it. But he feared he would not be successful.

Troubled thoughts whirled through his restless mind, and he was unable to sleep.

As he lay on his couch with his eyes closed, he worried that he might never find peace in his old age.

CHARLOTTESVILLE, MARCH 10, MONDAY, 8:10 P.M. JOHN

Arny was normally gone by the time I returned to my apartment each night.

He was either in town with his buddies playing poker or relaxing in the apartment I had built for him next door. His absence had become customary ever since M left. He would put a cold dinner in my refrigerator, ready to microwave, his work done for the day. And, as I said before, this was just fine with me. It meant I didn't have to deal with him and his questions, his observations on life, mostly his accusations about a certain woman. He never gave up. He bugged me every chance he had, on the phone, in my office, and in as many ways as he could find. He wanted to know why Monica was not in my apartment. He said he liked her. He missed her. He assumed it was my duty to have her living in my apartment for his entertainment.

I didn't quite see it his way. And I did not tell him about our rendezvous in New York. I knew this would simply encourage him. I kept that quiet.

So, when I entered my apartment that evening, I fully expected to have to scrounge in my refrigerator for a cold dinner. I was wrong, and my first clue was the unmistakable. Mouthwatering odor of steak cooking on the grill, immediately assaulted my hungry senses. And the only logical conclusion I could come to was that my friend, Arny, had planned an ambush. And for his ambush to succeed, a spy in my office was required; most likely, a security guard was in his back pocket. Arny had been called the minute I left my office and that's when he threw a steak on the grill.

Oddly, I wasn't irritated. I was almost glad. I hadn't seen him for days. And besides, the steak smelled really good, and I was hungry.

'Hi, boss,' Arny greeted me cheerily.

'Hey Arny, kind of late to be cooking dinner, isn't it?' I smiled.

'Got a couple of steaks, cornbread, and potatoes. Sound okay?' he asked, ignoring my comment.

'Sounds great.'

'How about a cold one?' he unscrewed the cap of a Molson, poured the beer into a clear glass, and returned to cooking.

I took a sip of beer, wondering how long it would take before he got around to his favorite subject. Not long, as it turned out. As soon as I began to relax, thinking maybe he would give me a break, not talk about her... he began. 'I talked to Monica today,' he casually mentioned, like it was an everyday occurrence for him.

Obviously, his reason for staying late to make me dinner was more than simply a desire to feed me warm food. Apparently, he was a man with a mission. I sighed, resigning myself to having to listen to his chatter if I wanted a hot steak dinner.

'You did?'

'Yeah, she seems happy,' he smiled.

'Anything else?'

'Not really, except something about how she and Charlie were working the case. Nothing new yet.'

'I see.'

I began to wonder if Monica had called to ask him to pass along the information, but Arny went into silent mode, giving nothing away, whistling as he worked, waiting.

Time passed. He knew I had to ask.

'So, how did you happen to talk to her?' I said.

'Oh, we talk all the time. I thought you knew.'

'No.'

'Yes, she and I are great friends. Didn't she mention this to you?'

'No.'

'Really,' a mischievous grin formed on his lips as he attempted to contain his delight.

I had the distinct impression a small conspiracy had been occurring behind my back for some time, but I said nothing.

He served dinner. It was delicious. Arny and I continued to chat; nothing important, mostly sports, the usual topic of discussion as we ate. It felt good and lifted my spirits considerably. But later, after he retired to his apartment, reality set in. My deeply disturbed state of mind once again regained control of my twisted brain. I needed some fresh air to clear my head, went outside on my deck dressed in a winter coat. It was a cold night, but it felt good. A glass of whiskey warmed my inner being while looking into a night sky full of stars.

Sure, it was great to know Monica and Arny were talking to each other, but why wasn't she talking to me? I wondered if she was still mad at me. Or was it something else? Was she in D.C. renewing an old love affair with Charlie? Was she simply out of my class? Gave me one last goodbye, mercy fuck, just to be nice. Wasn't this a line from a movie? Weren't all fucks, mercy fucks, from a woman's point of view? Be nice to a guy. Then time to say goodbye and off to her next life. Ta ta, hasn't it been fun?

The valley below my deck spread out in a fairytale-like vista of progressively shaded moonlit shadows. It was real, but it didn't look real in the dim light. A bright moon dominated the night sky. Thousands of sparkling lights shone in the clear air. I tried to imagine looking deep into the crevasses of infinite space, light years from Earth. But I knew I could not see that far. I was only looking into black voids between time-traveling beams of light, which quickly dispersed into my eye, fleeting energy beams from a star that might no longer exist.

I thought about my last night with Monica in New York. I wished I had not slept so deeply. I should have stayed awake. I should never have let her steal away in the morning, never let her out of my sight.

So what?

I couldn't control her. The fact is I controlled almost nothing.

My body cooled slowly in a cool night breeze. In a brief moment of absolute clarity, I realized that all my frustrations were nothing more than a waste of time. What will be, will be. I had only one choice: one vote in my future.

I could either directly involve myself in the events that were about to occur, or I could sit by in a state of mental paralysis and do nothing.

NEW YORK, N.Y., MARCH 13, THURSDAY, 8:55 A.M. JOHN

New York City traffic was tied up in knots when I returned.

Early spring road construction created traffic jams even more frustrating than normal. I resigned myself to the fact it would take time to drive from the airport to my Club and settled into the comfortable rear seat of Mike's Buick.

Lin had called a few days earlier to tell me Arthur was arriving early, several days before our board meeting. I didn't bother asking Lin how he knew this. He had his ways. He also told me he decided to come early, something about business in New York, I wasn't really paying attention.

With no real need to remain in Charlottesville, I informed Lin I would also arrive early. He approved. Said it would give us an opportunity to talk before the board meeting. I called my Club and moved up my reservation.

Mike's big Buick inched along in traffic.

'So, how are the Yankees shaping up this year?' I leaned over the front seat to ask Mike. I knew he liked talking baseball.

Mike answered by giving me a complete rundown of the Yankee's roster, player by player. I sat back, half listening while staring out the car window. A tall girl with long black hair and an open black raincoat flying in the wind strolled the sidewalk as I daydreamed about another lady, one with long red hair. Mike droned on in the front seat about the Yankees as we became stalled in traffic. The girl with black hair was making better time than Mike, walking with confident strides and athletic legs in black hose and high heels. Abruptly crossing in front of our Buick, she zigzagged through the mired traffic.

'She's a looker, eh boss?' Mike peered at me in his rearview mirror.

'She is indeed.' I smiled.

Finally, after easing past a construction zone, Mike hit his accelerator. His big blue Buick weaved in and out of traffic. He was a great driver. Although we did not exactly share a love for baseball, we did enjoy talking about race cars, Formula One racing cars in particular. Mike was Italian and he loved Ferraris with a passion. And like all Italians, he knew deep down he could have been a famous race car driver like Michael Schumacher. In his case, I believed him.

I thought about Monica as Mike concentrated on driving. She was somewhere in the city. I knew this because Charlie had called to tell me he was in New York. He casually mentioned Monica was with him. I guess he wanted me to know. I wasn't quite sure why. He asked if we could get together to review security for the board meeting. I agreed and thanked him after setting a time and place to meet.

Monica had still not returned any of my calls and I was trying to put her out of my mind, but it wasn't working. My meeting with Charlie was scheduled for tomorrow afternoon and I wondered if she would be in attendance. And what I would say if she did show up. Unfortunately, I had been spending most of my time thinking about her when I should have been preparing for the board meeting, but I wasn't, just couldn't do it.

However, Lin was. He had continued to lobby for me. He told me he was sensing some movement among board members. A few were reconsidering. He thought a vote to fire me might be closer than he had originally concluded. Arthur and Bob might not have the lock they thought they had. Lin now said he wasn't sure what would happen. It all depended on how the meeting went. I thanked him for all his hard work on my behalf. He was a good friend. I knew I had no chance to win without his support.

Lin was currently on an airplane flying across the Pacific Ocean and would be in New York later that afternoon. We had plans to meet as soon as he settled into his hotel.

I stared out the window of Mike's Buick as we traveled the streets of the Big Apple. It felt good to have returned to the activity of the big city. Charlottesville had begun to feel confining the last few days. Being in my office felt like house arrest, doing penance, forced to wait.

I took a deep breath.

'Hey boss, you okay? You're awfully quiet today.'

'I'm fine, Mike.'

'We're almost to your Club.'

'Thanks, Mike.'

My cell phone rang.

'John,' a familiar male voice said.

'Yes?' I answered, trying to identify the voice.

'John, it's Phillip.'

'How did you get this number?' I reacted in anger.

'That's not important, John. What is important is I want to talk to you.'

'Okay.' I tried to calm down.

'The last time we met, you asked me to help you. Isn't that right?'

'Yes.'

'Do you still want my help?'

'Of course.'

'Okay, Arthur and I have a solution which we think will be good for everyone concerned. We would like to discuss it with you. So... question is, are you willing to meet with us?'

'Are you kidding me, you and Arthur?'

'Why are you surprised, John?' he asked. 'Did you think Arthur couldn't be bought?'

'No, guess not.' I was stunned. 'Who bought him?'

'I'll tell you when we meet.'

'Why not now?'

'I'll tell you when I'm ready and not before. Now, do you want my help or not? Make up your mind.'

'What are you offering, Phillip?'

'All in good time. First, you must agree to meet with us. And John, while you are trying to decide... remember it was you who said you wanted it stopped. Well, we're willing to help, but only if you are willing to work with us. So... are you willing to meet with us to discuss it or not?'

My shit detector was rocketing up and down the scale as I talked to Phillip. Questions, too many questions, too many unknowns. Like, who was Phillip working with besides Arthur? And why did they want to meet with me now? And what did they want? Perhaps more importantly, should I agree to meet with them? Could it be a trap that would get me killed? But... what choice did I have? If they really were offering me a way out of this mess, I needed to at least hear them out... didn't I? No matter what the risk. Didn't I?

'It's a simple question, John, yes or no?' Phillip pushed me.

My mind whirled. I didn't know what to say. Finally, I said, 'Okay.'

'You in New York, right?' Phillip questioned.

'Yes.'

'Good, meet us for lunch at the Buddakan Restaurant on Ninth Street. It is a very public place. You don't need to worry. Nothing is going to happen there.'

'Okay.'

'And come alone.'

'Okay.'

'And finally, talk to no one... no one! Understand? Just be at the restaurant by noon. If you come alone, I'll join you. If not, you won't see me. You will see only Arthur, but he'll have nothing for you. Do you understand? He won't contribute anything. He'll act surprised to see you.'

'I got it.'

My phone fell silent.

Icy cold, I felt a deathly cold pass through my body despite perspiring in the warmth of the car's interior.

'Trouble, boss?' Mike asked, having monitored my facial expressions in his rear-view mirror.

'You could say that. I guess I have a date for lunch.'

'The red-haired chick?'

'No, I wish it was the lady.'

Mike agreed to drive me to my luncheon appointment after I checked in at my Club. My room was ready when I arrived. I slowly unpacked with Phillip's phone call playing in my subconscious while I organized my room.

His call had been completely unanticipated. Of all the possible scenarios which had run through my head during the previous week, of all possibilities I had tried to anticipate, this was one I had never considered. I didn't know how to react. I badly needed time to think.

I wondered what they wanted and why. What were they going to propose? I wanted to know, but I also knew I had an obligation to call Charlie first. Even though I was hesitant to involve him in this because Phillip had warned me to tell no one, I had no choice. I had promised Charlie I would keep him informed, and I couldn't go back on my word, not now, not if I wanted his help in the future. My hands were tied.

'Charlie,' I said into my cell phone after he answered.

'Yes.'

'It's John Van Laan.'

'Yes.'

'Charlie, I have a situation. Got a minute to talk?'

'Sure, John, one minute. What is it?'

'Phillip Palmer, he called. He wants to meet.'

'You're kidding,' Charlie reacted with astonishment.

'No, and apparently Arthur is joining us.'

'Arthur... your Arthur?'

'Yes.'

'Did he call you on your cell?' Charlie asked, immediately digging into details like any good CIA agent.

'Yes.'

'How did he get your number? It's unlisted, isn't it?'

'Maybe Arthur got it for him.'

'But Arthur doesn't have the number, does he?' asked Charlie, ignoring my suggestion. Apparently, the techno-spy in him was more interested in my cell phone security than he was in my current dilemma.

'Arthur had my number in the past,' I replied. 'But not since I changed it, not with everything which has been happening.'

'Didn't you tell your office not to give your number to anyone?'

'Yes... but why does this matter?' I asked, getting frustrated with Charlie's attention to minutia. I had bigger problems to solve than how Phillip got my cell phone number.

'I'll check it out. Someone gave him your number. I would like to know who. It could be important. Now, about the meeting, you can't go.'

'Why?' I asked, incredulous.

'You know why. These people are dangerous,' he said dismissively. 'When and where is the meeting?'

'Noon for lunch at a restaurant called Buddakan on Ninth Street.'

'You do understand the importance of staying alive? Don't you, John?'

'Of course.'

'You can't go anywhere near that meeting,' Charlie stated, no flinching in his voice.

'I guess.'

'No guessing, John.'

'But I have to go, Charlie. Don't you understand I've got to know what they will offer?'

In the background, I faintly heard M pepper Charlie with questions even as he was trying to ignore her.

'Hold on a minute, John,' Charlie demanded.

I waited, listening to Charlie explain my situation to M. I couldn't understand what she was saying, but it sounded like they were having an argument. Finally, he came back on the line.

'She wants to talk to you, John,' he said dismissively.

'Okay,' I replied, trying to be calm.

'John,' she said as soon as Charlie handed her his phone.

'Hi Monica, how are you?'

'Fine. You must not go to that meeting, John. You do know why, don't you?'

'Why?'

'Because you can't trust these people, it's that simple.'

'But they want to make a deal. If I don't go, I won't know what they have to offer. Maybe a compromise can be worked out which will be good for everyone. Can I afford to ignore them?'

'John, surely you don't believe them anymore.'

'What are you talking about?'

'John,' she sounded frustrated. 'It's not about just you or Phillip anymore. Or Arthur, either. It's about the economy of countries. It's about thousands of jobs, John. It's about control and power, nothing more, nothing less. They want you out, gone.'

'Okay, I get it. But don't I need to hear what they have to offer?'

'No, John.'

'No?'

'No, because you know the deal already, and it's not the deal you want. The only question for you is: do you want to live? Because the odds are if you go to this meeting, you won't come out alive.'

I didn't respond, my blood throbbing in my temples.

'Well?' she demanded.

'Do you want me to live?' I asked stupidly because I didn't know what else to say, regretting my words as soon as they jumped out of my mouth.

She paused before responding. 'John... that's a really stupid question... Here, talk to Charlie. And John, stay away from Phillip.'

She abruptly gave the phone back to Charlie before I could say another word.

'All right, John, this is how we play it,' Charlie stated. 'I'm going to send some of my people to the restaurant to determine if Arthur and Phillip actually intended to show. Let's find out first if they are really interested in meeting with you. Or if it was just a trap.'

'Okay.' I agreed, although clearly, I was not happy.

'Where are you now?'

'At my Club.'

'Stay there. I'll send a couple of my men over to cover you. They'll be at your Club within an hour.'

The line went silent immediately. He gave me no opportunity to object.

I thought about what he said, but only for a minute. Quickly finishing my unpacking, I headed for the door of my room. I needed to get out of there before Charlie's guys arrived. I assumed they would severely restrict my mobility, and I didn't want that, not now.

I mentioned to the doorman as I walked past, something about a couple of guys will be looking for me. Tell them I have some errands to do. Ask them to please have a seat in the lobby and wait for me to return.

I hoped this would stall Charlie's guys.

10:55 A.M. JOHN

I wasn't very good company, but Mike didn't seem to mind.

We went for coffee. I didn't have much to say. He did most of the talking. The hot coffee tasted good. I don't remember much else. I was too preoccupied, obsessed with my conversation with M and Charlie, wondering if I was making a mistake not going to see Phillip. As for Mike, he spent his time chatting in the background, trying to keep me occupied.

I like Mike. One of the reasons I like him is that he doesn't really need another person to have a two-sided conversation. All I had to do was nod or grunt once in a while. That's enough for Mike. He is one of the few men I know who can carry on a conversation with himself. That morning, the topic of his interest was New York politics. I wasn't listening. I glanced at my watch; it was almost lunchtime.

'Mike,' I suggested when I couldn't stand it any longer. 'You know a Chinese restaurant on Ninth Street, Budda something?'

'The Buddakan.'

'That's the one.'

'Let's go there.'

'Sure, boss, I know the place.'

I paid the tab for coffee and went outside in time to see Mike pull his Buick to the curb. I got into the front seat rather than the back. Mike didn't say a word. He drove as I explained the situation to him. I told him to find a parking place near the restaurant, close enough so we could see the entrance but far enough away so no one would notice us.

This wasn't going to be easy. Parking in New York is a puzzle not easily solved. Fortunately, Mike is a very resourceful guy. He found a place where we could see the front doors of the restaurant while parked in a loading zone. He said not to worry. He would move if he had to.

We could only vaguely see the people who were entering the restaurant. Ninth Street is five lanes wide, and we were on the other side of the street from the restaurant, which was okay with me. I just wanted to be near the place. But the truth was, it was killing me to be outside the restaurant. I really wanted to go inside and deal with Arthur and Phillip, but I had no choice. I had to listen to Charlie and M. Going against their wishes now could mean losing them. Still... I didn't like it.

The weather was gray and cold. Clouds had begun to thin, and occasionally, the sun broke through, warming the car's interior. It was well past twelve o'clock when we arrived. Phillip and Arthur could have already gone inside the restaurant before we got there. I tried to relax with nothing to do. I considered calling M's cell phone, but I didn't know what I would say.

Time dragged.

New York City pranced past our windows full of nervous energy while we sat in Mike's car. Everyone seemed intent on going somewhere, doing something. Everyone except me. Not because I didn't have anything to do, I did. And I could have been doing it and it might have been important. Instead, I was doing nothing... nothing except sitting patiently and wondering what was happening across the street.

'Mike, tell me if you see anything interesting,' I finally requested. I was bored and a little drained, hadn't slept well last night. I decided to rest.

I described Arthur and Phillip to Mike. Then Charlie and Monica, explaining my girlfriend and her partner would probably be driving a nondescript government car. I told Mike to be on the alert for them. I don't want them to know I was here.

'Just let me know if you see them.'

He nodded.

The warm sun shining on our car's interior felt good. I pushed a button for the reclining passenger seat to a down position, leaned my head back and closed my eyes.

1:54 P.M. JOHN

'Boss,' Mike said loudly for a second time.

I opened my eyes in a rush and sat up just in time to see a man duck into the back seat of a black limo that was sitting at the curb in front of the restaurant. The driver closed the door and walked around the car to get in the driver's seat.

'Is that one of your guys?' Mike asked.

'Maybe,' I replied. My eyes were still blurry.

The limo pulled away from the entrance to the restaurant and headed up the street.

'Mike, did you see a gold logo on the door?'

'Ya looked like a mountain inside a circle,' Mike replied.

'That's Bob's limo. Arthur never goes anywhere when he's in New York except in Bob's limo.'

I heard them before I saw them: motorbikes accelerating in a high-pitched whine, three crotch-rockets with riders wearing wildly painted helmets and brightly colored leather jackets. They screamed through the intersection, weaving in and out of traffic as if they were immune to death. I admired their speed and grace. Motorcycles are a normal part of the New York traffic scene. Still, I watched in fascination as one of the cyclists headed directly towards a car turning left into the intersection. The driver slammed the brakes and hit the horn. The cyclist never let up on the gas and smoothly leaned over to swerve out of his way. Riding his brightly painted bike with flashing chrome wheels, he quickly passed several cars as if they were standing still.

For a brief moment, I wanted to be him, free, young, and riding a motorcycle again.

I pushed the button to raise my passenger seat to a sitting position. Arthur was gone. There was nothing more to do here. It was time to return to my Club. I didn't need to wait for Phillip to exit the restaurant. If he was here, I was sure Charlie would put a tail on him. And the tail might spot us if we tried to follow.

'Hey,' said Mike. 'Is that your girlfriend's car coming up the street?'

I ducked down, catching only a glimpse of a black man and a red-haired woman sitting in a gray, nondescript Ford.

'Could be.'

'Want to follow?' Mike asked.

'No. Let's return to my Club.'

'Okay, boss.'

Mike started his Buick while rolling down his window for some fresh air. The open window made it easy to hear gunshots sounding like distant Chinese firecrackers, accompanied by squealing tires in full brake lock-up. A loud metallic thud followed like a canon shot, accompanied by more gunshots echoing across the canyon walls of the city.

'Sounds like automatic pistols,' Mike said easily, as if this was common knowledge in New York.

'Let's go.'

I didn't need to ask. Mike was already on his accelerator, then the brakes. His big Buick hesitated for an instant before completing a neat U-turn when Mike spotted an opening, jumping into traffic, barely missing a car speeding up the right lane. Swerving left to avoid a slow-moving car, Mike looked for holes in traffic and open lanes as he raced up the street towards the last echoes of gunfire.

A flashing red light appeared ahead as we approached the intersection of Fifteenth Street. Cars were already stopped on the road, their red taillights warning us. Mike hit his brakes hard. I braced myself against the dashboard, anticipating an impact. His Buick slid to a stop inches from the rear bumper of a stalled van. The intersection was completely stalled. We were stuck half a block from the flashing red light seen reflecting off storefront windows.

I got out of the car and started walking towards the red light. In a state of paranoia and fear, I was worried. Arthur's limo had been followed by Charlie and M's Ford. They had both driven in the direction of the gunfire. I told myself not to think negatively. It could have nothing to do with M or Arthur. There was no need to jump to conclusions. Walking at a fast pace, I stayed off to the side, near the buildings, knowing I shouldn't be here, trying to blend in with the crowd. I didn't want Charlie or M to see me.

With the sounds of gunfire and harsh metal crashes still echoing in my ears, I wondered who was shooting and who had been targeted. Who was wounded, and who was still alive? I had to know, hoping against hope Monica was not involved as images of torn metal and ripped bodies rotated through my mind's eye.

Gawkers came running, coming from all directions, bumping and pushing. The scene got crowded near where a red light was flashing from the roof of a gray Ford parked in the middle of the street. It had to be Charlie's car. Thankfully, I saw no damage to the car and no wounded bodies. But I didn't see her. I still didn't know if she was okay.

Pushing and shoving, I moved ahead, less worried now about being seen and more worried about what had happened, trying to get closer. Bodies pressed, New Yorkers, no etiquette expected, none given. Sweet perfume and sour sweat mixed with the pungent odor of hot evaporating radiator fluid dripping on the pavement as I got closer. Straining to get close, yet not sure I wanted to be there.

I have never run to tragedy, never chased fire engines, never stopped at an accident scene except to help. Life contains too much pain to look for it. Usually it follows you, finds you without searching for it. But this time I could not stay away. I had to know what happened. Too much was at stake.

A brief glimpse of a wrecked car could be seen through the crowd. It was a long black limo parked at an odd angle in the road. Its hood was bent, inserted into the side of a parked yellow taxi cab. People were milling around. A man shouted to stand back, give air. A barrier quickly formed ahead, a circle of humanity surrounding a tragic spectacle. The crowd pushed, congesting, tightening, strangling the scene.

Getting closer, a big, tall man in a long coat briefly moved aside, creating a small opening in the edge of a circle of adrenalin junkies who had run to witness the suffering of other humans. I shoved into the opening. The big man pushed back, unwilling to give space. I held my ground.

Broken glass, glittering like a thousand diamonds shining in the sunlight, littered the black pavement. The back door of the wrecked limo was open wide. A gold logo, Bob's logo, was painted on the door. Multiple neatly round holes pocketed its black sheet metal, marring the otherwise smooth surface. Instinctively, I looked away for a moment, reluctant to see the carnage, whispering a short prayer before looking up again. A body was lying on the street near the limo, not moving, legs sprawled in an unnatural position. Mostly covered by a black coat, no one was attending to this person. Pools of blood could be seen seeping slowly from under the coat, extinguishing reflections from some of the shining crystals of broken glass on the street. A tuft of curly hair was the only clue to the identity of the dead person. Had to be Arthur.

That's when panic took over, my heart beat racing; I needed to go, get out of there. Didn't want to see anymore, but looked up anyway, one more time, briefly.

A tall black man dressed in a dark blue suit coat was standing near the body with his back to me. He could be Charlie, acted like Charlie. I couldn't see his face as he attended to the driver of the limo, who was slumped over its steering wheel. I recognized the hurt man. He was Bob's chauffeur. I knew him because he had often driven me. That's when I saw her standing near the limo, with red hair and a raincoat. Monica was okay, not hurt. That's all I needed to know. It was time to leave.

No doubt, it was Arthur's corpse lying on the street in a pool of blood and glass under a coat. And he was obviously dead, not moving, no one looking after him.

Abruptly pushing out of the crowd with no concern for the people I pushed, I had to go. Finally breaking free of the tragedy junkies, I slumped over for a moment, sick to my stomach. A couple of deep breaths of fresh air helped. Enough to regain my composure. Mike's car was still stalled in traffic. I am heading in that direction, blending in with the crowd as much as possible, not trying to understand. I was too physically ill to process what I had just witnessed. People rushed past me as I headed against the tide of thrill seekers, trying to stay out of their way.

A gentleman, Asian looking, momentarily caught my eye. He was a short man, didn't seem to be in any hurry. I thought this odd, him standing there very still, looking in my direction as people hurried past. I stopped, glanced around, thinking he must be looking at someone or something behind me. Nothing unusual attracted my attention, nothing worth stopping to see.

When I turned, he was gone.

2:20 P.M. JOHN

'What happened?' asked Mike.

'It's hard to know,' I replied, words coming fast in staccato tempo. 'The limo you saw. It's wrecked, shot up. A body is lying next to it on the street. Person looks dead. I think it is my friend Arthur.'

I was trying to be calm, control my breathing, and slow my heart rate. But it wasn't working. I was too hyped up, death too near.

'They whacked your guy Arthur?' Mike asked in his Italian lingo.

'Yes, I think so.'

'Man... that's cruel.'

'Can we get out of here, Mike?'

'Sure.'

His Buick was trapped in the intersection. Cars surrounding it, stationary, couldn't break free. Mike leaned out of his window and started yelling instructions at the other drivers. I sat in the passenger seat, very still, wanting badly to be away from this latest version of hell.

'Yeah, yeah, yous, move it,' Mike yelled. 'You... yes, you lady, turn to the left and go!'

Finally, he got out of his Buick and started waving his arms, giving directions like a traffic cop. I watched, only vaguely aware of what was going on. Cars began to move slowly. Mike got back behind the driver's wheel and inched his way past a few stalled, brain-dead drivers, finally breaking free of the traffic jam.

'Where to boss?' he asked.

'Don't know.'

I thought for a moment and then told him to return to my Club. That was where I was supposed to be, where I should have stayed. I wished now I had not come. Mike headed uptown.

'No hurry, Mike,' I said after a moment.

'Okay. So, what really happened?' Mike asked.

'I wish I knew,' I was finally regaining some composure.

We drove in silence as Mike expertly weaved expertly through afternoon traffic.

'Maybe we should stop for a drink,' Mike said. 'You look like you could use one.'

'Sure, it's early, but why not?' I replied, thinking I must have looked pale.

My cell rang. I fumbled to get it out of my pocket.

'Hello,' I said rather feebly.

'John.'

'Yes, Monica,' I recognized her voice.

'John, there has been a shooting.'

'Yes.'

'Arthur has been killed.'

'Oh,' I replied, trying to sound normal.

'You don't sound surprised.'

'I am. How did it happen?'

She described in detail how men on motorcycles shot at Arthur's limo, forcing it into a parked taxi cab. One of the cyclists calmly got off his bike and emptied an automatic pistol into Arthur before he could escape.

'You're sure it's Arthur?'

'Yes, I'm sure. His driver confirmed it.'

'Is the driver all right?'

'He's wounded, but I think he'll make it. Why do you ask?'

She was right to ask. I wouldn't have asked this question if I hadn't seen Charlie attending to him at the scene. 'I know him. He has driven for me many times,' I replied, hoping she wouldn't read anything more into what I said.

'You seem to be taking this pretty easy,' she commented.

I didn't know what to say to her. Truth was, I was mostly in shock.

'Are you okay?' she asked when I didn't answer.

'I'm fine.' I lied. Truth was I was anything but fine.

'This changes everything, doesn't it?' she commented.

'Yes, I suppose it does.'

I knew I was still acting too calm, but I couldn't adjust.

'Where are you?'

I guessed she asked because she heard traffic in the background.

'Went to lunch, I'm returning to my Club.' I half lied.

'Oh, do you have Charlie's guys with you?'

'No,' I said, knowing I couldn't bluff my way out of this one.

'Why not?' She sounded frustrated.

'Those guys didn't look like good lunch companions.'

'John, when are you going to understand how serious this is?'

'I'm with Mike. He's my bodyguard.'

'Who's Mike?'

'Mike is a big Italian guy who drives for me. He's a lot more fun than those CIA stiffs.'

'John...'

'Drop it, M.' I finally got mad.

She didn't respond. Then she said, 'Someone has to call Bob. Do you want to do it?'

I hadn't thought about Bob, but I knew my answer. 'No,' I simply replied to her, knowing I didn't want to deal with Bob, not now. I might get angry and say something I shouldn't.

'Okay, I'll do it.' She seemed to understand.

'Thanks.'

'John,' I think she was going to say something more, but I heard someone talking to her in the background. I assumed it was Charlie. 'We'll talk later.'

'Okay.'

Her phone went silent.

'Who was that?' asked Mike. He had heard only one side of my conversation.

'My friend, Monica.'

'She tell you what happened?'

'Yes, Arthur was killed by those motorcyclists we saw,' I replied. 'Forced his limo off the road and killed him in cold blood. He never had a chance.'

'Sorry.'

'Yea.'

A bus roared by, throwing exhaust fumes in the air as we waited at a light. People were casually crossing the street as if nothing had happened. They didn't know Arthur was dead, his blood slowly drying into the asphalt. They weren't sad, mourning for Arthur like I was. Okay, now I knew he had betrayed me, but at this moment, I tried not to think about him in this context. I wanted to remember the good times. The times we laughed and worked and built a company; the good times. What the hell went wrong, I wondered. Wasn't it enough to be successful and happy? Didn't we achieve our ambitions? We had it all, Arthur. Damn it. So why, Arthur? Why did you turn against me?

A pretty blond crossed an intersection in front of our waiting Buick. Her black leather jacket was open to the spring sunshine. She wore a loosely fitting white blouse, mostly unbuttoned, and a short skirt revealing a confident walk with beautiful long legs. I momentarily wished she would turn and smile at me, offering me some joy on this bleak day, but she simply continued across the street as if I didn't exist. She didn't know me, didn't know my friend Arthur was dead, didn't care.

I sat in Mike's Buick, seeing an ambulance in my mind's eye, lights flashing. A black body bag was zipped over Arthur's unseeing eyes. Medics lifted his limp body onto a gurney.

The light changed, and Mike accelerated through the intersection as images of tragedy roamed through my head. My eyes viewed nothing of my current reality. It was locked on a death scene, broken glass sparkling in the afternoon sunshine, dark blood seeping over dirty black pavement, extinguishing the light reflecting off the shattered glass. Dull holes in the shiny metal of a limo, an open door, a motionless body lying on the street; pictures, pictures racing through my mind.

Mike drove, looking for a bar.

I thought about Phillip and Arthur. Now I knew they were in it together. Phillip had said as much when he called. I would have learned more if I had accepted his invitation to lunch. But then... perhaps... I would have been lying dead on the street instead of Arthur; my number was called instead of his. M was right. I needed to stay away.

And Arthur, it seemed had paid for his blind ambition with his life. Whoever was in charge of this mess apparently never had any intention of giving Arthur what he had been promised. After I failed to meet with him, they must have concluded they didn't need him anymore. He was a liability, not an asset. He probably knew too much. He needed to be silenced. Whatever the reason, Arthur was dead.

Poor Arthur, he never understood the big picture.

2:55 P.M. JOHN

'Boss,' Mike said with an urgent edge to his voice.
'What?'
'Behind us, a couple of motorcycles.'
I jerked my head around. Mike was right. Two helmeted motorcycles weaved in and out of traffic behind us, coming fast, racing motorcycles with bright colors on the driver's helmets. They could have been a coincidence, but I didn't think I should wait around and find out the hard way.

'Lose them, Mike. They look like the guys who killed my partner.'

Mike hit his accelerator, making a quick left turn into an intersection in front of oncoming traffic; horns blared, and tires screeched. The big Buick swerved through a small opening, darted past startled pedestrians, and roared up a side street. I looked behind, hoping the motorcycles had gone straight, ignoring us. But they turned, engines winding in a high frenzy scream.

'They're still coming!' I yelled.

'Damn!' Mike's full attention was on the road ahead. Alternately, he hit his brakes and accelerator, swerving in and out of traffic lanes. I glanced back again to see the motorcycles gaining ground. As good a driver as Mike was, a lumbering, luxurious Buick was no match for two-wheeled racing bikes in heavy traffic. We needed help and needed it fast. I pulled my cell phone out of my jacket pocket and speed-dialed M's number. She answered quickly, to my relief.

'M, it's John. We have a problem.'

'What?'

'Please listen carefully,' I lowered my voice to just under a scream. 'Two motorcycles are on our tail, closing fast. We are trying to lose them, but they're catching us. We're unarmed, and I'm afraid they are the same guys who killed Arthur. Do you understand?'

'Where are you?

'At the corner of Eighth and ...' A street sign passed before I could read it.

'And Thirty-First,' Mike helped.

'And Thirty-First,' I repeated into my phone.

M didn't immediately answer. I could hear her talking loudly to Charlie in the background.

Mike jammed his brakes and swerved to avoid hitting the back of a slow-moving car causing me to jerk forward. I had not anticipated his move and had to lean on the dashboard with my free hand to avoid hitting my head on the windshield, momentarily losing hold of my cell phone. The Buick rocked from side to side in its haste to escape as I attempted to grab my phone, which was sliding across the floor.

I got it in time to hear her say, 'Charlie says to keep going as fast as you can.'

'Believe me, we are.'

"And stay on your phone. Give me your locations.'

'I'll try. We are turning on Thirty-Fourth.'

Mike was working his horn like a siren, desperately hoping to warn traffic ahead. Some drivers heard and moved out of our way. But other drivers were brain dead, unconsciously ignoring his horn as Mike's Buick thundered past, narrowly missing them.

'Thirty-Fourth and Ninth,' I yelled, watching cars in a blur, hoping M could hear me above the sound of his horn and the tires screaming in protest.

'We're coming to you,' she said.

But so were the motorcycles. The high-performance machines were eating up the distance between us.

'Mike,' I warned. 'Taxi on your right!'

'Sorry, boss,' he swerved hard left to avoid a taxi at the last second, darting into an open lane of oncoming traffic and then back to the right to avoid hitting a car head-on.

The sound of high-pitched motorcycle engines suddenly wound up beside us, one on each side, their brightly colored helmets flashing in the sunlight. Our pursuers were on us like two cheetahs on a big old bullcow.

A large bus came up fast.

Mike brushed off the motorcycle on his right by heading right for the bus, forcing the cyclist to hit his brakes to avoid crashing into the back of the bus. Mike swerved at the last second into traffic to pass the bus. A car was coming in the opposite direction, cutting off our lane. I held on to the dash, knees braced for an anticipated impact. The bus attempted to slow down but couldn't react in time. It hit our rear bumper when Mike swerved in front of the bus to avoid the oncoming car. The impact of the bus sent us fishtailing into a side street. Turning the steering wheel against the spin, Mike fought for control. Parked cars came up fast. His Buick bounced off the side of one of the cars. My head jerked in the collision. Metal cursed against metal in a moment of shrill exasperation as we slid past the car. No stopping, Mike accelerating down the street.

The big bus temporarily blocked the cyclists. They were forced to go straight through the intersection. We had escaped. I took a breath. I was still alive.

'Nice move, Mike.'

He turned at the corner of Tenth and Thirty-Fourth as I yelled street names into my cell phone.

'We may have lost them.' I said into my cellphone. But a brief glimpse of cycles in our rear window confirmed the fallacy of my statement as we turned at the next intersection.

'No, scratch that,' I yelled. 'They're still coming.'

'Okay, listen, John,' Monica said. 'Tell your driver to try to get to Fourteenth Street off the West Side Parkway. We'll meet you there. We're coming from the other direction.'

I repeated her instructions to Mike. 'Do you think you can get there before they catch us again?'

'I'll try,' Mike replied tensely, fear invading his otherwise confident voice.

His Buick turned onto an entrance ramp to the Parkway, passing cars on the shoulder where no car should be driven. The motorcycles were coming fast. They saw us turn and followed. Fifty, sixty miles per hour. I glanced momentarily at our speedometer as cars slid behind us as if they were stationary obstacles parked on the road. Mike's Buick was more competitive on an open road at speed. Still, the cyclists were gaining on us.

'Almost there!' Mike yelled, weaving through traffic.

'Did you hear that? We're almost there!' I yelled into my cell phone.

'Yes,' she replied, talking to Charlie at the same time.

The intersection at Fourteenth Street came up fast, too fast for our big Buick. Brakes in a full slide, tires stuttering across the pavement, burning rubber. Leaning to one side, the Buick scrubbed off speed in a four-wheel drift, which would have made Michael Schumacher proud as we turned at Fourteenth. I held on, white-knuckled, hoping, praying as we slid through the intersection towards some parked cars, which forced a decreasing radius turn. Hitting one of the cars, sparks flashed off the fenders. Holding onto anything I could grab, my seatbelt tightened around my chest as we raced down the road.

'We're at Fourteenth. Where are you?' I screamed into my cell phone as I wildly scanned the road ahead, looking for a grey Ford. It was a big intersection. I saw no Taurus with a red light flashing, no help in sight.

'We're almost there, John. You made it there faster than we anticipated,' Monica said into her cell phone.

'We can't stop M, can't wait for you. They'll kill us if they catch us.' Pictures of a black coat covering a dead body in the street raced through my mind.

'Keep going. We'll get to you.'

'Corner of Fourteenth and Ninth,' I yelled the location of the next intersection as the motorcycles ate up the distance between us now in big chunks.

'Double back,' M yelled into her phone. 'Turn left down Eighth and come back to us.'

Mike slid into the corner after I gave him Monica's instructions. A few startled pedestrians scattered. Traffic was graciously sparse in this part of town, but this helped the cyclists more than us. We turned at Fifteenth hoping we were heading towards Charlie, but the painted helmets were on us before we made it, engines whining, closing in. Mike swerved to the right blocking one of the bikes behind us, allowing the other bike to scream up our left side.

A red light flashed blocks ahead... had to be Charlie... too late to help.

Mike swerved left banging the other bike on the handle bars. The rider regained his balance, slowed and reached into his coat for a gun while accelerating up the road beside us. Coming up on our right, the other bike trapped us on our left.

'Hit the brakes, Mike,' I yelled as they tore up beside us. 'Now, NOW.'

The Buick nosedived into a four-wheel drift, tires screaming and smoking as it slowed. The bikes flew past, not anticipating our move. Charlie's gray Ford could be seen coming, a red light flashing on the roof, still too far away to help. Mike jammed his accelerator, heading directly towards one of the slowing cyclists who turned his black helmet visor towards us. He leaned forward when he saw Mike's Buick bear down on him, his accelerator turning in his hand, front wheel up, but not before Mike hit him with the Buick's fender with a glancing blow, sending him sliding, sparking across the pavement on his side.

The second cyclist, pistol in his hand, fired a volley of shots in rapid succession. Window glass shattered, exploding into shards of light. I instinctively ducked down to avoid being hit.

'Go to the flashing light, Mike,' I yelled.

Mike turned his wheel and accelerated up the street, bouncing off the bumper of a startled taxi, his Buick jamming into lanes of oncoming traffic looking for cover, fishtailing down the street around cars, approaching Charlie's Ford. Charlie's car slid to a stop in the middle of the road as Mike passed him with his brakes in full lock, finally stopping.

Charlie jumped out of his car and aimed his gun at an approaching cyclist. Our assassin abruptly slowed when he saw Charlie, acknowledging this new reality through the anonymity of his shaded visor. Turning sharply, he accelerated away. The other bike, the one Mike had hit, was already gone. I breathed deeply. Charlie lowered his gun.

Mike had his head down against the steering wheel, white knuckles still in a death grip.

'It's over, Mike,' I said.

He slumped back into his seat in sheer exhaustion and relief.

I looked up to see Charlie reaching into his Ford for a phone. M got out of the passenger side door.

I opened the door of Mike's Buick, which wasn't easy. The side of the car was badly beaten up. It took some effort to get the door open. After getting out, I stood stationary in the middle of the street. My knees felt weak. I didn't know if I could walk. Cars slowed; drivers turned to look as they passed. In a dream, she walked to where I was standing next to our beat-up Buick and put her arms around me, burying her head in my coat and holding me tightly. The quiet comfort of her body felt good. Holding her, touching her hair, I didn't want to let go.

Finally, she pushed me back. 'I don't think I'd better leave you alone again,' she smiled, a single tear sliding down her cheek which she wiped away. 'You're always getting into trouble.'

I embraced her again. 'That's fine with me,' I said.

Mike was surveying the damage to his Buick when I approached him. The rear side window had been shot out, and more than a few new restyling features had been added to its sheet metal, including the whole left side of his Buick. It was badly disfigured.

I gave him a big hug. 'Thanks, man. That was close. I owe you one.'

'I thought we were road kill,' he chuckled.

'Don't worry about the car,' I said. 'I'll buy you a new one.'

'Okay, but what am I going to tell my boss?' he snorted. 'I called in sick today.'

I laughed more from relief than anything else. 'I'll phone him and explain everything. Maybe Charlie can help; tell him we were on a special mission for the CIA.'

'Good. Yeah, that might work.'

'If he doesn't buy it, you can work for me.'

'I'd like that.' He smiled and laid a huge hand on my shoulder.

'Consider it done.'

M stayed close.

Charlie finally joined us in the street.

'I could use a drink,' I said to him. 'Do you suppose we could get out of here?'

A plain Jane Ford drove up. Two suits got out.

'Just a minute,' Charlie replied before going over to talk to the suits.

Two NYPD patrol cars arrived on the scene as they were talking, sirens screaming, lights flashing.

Charlie walked up to a couple of NYPD cops who had exited their car. He flashed his credentials and said something to them, after which they had a short discussion that didn't sound too cordial. I couldn't hear what they were saying, but it definitely got heated, and then everyone got quiet. I found M's hand and held it while watching the uniformed NYPD cops get in their cars. Flashing lights were turned off. They drove away.

The two suits approached us with Charlie.

'This is Ben and Matthew.' Charlie introduced his guys to me. 'They work for me. They are CIA. They'll be your security detail while you are in New York. From now on, they'll go everywhere you go... That okay with you John?' He looked directly at me. It wasn't a question.

'Yes, okay,' I conceded.

'I thought it might be,' he smiled.

4:25 P.M. JOHN

On warm days, the uptown restaurant opened its front shutters to let in some fresh air and sunshine.

A few tables were set outside on the sidewalk. Brave souls occupied these fresh-air havens. Our group retreated past a long bar to a table in the rear, where it was warmer and more secure. Soft lights provided a measure of anonymity and comfort. The restaurant was well-occupied even though it was early for dinner.

My nerves were strung tighter than a guitar. I might be cool under fire, but when the danger is over, I don't do well. I couldn't stop thinking about how close I came to dying. Had things gone just slightly differently, my blood may have joined Arthur's, staining the streets of New York City. Truth was, I had dodged too many bullets lately, and the odds were beginning to stack up against me. By all rights, I should have been dead. I was not. But the cumulative effect of the near-death experiences was taking a toll on my mental health.

I didn't bother to look at a menu, simply asked for a whiskey when the waitress arrived. I shrugged when she asked what brand I preferred. 'Don't care, just make it a double.' I took a sip as soon as the whiskey was placed in front of me.

M's hand was still firmly in my grip where it had been when we entered the restaurant. After observing her graciously trying to open a menu with one free hand, I let go. Charlie smiled, observing my needy behavior with obvious amusement. I ignored him and took another sip of whiskey, allowing the warm liquid to drift down my throat.

'Okay,' Charlie looked directly at me. 'Can we talk now?'

His eyes told me something didn't add up in his mind. I think he knew. It was time to come clean. Before anyone could say another word, I admitted I had been at the scene and saw Arthur's dead body on the street. Mike nodded in agreement.

'You were there?' M asked incredulously.

'Yes.'

'Why did you think it was Arthur?'

'Because we saw him come out of the restaurant and get into Bob's limo,' I continued.

'You were at the restaurant?' M asked, amazed at the depth of my presumed stupidity.

'Yes. We followed your car up the street after hearing shots.'

'You did what?'

'We followed you. I saw the whole mess, the limo, Arthur's body covered with a coat, everything.'

'But you didn't bother to tell us you were there.' M noted.

'No.'

'Why not?'

'I didn't want to stick around.' This was true to a degree. The scene had made me sick to my stomach. But she had a different perspective. One not so complimentary.

'You mean you didn't want me to see you,' she nailed the real reason I got out of there.

I didn't reply, couldn't; she was right.

M and Charlie continued to pepper me with questions. I patiently tried to answer all of them and tried to justify my aberrant behavior, but I guess I wasn't too successful. It was clear they were not pleased, especially M.

'Okay, I should have stayed at my Club,' I finally apologized. 'But in my defense, I didn't go inside the restaurant as you ordered. I wanted to, but I didn't. I stayed outside as ordered. That should count for something.'

'You just about got yourself killed,' Charlie countered tersely.

'Point taken.'

Everyone was quiet for a moment.

'So, what now?' I asked, attempting to change the subject.

'We wait for a break,' Charlie replied.

'But the Thais, I told you they are involved.'

'What do you want me to do, John?'

'I don't know. Arrest someone.' I said in exasperation. I was tired. I had almost been killed. I wanted something done, anything.

'Arrest who?' he argued. 'Sure, we can join the dots by circumstance, but that's not enough to arrest anyone. And who should I arrest even if I wanted to, the whole country of Thailand? Right now, we don't know which Thai is involved.'

'Did you talk to Bob?' I asked M, momentarily ignoring Charlie.

'Yes,' she answered.

'How did he take it?'

'He was surprised and shocked.'

'Was he faking it?'

'No, I think he was genuine. He asked how I knew. I told him I was not allowed to say. He didn't sound too happy with my answer.'

My cell phone rang. I clumsily dug it out of my coat pocket, answering it as quickly as possible, wanting to put an end to its obnoxious noise.

'Hello?'

'John?' he said like it was a question.

'Yes.'

'It's Lin. I'm driving in from Kennedy Airport. I'm calling to let you know I have arrived safely,' he explained.

In the excitement, I had forgotten about Lin. 'Trip, okay?' I asked, urgently trying to decide what to tell him.

'Yes, it was a good flight, John.'

'I'm glad. Look, I have something to tell you.' I swallowed. 'Arthur's dead. It happened this afternoon.'

'Oh,' Lin said in his usual impassive manner.

'He was gunned down in cold blood. He never had a chance.'

'Sorry.' Lin sounded genuine.

'There's more. Phillip earlier invited me to have lunch with Arthur and said they wanted to offer me a deal.'

'Arthur and Phillip, they were working together?'

'Yes.'

'What did they offer?'

'I don't know. I didn't go.'

'You didn't go?'

'No.'

'Why?'

'Didn't think it was safe,' I half lied, smiling at M.

'I see,' he said coolly.

I didn't reply.

'You were right about Arthur after all?' Lin observed.

'I guess, but it doesn't matter anymore. He's dead.'

'You were not harmed?' Lin asked.

'No. I told you I didn't go anywhere near Arthur.'

I decided not to tell Lin about my close call with death on the streets of New York City. That could wait. I wanted Lin to focus on Phillip and Arthur, the co-conspirators directly involved in the problems of our company.

'Yes, of course. I'm glad you were not hurt,' Lin replied, still concerned about my welfare.

'I'm fine, Lin,' I replied. 'Can we talk about something else, like how this will affect the board meeting? Obviously, everything has changed. So, what do we do now?'

'I do not know,' Lin replied.

'Should we draw some connection to the Thais at the meeting.'

'Yes, the Thai are a problem,' Lin observed. His cell phone transmission began to break up. 'We need to talk, John. Where can I meet you?'

'Meet me at my Club.'

'When?'

'I should be... Hold on, Lin,' Charlie was madly waving his arms to get my attention. I put my hand over my cell phone.

'You and I and Mike here need to pay a visit to the NYPD,' Charlie explained rather pointedly. 'They have a few questions. I promised I would bring you in today. I told them you needed to calm down first. But you have to talk to them before you do anything else.'

I looked at Charlie with disgust. The last thing I wanted to do was to talk with some cops. I think he read my mind.

'Look, John, this is not a request.'

I could feel my shoulders begin to tense. 'Lin, it seems I have something I need to do first. Where are you staying?'

'I'm at the Plaza.'

'Okay. I'll call as soon as I'm done.'

'What do you have to do?' Lin asked.

'I'll tell you when we meet.'

'I will wait for your call,' he hung up.

6:10 P.M. JOHN

Police stations are like some other public buildings such as hospitals and court rooms; places to be avoided like a plague if you can.

Blank stares followed us when we arrived in the building's crowded halls, faces probably wondering what terrible deed brought us to this place of no hope. A young mother was sitting on a bench with a small child on her lap. The child's stringy brown hair was matted to her young head, and she was whimpering softly as if she knew crying wouldn't help. I wondered what had brought this mother to this non-descript hall with its dirty gray carpet. Why was she in this merciless building and not home caring for her child? But then, perhaps the young woman couldn't answer my question any more than I could.

Our group was ushered down the halls by a detective. I had already forgotten the man's name even though he had introduced himself. Detective Al or Hal or something, I couldn't remember. He took us to a sparsely furnished, one-table room surrounded by several chairs. The cop ordered Charlie and me to sit. Mike was taken to a separate room.

Charlie was with me because he insisted on accompanying me during my interview and told the cop he wasn't going anywhere. This didn't make the detective happy, not too pleased with either of us. I guess I couldn't blame him. We probably meant a stack of paperwork for him.

I had regained some semblance of mental stability by the time we arrived. Whiskey and food at the restaurant helped. M was waiting in the lobby. Charlie didn't want her involved, probably to keep her name out of a police report. No doubt, he wanted to avoid explaining to his CIA bosses why a female civilian was in his car at the time of the shooting. At least, that was my take on the situation.

The interview with the detective, whose name I could not recall, was just the first of many interviews I endured in the windowless interrogation room painted an ugly lime green color. The room became claustrophobic after a while. Once the door was closed, I felt trapped. A pen-scratched table occupied the center of the room. The walls were smudged and dirty. I wondered who had been questioned at this table before me. How many tragic and haunting stories lingered inside these walls?

Charlie stayed at my side through it all, probably concerned I might screw up his preplanned explanation. His cell phone buzzed constantly the whole time, giving him updates on Arthur's murder and other working cases. He was a busy guy. The cops who were interviewing us were not too pleased with Charlie's phone. They asked him several times to turn off his fucking phone or take the fucking thing out of the room to answer calls. He calmly explained he was CIA and he was not going to turn off his fucking cell phone or take his fucking phone out of the room. His fucking phone was for official CIA business. Get used to it.

It got funny a few times and I had to admit I gained a new respect for Charlie through these interviews. He was great. During questioning, I occasionally paused and looked to Charlie for help. I either didn't know the answer to a question, or I was afraid I would give the wrong answer. He would kindly take over at that point and patiently answer for me, occasionally telling the cops the information they were seeking was confidential, part of an ongoing CIA operation. That did not make the officers very happy.

'Why don't you let Mr. Van Laan answer the question?' one detective observed coolly.

'Mr. Van Laan is answering all the questions which are within his ability to answer.' Charlie explained. 'There are some answers neither he nor I know. I'm sorry.'

'And why is that?' asked a cop.

'Because the bad guys haven't called recently to tell us the answers,' Charlie retorted. 'As soon as they do, I'll tell you what they said.'

The detective grunted in exasperation. 'Seems there's a lot you boys don't know.'

Charlie didn't respond; they simply met his gaze squarely.

'The guy who was gunned down on Ninth Avenue this afternoon. Do you think his murder is connected to the guys who were chasing you?' a cop asked, referring to Arthur's death.

I started to answer, but Charlie took over. 'Look, detective, the guy who was murdered was a business partner of Mr. Van Laan. And the guys who tried to chase down Mr. Van Laan were on motorbikes, similar to the guys who killed his partner. Their M.O. was the same. So, why don't you answer your question yourself?'

Time dragged.

After telling the same story for about the fifth time, the novelty wore off. I was getting tired. The tedium of answering the same questions over and over was making me irritable. I sensed the cops knew Charlie had advised me to hold something back. They also knew Charlie was a pro and would understand the game they were playing. I was the obvious target of their interminable grilling. They were trying to get me to make a mistake. It helped to have Charlie with me. He remained calm through it all and served as my example.

In between interviews, he said we simply had to outlast them.

8:05 P.M. JOHN

Escaping the unyielding stone-cold police building occupied by people in blue uniforms with badges was a relief.

Night air felt fresh and clean when we finally got outside. I took a deep breath and looked up at the outline of New York's skyscrapers against a dark night sky, trying to clear my head of the dripping ooze of human frailty that seemed to permeate every pore of that public building. The one thing I wanted to do less than any other at that moment was to answer one more exasperating question about what happened. But I knew Lin had been waiting patiently for me to get back to him. I called him on my cell phone as we walked and suggested since it was late, we meet him in his hotel room to save some time. He asked me who else was coming when he heard me use the word 'we.' I told him, Monica.

'You don't need to bring her,' he suggested. 'We have much to discuss. She will get bored.'

'She's coming,' I said sharply, venting some inner, pent-up frustration. I guess I said it forcefully because when he started to object again, he stopped, aware it would do no good.

I knew I should not have acted so frustrated. His negative reaction to her was simply his normal Chinese aversion to mixing women and business. I didn't care. I did not want to be separated from her again, not after what happened the last time. But the real truth was that it was Monica who had insisted on coming with me. It wasn't my idea. Although I had to admit, I was happy she asked. I think she read my mind. She must have sensed I wanted her by my side, and I hoped she felt the same way.

However, Charlie objected, didn't think she should go and he told her so. But when she gave him one of her killer looks, he backed off. I quietly thanked her as we walked to his car.

As we drove to the Plaza, I explained to Charlie that we were going there to update Lin. We needed to discuss the ramifications of the recent events for the board meeting. M could report to him if anything interesting was discussed. He decided this would be okay but insisted his two CIA bodyguards wait in the lobby of the hotel and escort us to our respective hotels after we finished. I didn't object.

Although I was tempted to ask Charlie if it would be okay for M to sleep with me at my Club tonight, but I kept my mouth shut. I knew M would not be too happy if I posed this indelicate question.

However, I did ask Charlie if I could tell Lin about the CIA's involvement. Initially he said no, but when I explained Lin had been my one friend in all this mess and I trusted him. I needed him to understand everything so he could help me with my board.

Charlie reluctantly agreed after I assured him Lin could keep a secret.

8:20 P.M. JOHN

By the time we arrived at the grand entrance to the Plaza Hotel, I was dead tired and seriously hungry.

I had eaten very little at the restaurant earlier that afternoon. Only picked at my food and sipped some whiskey while generally trying to calm down. From the lobby I called Lin's room and suggested we meet in the hotel restaurant so I could get something to eat. Said I had been busy, no time for dinner. He suggested room service instead. This way we could talk in private.

I agreed.

Lin welcomed us at the door to his suite. I shook his hand warmly in a small hall leading into his suite of rooms. I was beginning to feel better by this time. Just being out of the police station had given me a lift.

Lin's suite was larger than any I had previously seen at the Plaza. The decor was more subdued than the extreme luxury normal for this hotel. Apparently, the Plaza offered some rooms tailored to the exclusive tastes of guests from different cultures. Although the room did not appear to be oriental, I knew it suited Lin's tastes. The wallpaper in the sitting room was a thin pale green and maroon-lined design over a subduedly tinted silver background. The furniture was simple in design, made of elegantly polished wood and upholstered cushions, sitting quite low to the floor in an obvious attempt to cater to Asian preferences.

'This is a very nice room,' I remarked to Lin. 'I don't think I've seen one like it in this hotel.'

'Yes, I request this room when I come to New York.'

'You secured it on short notice.'

'It's very expensive. Usually, it's available.'

M curled up on one of the low couches. I sat down beside her.

'Would you like a drink?' he asked while standing across from us, separated by a wood serving table.

I suggested wine.

A small cabinet against the wall contained glasses and single-serving bottles of red wine. Lin found two wine glasses and gave us menus for room service.

'Why don't you look at the menus while I pour your wine?' he suggested.

Oddly, he seemed to be in no hurry to hear about Arthur's death. But then, his behavior was normal for him. All things were accomplished in a proper order in Lin's world. Dinner was important, ordered first. Talk could wait until later.

After a few sips of wine, the accumulated mental damage caused by a stress-filled afternoon of absolute terror evolved into a heavy fatigue that settled into every sinew and muscle fiber of my body. I leaned back and rested on a couch while my over-anxious nervous system slowed to a dull, headache drumbeat.

M took over the burden of conversation. She must have sensed how tired I was. She began by telling Lin about Phillip's call and her insistence I not go. As she talked, I rested, content to listen to the sound of her voice while observing the softly flowing silhouette of her body. I hoped her coming with me this evening meant we were permanently together again. I hadn't asked her if this was true. I guess I was afraid to ask, afraid her answer might not be what I desired.

Maybe later... I made a mental note to ask her later.

Not having to carry the lead in the conversation allowed me a unique opportunity to observe Lin as she talked, something I normally had no opportunity to do. As was his custom, he sat passively upright, sipping tea, giving nothing away, no clues to what he was thinking or how he felt, looking stone-faced, almost disinterested, smiling only occasionally. I was glad he was my friend, and I never had to negotiate with him because I knew he would be a superior opponent.

As M continued, I looked away for a moment, shutting my tired eyes for a few minutes of badly needed rest. Truth was, I had no desire to relive the afternoon's events one more time. Instead, I pondered why Arthur had turned on me. Couldn't just be money. He made a lot of money. Plus, his wife was very wealthy, or so he said, old money according to him. So, his reasons for turning on me must have been something else; perhaps something I did to upset him. I wondered if I ignored him one too many times when I should have been paying attention. Did I belittle his ideas too often? Did I poke fun at his British humor more than I should have? What clues to his puzzling behavior had I missed? He had a big ego. I knew this, and I knew it was sometimes difficult for him to work for me, but the job was his choice. He could have quit anytime if he didn't like it.

We didn't always agree, but I couldn't help it. I had to disagree with him on occasion, like when he made unsolicited suggestions out of the blue at a board meeting. Arthur didn't always see the big picture. His bright intelligence frequently got bogged down, mired in some minute detail. There were times when I had to say no to him. His ideas would have taken hours to discuss and we didn't have hours at a board meeting. Later, after our meetings were over, he would often come up to me with a jolly remark or a pat on my back. I assumed he had forgotten about our disagreements. Now, as I looked back, I wondered if this was true. I guessed I should have been more sympathetic.

But then, perhaps I was wrong. Perhaps this was just about money. Perhaps someone offered him more money than he could turn down?

I stood to stretch my legs.

Lin had started a pot of coffee at my request. Caffeine was required. I was fading fast, and we still had work to do. I poured a cup while overhearing M describe how she and Charlie waited outside the restaurant, wondering if Phillip would show.

Lin politely interrupted. 'Who is Charlie?'

'Charles Stewart works for the CIA,' M explained. 'He's a friend from my law school days. I asked him to assist John and Gemstones International in learning who is behind the problems of your company. He has been a tremendous help.'

Lin's body language actually seemed to react to this new information. His normally inscrutable Chinese stoicism broke down, if only for a brief moment, not much. I probably wouldn't have seen it if I had been talking to him. But because I was simply observing, I could clearly see the muscles in his back tightening. He sat up straighter than usual and stared intently at Monica, giving her his full attention, something he seldom gave any woman.

'CIA?' Lin asked, a small frown forming on his normally placid features. 'You didn't tell me the CIA was involved, John.'

'Charlie wouldn't let me tell you or anyone on the board,' I explained. 'He was afraid this information might be leaked and affect his inquiry. I'm sorry, Lin, but my hands were tied. The only reason you're being told now is because I expressly asked Charlie for permission. In light of what happened this afternoon, I thought you should know everything.'

'I didn't think we had secrets,' he responded coldly.

'It wasn't a secret, Lin. It was privileged CIA information.'

He was silent.

'Lin, please try to understand. I couldn't turn down his help. You know this as much as anyone.'

I paused, giving Lin time to process this new information, waiting for him to respond. When he didn't react, I continued, 'I guess it all seems pretty obvious now. But before today, we couldn't prove anything.'

'I wish you had told me about the CIA, John,' he replied.

I felt bad like I had somehow betrayed him.

'Would it have made a difference?' I asked.

'It could have,' Lin replied.

I had no idea what he meant by his remark, but I decided to let it go. I had other things I wanted to discuss.

M looked slightly embarrassed, her eyes darting from me to Lin.

'Please, go on,' Lin finally said to Monica, once more retreating to his usual stoic behavior.

She looked at me.

'Go ahead,' I said. 'Tell him what happened next.'

'Phillip met with Arthur in the restaurant, but not for long,' she explained.

'How do you know that?' Lin asked. 'You said you were in a car outside the restaurant.'

'Charlie had men inside.'

'And they saw Phillip? You are sure it was Phillip?' asked Lin.

'Charlie's men were given his description.'

'Remember, I told you Phillip initially set up this meeting,' I interjected, becoming frustrated with Lin's fixation with detail. I was tired. I didn't want our discussion to drag on. I wanted to quickly move to more important questions, like how to deal with the board.

'Yes, yes, you did,' Lin answered.

'Phillip has been traveling under an assumed name, using a diplomatic passport,' M continued. 'The CIA has been tracking him for us. We temporarily lost him after John met with him in New York.'

'You met with Phillip the last time you were in New York?' Lin turned to me.

'Yes, but I got nothing from him.'

'I don't remember you telling me about this,' Lin accused me.

'Nothing to tell,' I replied tersely. 'I learned nothing from him.'

'I see.' Lin took a sip of tea.

This was the second time I had kept something from him. I never gave it a thought at the time. The meeting had been a disaster. I put it out of my mind.

'You waited for Arthur to come out of the restaurant?' Lin returned his attention to M, temporarily ignoring me.

'Yes,' she said simply. 'We followed his limousine. Two motorcyclists passed us and caught his limousine. One of the cyclists shot the driver through the window, forcing the car off the road. The limo slammed into a parked cab. Arthur tried to run, but he didn't get far. A second rider killed him as soon as he got out of the car. He staggered into the street for a few steps before falling over, dead. His killers escaped on their bikes in the afternoon traffic. Unfortunately, it all happened very fast. We didn't have an opportunity to intervene.'

No one spoke.

'This is very bad,' Lin finally remarked.

M quietly sipped her wine.

I sat down beside her.

'It changes everything for our board meeting,' I observed, hoping to move to the issues I wanted to discuss.

'Yes, it does, John,' he replied.

'What do think our strategy should be?'

'I don't know,' Lin said in an almost inaudible whisper. 'The CIA,' he questioned. 'How much are they involved?'

'Up until recently, they had only a small interest,' M explained. 'Mostly as a favor to me. Now they are very interested.'

'Why?' Lin asked.

'Because they suspect a foreign national is involved, someone highly placed in the Thai government.'

Lin was silent.

'There's more.' I decided to reveal everything so we could discuss how to bring the information to our board.

'More?' he questioned.

'Tell him what happened to me.' I looked at M.

She told Lin about my close call with motorcycle killers. Lin seldom took his eyes off her as she replayed my story.

I sipped coffee, listening, reliving the afternoon, pictures running rampantly through my head as M talked: Arthur lying on the street under a black coat, screeching tires of the Buick as Mike expertly weaved his way through traffic, the high whining scream of motorcycles, the cyclist who stopped after Charlie pulled his gun and sighted him. The helmeted attacker had turned and briefly looked straight at me, indicating, I suppose, that he regretted having to leave before he could kill me. Smoke rose from the rear tire of his bike as he accelerated through traffic. There was nothing Charlie could do to stop him. An errant bullet could have easily injured or killed an innocent bystander. And finally, the immense relief I felt as I watched the biker disappear.

'You escaped, John?' Lin asked, suddenly turning to me as if questioning my very existence.

M answered his question for me, explaining how she and Charlie had been able to intercept the cyclists and chase them off.

'I see. So, you are lucky to be alive, John,' Lin stated with absolutely no emotion.

'Yes,' I replied, admiring his calm composure.

Lin stared at nothing, seemingly lost. I made one last effort to get him to focus.

'So how do you think we should handle this new information at the board meeting?' I asked.

'Yes, yes, what to do at the board meeting,' he replied, pondering my question. He abruptly stood, turned, and looked at his chair as if he wanted to sit down again. Changing his mind, he continued to stand, stand very still, very rigid. He seemed distracted like he had too much to think about. I had never ever seen him act like this before.

M looked at me with a question on her lips, perplexed, uneasy, as if she wanted to leave. Lin's behavior was obviously bothering her. It was bothering me also.

'It's late,' I decided hastily. 'I think I'll skip dinner. I don't know about you, but I'm not sure I'm capable of making any rational decisions tonight. Perhaps it would be best if we got some rest and met early for breakfast at my Club.'

'Yes, good,' Lin said. 'Meet at your Club in the morning. Yes.'

A knock on his hotel door startled him. He turned to the secluded hall leading to the outer door. 'Your dinner?' he questioned and disappeared down his hall.

Voices, two men talking, not English, some foreign language. The voices sounded excited as if they were disagreeing. The door could be heard hitting a wall hard with a bang.

I looked at M.

She immediately began to fumble with something in her purse.

'Charlie said to call if anything unusual happens,' she whispered to me as she pressed a preset number on her cell phone, shoving it quickly into her open purse when Lin reappeared with Phillip following close behind.

'Hello, John,' Phillip smiled, 'I thought I'd pay you a visit since you decided not to grace us with your company at lunch today.'

'Phillip,' I tried to conceal my astonishment. 'Sorry, I was occupied.'

'I'm sure you were,' he sneered.

I looked at Lin.

He stepped back without acknowledging my silent question.

8:50 P.M. CHARLIE

His cell phone rang.

Charlie put down a report he had been reading and looked at his phone's caller ID.

It was Monica, and he immediately assumed she was calling to give him a report on what John and Lin had discussed. Or maybe to ask a question. Casually picking up his phone, he clicked the call button and said hello.

She didn't answer.

He said hello again, this time louder... then listened... expecting her to return his greeting.

Nothing, no words of greeting spoken, only strange noises in the background, people talking. Words he couldn't understand.

Assuming at first it was a wrong number, he was tempted to turn his phone off. But after glancing once again at the caller ID, he recognized her number.

'Monica, say something.'

Nothing... again, she was silent.

Background noise, a man speaking, sounds crossing a telecommunication gap between his and her phone. Charlie could understand some of the words, but not enough to know what was being said. It could be John talking, sounding a little like him. Then another man spoke fainter. Charlie didn't know who and couldn't really hear the voice well enough to understand anything the man was saying.

Interested now, intrigued and mystified, Charlie continued to listen, beginning to comprehend some of the words in a conversation, mostly words spoken by either a woman, probably Monica, or a man, probably John.

They seemed to be closer to the phone than other voices.

8:52 P.M. JOHN

Following Phillip into Lin's hotel room were two Asian men dressed in expensive suits, starched white shirts and silk ties.

Young and fit with broad shoulders, they uttered not a word, stepping aside politely to allow a shorter gentleman enter behind them. The man bowed in our direction. M followed my lead by standing and returning his greeting.

'Good evening,' he said in good English with a clipped Asian accent.

'Good evening,' I replied.

The man clearly wasn't Chinese. He had to be from somewhere else. Thailand immediately came to mind. He walked slightly bent over at the waist with an almost indistinguishable limp, like he was suffering from some kind of a physical injury. His oval face was surprisingly free of wrinkles making it difficult to determine his exact age. His limp made him appear to be older, but after a second glance, I wasn't sure he was old at all. He could have been middle-aged or even younger. His most distinguishing feature was his eyes; dark, so dark it appeared light might never pierce his retinas. A permanent smile crossed his thin lips. Dressed fashionably in a western-style suit, not flashy like his young friends, but with a hint of subdued luxury, I couldn't shake the idea I had seen the man before.

'And who might this be?' Phillip said while rudely staring at Monica.

'This is my friend Monica Sorensen,' I replied.

M extended her hand and said with some sarcasm. 'I've heard so much about you, Mr. Palmer.'

'All good, I'm sure; I mean everything you've heard about me from John,' he laughed. 'I'm sure he was very complimentary.'

M smiled knowingly at Phillip, who turned to his associate.

'It is my pleasure to introduce Mr. Nue,' Phillip said. 'He and I are partners in business. We've come here tonight because we have a proposal for you, John.' Pausing before continuing, 'We would have discussed it with you at lunch, but you chose to decline our invitation. However, we are confident if you had known what we were offering, you would have chosen to grace us with your presence.'

'Perhaps you and Mr. Nue would like to sit.' I motioned towards chairs on the other side of the serving table, thinking they were here now. I could, at a minimum, listen to their proposal.

Phillip turned to Lin. 'Aren't you going to offer us something to drink, Lin?'

Lin had taken a few steps back, standing against a wall during our introductions, observing everything, saying nothing as if he was attempting to melt into the wall. 'Of course,' he showed no emotion.

'I'll have a Coke,' demanded Phillip.

'Mr. Nue, may I get you something to drink?' Lin turned to Nue, ignoring Phillip's request.

Nue waved him off. 'Please sit down, Lin. We have a business to conduct. It is late.'

It was how they spoke to each other, Lin and Phillip and Nue, with an air of familiarity as if they were well acquainted. I began to fear they had some sort of connection and in a gesture which seemed to support my concerns, Lin placed a chair behind and to the side of Nue. I couldn't help but wonder if he did this intentionally to indicate his place in our discussion, no longer on my side of the room.

The two suits who arrived with Phillip and Nue, remained standing very still. Two sentinels on either side of the room. No expression crossed their motionless faces and they did nothing to acknowledge my glances as their dark presence hung over the room like a shroud. Apparently, their place in our discussion needed no explanation.

Nue noticed me staring at them. 'Do not be concerned about them, Mr. Van Laan,' he said. 'They are no threat to you.'

I didn't reply, thinking they sure looked like a threat.

'I would really like a Coke, Lin,' Phillip again pressed Lin.

Lin rose and asked M if she would like another glass of wine, ignoring Phillip.

'Thank you, Lin, but that's not necessary,' she answered with muted sympathy.

Without comment, Lin retrieved a can of Coke for Phillip from a small hotel refrigerator and handed it to him.

Phillip began, 'Before we continue, I think John should know that our proposal comes from Lin as well as my associate.'

I stared at Lin, now fully aware of his deceit. He had his back to me at the time, searching for a glass of Phillip's Coke. When he had found one, he gave the glass to Phillip before returning to his seat behind Nue without returning my gaze.

I didn't want to believe Lin was involved with these men. It made no sense to me even though it was now clearly true. And who were these guys anyway? Mr. Nue and his companions certainly looked Thai, especially the two sentinels, wide eyes, features common to Thai people. But Nue looked different. Like some stray blood had found its way into his gene pool, perhaps a hint of Chinese ancestry.   This thought gave me no comfort. I began to wonder if I am sitting across from the high government official Charlie had mentioned.

Instinctively, I moved closer to M. I was happy she was with me.

But I also knew it would have been far better for her to be somewhere else, somewhere safe.

9:01 P.M. CHARLIE

Charlie couldn't use his cell phone to place a call.

His instrument of communication was currently in use listening to a conversation he could only faintly hear in the background. Frantically digging through his briefcase for a list of cell numbers, specifically numbers for his guys, the CIA agents who were assigned to protect John and Monica. With the list in his hand, Charlie scrambled to the hotel desk in his room and dialed, using an outside line, making sure to hit the correct numbers.

'Bill!'

'Yea boss,' Bill replied.

'Anything going on?' Charlie asked impatiently.

'No.'

'Where are you?'

'Sitting in the lobby of the Plaza waiting for them to come down, just like you ordered.'

'Have you seen anything unusual?'

'No.'

'Anyone come in lately; look odd or different to you?'

'No.'

'Think Bill, did you see anyone who looked like they could be from the Far East?'

Bill hesitated. 'Maybe, some guys, four to be exact. Three of them looked like they could be Vietnamese. Other guy was a white Caucasian. They were well dressed. We assumed they were hotel guests.'

'Damn.'

'What is it, boss?'

'Get up to the room where John and Monica are. What's the number?'

'Room 3012,' Bill replied.

'Right, go there now,' Charlie said, writing down the room number on a pad of paper and shoving it in his pants pocket. 'Don't do anything until I get there, understand.'

'Yes, sir,' Bill answered curtly. Bill had been in the Army, former Special Forces, and didn't have to be told twice.

'I'll be there in a few minutes.' Charlie said.

Putting on his coat, Charlie grabbed a small hard suitcase which always traveled with him. It contained special tools and weapons to be used in emergencies. With his cell phone still pressed to his ear, he awkwardly fumbled with the latch on his hotel room door. Placing the suitcase and phone on the floor, he needed both hands to get the door open.

Grabbing his suitcase again, he slammed his door shut with his foot and ran down the hall towards an elevator.

9:03 P.M. JOHN

'Mr. Nue,' I interjected. 'Perhaps before we continue, you might do me the honor of telling me who you are. I am acquainted with the other gentlemen in the room, but I do not know you or your companions.'

'Learned that from me, didn't you, John?' Phillip butted in obnoxiously. 'It's always important to know who you are talking to.'

'Yes, I learned a lot from you, Phillip. But, unfortunately, you learned nothing from me.'

'Nothing to...' Phillip began to reply.

'Please be quiet now, Phillip,' Nue interrupted him.

Phillip immediately shut up.

'Mr. Van Laan,' Nue continued. 'It is not important who I am. What is important is that Mr. Palmer and Mr. Hung-Chao can verify everything I tell you is true.'

'Mr. Nue,' Lin politely interrupted. 'May I have a word with John before you continue?'

Nue nodded to Lin.

Speaking directly to me for the first time since these men entered his room, Lin's voice once again assumed the methodical tone I was accustomed to hearing. It was apparent he was resigned to the fact I now knew he was involved with my enemy in everything. He didn't need to say it.

'John,' Lin began. 'Mr. Nue is a high-ranking official in the Thai government.'

Lin paused to let this information register. He knew I would immediately understand the significance given a moment to think about it. I did. The words Thai and ranking government official were all I needed to hear. It confirmed what I already feared.

'The only other information you need to know about Mr. Nue is that he has the resources to do whatever he proposes tonight,' Lin continued.

'That's it?' I responded irritably. 'Nothing else you wish to tell me?'

Lin did not reply, so I asked him directly, just to hear him admit it. 'Have you been working for Mr. Nue all along?'

'Yes,' Lin said quietly. 'I don't expect you to understand, John. But I never had an alternative. I am half-Thai by birth. Mr. Nue is my cousin. As much as I respect you, my loyalty was always to my family and my country first.'

'But then why...?'

'Why did I help you?'

'Yes.'

'I wanted you to succeed. I hoped I could find a way...'

'How? How did you ever think that was possible?'

'I'm sorry.' Lin met my gaze directly, sounding genuinely regretful. 'I know now it was not possible.'

'And Phillip, he's one of your partners in this deadly game we have been playing?' I asked without looking at Phillip.

'Not in the way you imagine, but the answer to your question is yes,' Lin responded.

'What's Phillip's role in all this?' I asked.

'That is not something you need to be concerned about,' Lin replied calmly.

Nue sat content on a couch throughout this exchange. It was obvious he was comfortable having Lin speak for him. I began to wonder if this was not the first time Lin had acted as his spokesperson.

Phillip opened his mouth to say something, but Nue raised his hand.

'Quiet Phillip, we will talk later,' Nue said with finality.

Phillip sat back in his chair, oddly submissive, not something normal for him.

Nue then turned his full attention to me. 'Please understand, Mr. Van Laan, when Lin is speaking, he is speaking for me.'

I momentarily turned my attention to Nue's two stone-faced enforcers, who were standing near the hall entrance like human statues. I found M's hand and held it tightly. I knew she was scared. I was also. The more time I had to evaluate our situation, the more concerned I became.

By this time, Phillip had moved on. Having been put down by Nue, he was compensating by living in another one of his imagined realities.

Lin also had become quiet, obviously content to now let Nue carry the conversation.

'Mr. Van Laan,' Nue continued, 'I have observed your career for some time, and I want to compliment you. Your work is most impressive. You have accomplished much good for the sapphire industry. You have raised the prices of the gemstones to levels I never thought I would see in my lifetime. And your company has been good for many people in many lands. I want you to know I respect you for your accomplishments.'

I didn't respond, thinking apparently it wasn't good enough to stop trying to kill me.

'But unfortunately, your company has caused many problems for my family and my country,' he continued. 'When you began, we thought perhaps we could find a way to work with you. But your association with certain elements in Sri Lanka made this impossible. We needed to find another solution.'

'Is this why you had my friend Vidu murdered?' I interrupted him.

'His death was regrettable.' Nue continued without emotion. 'But if you could ask him now, he would tell you he understood the risk he took when he built his factories.'

'Does that justify his death?' I felt my face flush with anger.

'Justice is a complex issue,' Nue answered. 'For instance, is it just for people in my country to have lost their jobs? Their children are crying in their beds now because they are hungry and have no food. They are crying because of what you have done. Is this justice, Mr. Van Laan?'

I didn't answer.

Nue continued. 'But please, let us put these concerns aside for a moment and continue to find a solution to our problems. But before we do, I want to personally apologize to you for all the trouble you have recently endured.'

Again, I said nothing, knowing I might lose control if I responded. I decided to let him have his say first.

'You have proven to be very resourceful, Mr. Van Laan and I am happy you have endured. And to you, young lady.' Nue turned to M. 'Please allow me to express my sincere regrets for the difficulties this may have caused you.'

'Your pathetic attempt at an apology is not acceptable,' Monica immediately responded her voice tight with subdued rage. 'You had no right.'

Nue appeared momentarily shaken by M's rebuke.

I smiled, guessing he didn't appreciate being criticized by a woman.

M stared at him

'I am sorry,' he said.

'I have a hard time believing you,' she responded.

Nue momentarily looked unsure of how to proceed. Then, he smiled faintly, thinking about his uncle, Luang. He knew the old man would be happy with what he was doing.

'Let us move on to more important business.' Nue turned his attention to me. 'Mr. Van Laan, you will be pleased to know we wish to propose a pleasant solution to our problems.'

'Good,' I said, stifling a laugh, appalled by what I was hearing. The man had tried to kill me. Now, he was dismissing my life as though it was simply an introductory paragraph in a business deal.

Nue smiled placidly. 'However, first, you must understand that your company cannot continue under your control. The time has come for Gemstone International to move on without you, Mr. Van Laan.'

He waited politely for my reaction.

'I don't suppose I have a say in this matter,' I finally responded.

'That will not be necessary. After you hear our proposal, you will appreciate the wisdom of our decision. May I continue?'

'Please do.' I was curious to learn what he would propose.

'Mr. Van Laan, we have placed a sum of five hundred million dollars US in a bank account under your name alone. No co-signature is required. This is money only you can access. It is payment for your stock in your company. The money is yours now. We cannot take it back because we are confident that will not be necessary.'

He paused before continuing, assuming I would be impressed by the generosity of his offer. In truth, it got my attention, but I tried not to react visibly.

'Also, we are offering you a consulting contract worth one million US dollars per year, payable to you until the year of your death, or for a minimum of thirty years. The only condition to your receiving this money is that you must refrain from working in the colored stone business during the term of the contract. And please understand that if your death occurs before thirty years have passed, the money will continue to be paid to your estate. The contract is fully funded by an annuity which has been purchased. Therefore, you do not have to fear being killed to stop the contract from being honored.'

He waited, I assumed, to allow me time to consider the enormity of his offer.

When I said nothing, he continued. 'Phillip has informed us you have a mutual friend in your hometown who is your attorney. Your friend received a package by special courier this morning. A letter attached to the package specifies it to be opened only after you have called or in the event he receives word of your death. The contents of this package contain documents detailing our proposal. We have done this, so you know we are completely serious. The documents inside the package include the number of the bank account under your name where the money is being held. And, of course, the account is completely confidential. I am sure you understand the importance of this measure.'

I didn't respond. It all sounded too neat and tidy. They had gone to a lot of trouble but for nothing. I had no intention of agreeing to any deal.

'We assume your lawyer friend in Grand Haven has your power of attorney,' he said.

'Yes, how did you know?'

'We guessed. You are a single man of means. Usually, under these circumstances, you need someone to act for you in the case of your death. Phillip assumed your attorney friend would play this role. Am I right?'

I nodded, thinking the word death had been mentioned too many times in our conversation. It was no coincidence; spoken to make a point.

'So, please understand. This money is in your possession now. Your lawyer's signature on the documents is as good as yours. The money belongs to you under any and all circumstances at this time.'

He paused again.

I said nothing.

'I have in my briefcase a copy of everything your lawyer has received,' he continued. 'Would you like to review the documents and call him?'

He stared at me, waiting for my response. 'Mr. Van Laan, this is a very generous offer. I am completely confident you will agree. Do you have any questions?'

I didn't know what to say. Even if I wanted to accept his offer, which I didn't, I had nothing but his word. I would need absolute confirmation from the financial institutions involved before I knew for sure he was telling the truth. And I would need to talk to David in Grand Haven to be sure he had received a package. These issues and Nue's several subtle references to my death ran through my mind as he talked. Although he made it sound simple, in fact it was very complicated, nothing to calm my nerves.

However, Nue appeared unconcerned. He proceeded to take papers out of his briefcase and place them on the table in front of me. A quick glance at the documents revealed bank account numbers. Five hundred million dollars was written several times in the documents. A letter of credit from a Swiss bank was also included as a backup for his proposal. He had thought of everything.

He again asked me if I would like to call David to confirm the transaction. I looked at Lin. Lin nodded. Somehow, I knew I didn't need to call David. The money was mine. Nue was not lying.

'One thing I don't understand,' I asked. 'If this money is already in my possession, why did you send your motorcycle goons to kill me this afternoon?'

'You were never in any danger,' Nue responded.

'So why send them?'

Nue stared straight ahead, saying nothing, waiting for me to understand.

'You sent them to soften me up for this?' I finally responded. 'When I didn't go to lunch, you thought I needed some convincing. Is that it?'

'It is not important now. What is important is to conclude our business here tonight,' Nue said. 'Just one formality remains your signature affirming your resignation as the CEO of your company and the forfeiture of your stock in your company to us for the sum of one dollar.'

'You mean five hundred million...' I replied.

'My word is good,' Nue replied. 'The number of the bank account containing your money is on the table in front of you. And as you can see, I have included a bank letter of credit to back up our offer. If you wish, you can call the bank in Switzerland now to confirm its existence. I have a bank official waiting if you desire. When you are talking to him, please ask him to explain that your money is untraceable.'

Nue found the 'Letter of Credit' with the name of the guaranteeing bank. A bank officer's name and his telephone number were at the top of the page. He pushed the document towards me.

His deal was as close to a tax-free gift as international law allowed. It would be strictly my choice if I wanted to declare it or not. Of course, the US government wouldn't see it this way. They would demand I declare it if they learned of its existence and pay income taxes, a lot of taxes. But as long as I didn't spend the money in the US or the IRS got wind of its existence, it was mine to give away or spend on anything I chose.

'John, may I apologize to you for everything which has happened,' Lin interjected at this point in the conversation.

'Little late for apologies, isn't it, Lin? And way too late for Arthur.'

'Arthur's greed killed him, John.'

'I suppose. Couldn't really help himself, could he?'

'You know that's true,' Lin responded without emotion.

'For his indigressions, he had to die?'

'An adjustment was required. It was time to move on without Arthur. He was no longer necessary.'

'And you, Lin. I suppose you will run the company now.'

'If Mr. Nue wishes,' Lin said.

'And Phillip?' I asked. 'What will happen to Phillip?'

'Not your concern,' Lin answered.

I thought perhaps mentioning his name would bring Phillip to life. He normally didn't like being left out of a conversation. But he sat quietly, saying nothing, lost in thought, effectively eliminated from our discussion. This was not like Phillip. When important business was being discussed, he liked to control the conversation. But then, Phillip was a skilled survivor.

He sat quietly, insulating himself by inhabiting an imaginary world.

9:15 P.M. CHARLIE

Charlie anxiously hit the elevator button several times in the lobby of the Plaza Hotel while attempting to catch his breath.

His hotel was a few blocks away. He had run the entire distance to the Plaza, didn't bother to wait for a taxi, grabbed his weapons case, and headed out his door with his cell phone glued to his ear.

Too much noise surrounded him as he ran down the sidewalk: people talking, buses accelerating, horns honking; he couldn't hear enough of the conversation in the background to know precisely what was happening, but from what little he could hear of John's voice, he knew John was in trouble, big time trouble.

Okay, slow down, he said to himself while waiting impatiently for the Plaza elevator door to open. Fumbling for the piece of paper in his pants pocket, he took it out and looked at the room number written on it while still trying to hear what was being said inside a room upstairs.

Monica was inside. He knew this for certain. He had recognized her voice several times. Silently cursing himself now for allowing her to go with John.... Shit, he should have known better. He did know better. He should have never let her go.

Relax; nothing has happened, not yet. No need to get excited. But he couldn't help it. He was scared.

His experience told him the situation in room 3012 was a disaster waiting to explode.

9:16 P.M. JOHN

'Okay,' I replied. 'Let me see if I understand your offer.'
Nue smiled.

'I assume you already control Arthur's stock,' I continued. 'With my twenty-five percent stock added to Arthur's ten percent and Lin's ten percent, that's forty-five percent. You only need one or two other stockholder's cooperation to reach fifty-one percent, and you take control of the company.' I paused. 'And I suppose you already have the other stockholders in your back pocket.'

'You understand our position perfectly,' Lin answered my question.

'It is time for your signature, Mr. Van Laan,' Nue pressed calmly. 'Would you like to call the bank in Switzerland first? Or talk to your friend in Michigan before you sign?'

'No, I do not think that is necessary.'

'You do not question my offer?' Nue asked.

'No, should I?'

'No, you should not. I would not be here if I was not serious.'
I didn't respond.

He pushed a single-page document across the table toward me. Taking a pen out of a pocket in his suit coat, he calmly placed the writing instrument on the table next to the document.

'Please sign here.' Nue pointed to a line at the bottom of the page where my name was typed below.

'Hold on just a minute,' I countered. 'Your offer is very generous, Mr. Nue. I want to thank you. But what you are asking from me is not so simple. You need to understand something first. This company has been my life's work, and it was never all about money. Making money was never my goal. The money I receive is simply the prize given for being successful. But money is not why I work. I work because I like what I do. And just maybe, I don't want to give it up. Can you understand that?'

'Very interesting, Mr. Van Laan. And I do understand, believe me. But this does not solve my problem. My problem is providing work for the people in my country. They need jobs for our country to grow and become strong. Colored gems have historically been one of our country's most important industries. Your company will help Thailand's economy grow. So, you see, it is very important you sign the paper.'

'What about Sri Lanka?' I questioned. 'Don't the people in Sri Lanka also need jobs? Why should their gemstones be sent to Thailand for cutting and polishing? Why should they not benefit from the sales of a natural resource that belongs to them?'

'That is true, but Sri Lanka is not my concern, Mr. Van Laan. Only Thailand is.' Nue answered before continuing after a pause. 'But allow me to take a moment to answer your question. Don't you benefit now from Sri Lanka's resources? So please tell me why you should share in their natural resources any more than me? Why do you accuse me of doing what you now do?'

'I take only a small percentage for a service I supply to them,' I answered.

'And how is this different from what I am proposing?'

'It is different because they are willing to pay me for my services. Something which was not true for you.'

'This business historically belongs to Thailand, no one else.' Nue responded.

'I don't agree.'

Nue said nothing more. Apparently, our discussion had come to an end. I looked at M, stalling for time.

'What do you think, Monica? You're my legal advisor.'

'It's your decision, John. I can't make it for you. But if you really want my opinion, I think you should tell him to go to hell,' she said with emphasis.

Her comment finally woke up Phillip from his trance. He actually smiled, admiring her guts. However, Nue did not react. He continued to sit stoically in his chair, his back straight, never flinching. And Lin, as was his way, was also unmoved by her remark.

'And if I don't accept?' I asked Nue, even though I feared I knew the answer.

'Mr. Van Laan, we intend to control this industry. In order to do this, we need your company. Certainly, you can understand this better than anyone.'

'May I have time to think about your offer?'

'John,' Lin interjected. 'There is nothing to think about. The money is yours now, today.' He paused, 'And the alternative is unacceptable.'

'And what might the alternative be?'

Lin began to reply.

Nue raised his hand to silence him. 'I do not think this conversation is necessary.'

'You kill me?' I said, looking at his bodyguards. 'Is this why these goons are here...? To kill me if I refuse to sign.'

'Mr. Van Laan, I believe I have been absolutely clear in this matter,' Nue said, his voice sounding composed as if he was discussing a common legal contract. 'You are a smart man. Surely, risking your life... or the life of your girlfriend is not worthy of discussion.'

The room became silent. I felt M's hand in mine and gave it a squeeze. Nue was right. I had no alternative. Even if I chose to risk my life, I could not gamble with hers.

'Your signature now, please, Mr. Van Laan. It is late. I wish to go to bed.' Nue spoke his words very softly with no implied threat in the tone of his voice. But that didn't stop the scent of death from hanging over the room. The two sentinels standing at attention were a threat by their very presence. I assumed they had guns and would use them if necessary. One word from Nue and we were dead, here or somewhere else, like in a river.

I leaned over the table to pick up Nue's pen.

An ear-shattering explosion erupted, sending wood splinters flying across the room from the direction of the hall, followed by the sound of a door crashing against a wall. The lights went dark.

We were enveloped in a vague, dimly lit room, illuminated only by a thousand city lights weakly casting shadows through the hotel windows across a harshly confused room. My ears screamed in protest to the blast as an acrid grey-gray gas seeped into my lungs. Coughing, I couldn't stop coughing. Gunshots echoed off the walls of the room accompanied by red tracer lights darting through the dull gray gas, searching for targets. A shadow of one of the bodyguards fell near a window. M rammed her shoulder into my chest, driving me off the couch where we were sitting, falling on top of me when we landed on the floor. Lin cried out somewhere in the mayhem. M flinched, driving her nails into my back. Warm liquid began to drip on my face in the semi-darkness. Her body tightened, then relaxed as I held her.

Shouts and the crack of gunshots continued to pierce the gray confusion for what seemed an eternity.

CHARLOTTESVILLE, VIRGINIA, APRIL 17, 7:35 P.M. JOHN

Arny sat across the kitchen counter from me, sharing a couple of beers and dinner: steak and potatoes cooked by him on an outside grill.

Food was delicious, as usual, but I was not very hungry, picking at my dinner, more interested in drinking beer and half-listening to his feeble attempt to entertain me with a gift of gab. His hapless New Jersey Nets had been beaten again by my rowdy Pistons and he was busy complaining about the refs as was his usual custom.

Charlottesville was in its full spring-blossom glory, filled with flowering dogwood trees spreading new color across a previous dingy, brown-gray winter landscape. Brilliant fresh white and pastel pink blossoms were interspersed with glorious shades of purple redbud trees that had been flowering for several weeks.

All this spring splendor had very little positive effect on me. Even on the days when I took time to play golf with my buddies, their camaraderie cheered me for only a short time. After drinks and happy talk at the club's bar was over and it was time to drive home, home to an empty apartment which never seemed so empty before.

In my thoughts and dreams, I have relived the night she died countless times since it happened. When Charlie received a call from M's phone, he ran to the Plaza. Although he could only hear bits and pieces of our conversation from the phone in her purse, it was enough to make him decide we needed to be rescued. Especially after he heard me say something about being killed if I didn't sign. The door to Lin's hotel room was blasted open. Ear-shattering, disorientating explosions followed, accompanied by tear gas and gunshots. M was hit by a stray bullet to her head. She died instantly, falling on me, her warm blood dripping on my face as I held her for one last time.

A plane was chartered to return her body to her hometown of Columbus, Ohio, where she belonged with her family. Her parents were kind to me, but I knew they didn't understand. I didn't either. They had many obligations to fulfill during the days before her funeral. They couldn't spend all their time with me and for the most part, this was fine with me. I wanted to be alone. Besides, there were moments when I thought they looked at me in a way that indicated they blamed me for her death... And for long, excruciating minutes, I felt they were right.

Monica's funeral was held in a large gothic Methodist church filled with bright afternoon sunlight streaming through the church's elaborately colored stained-glass windows, casting a warm glow over wooden pews filled with mourners dressed mostly in black. Rich chords resonated from rows of brass organ pipes, echoing off the towering brownstone walls of the imposing church. Monica had been a very popular girl in her hometown, a former cheerleader and honor student at her high school. Friends from high school, college, and law school attended her funeral. The church was full. It was her church, her home, her people. I could feel her spirit in this place.

Her funeral made me wonder if death was not an end as we are taught to think. Made me wonder if our bodies are really nothing more than vessels born to carry our spirits for a brief time. And this is why it is so hard for us to live; because we are, each of us, spirits interned in a corporal body that inhibits our movement, holds us, and encases us like the cold, hard snow of an avalanche packed tightly around our eternal souls? We often yearn to fly on the wind, to soar like birds, to streak through the far reaches of space, to walk with God through valleys filled with knowledge and beauty, becoming one with love and mercy and grace. But instead, we are caught in a trap, held tightly by our carnal bodies for a time of suffering and longing to be free.

As I looked around her church, I imagined holding Monica's hand one more time, just once more, while resting in the presence of her smile. Tears fell as I thought of her; tears I chose not to wipe... tears falling freely... a physical tribute to her, to her spirit and her grace.

I didn't sit during the service. I couldn't. I chose instead to stand in the rear of the church, listening to a minister drone on from the pulpit, not comprehending anything he was saying. Thinking instead about something M had once mentioned about death, about why good people die first. I think we were talking about Vidu's death at the time. I couldn't remember her exact words, but they were something like 'an early death is a reward for a life well lived.'

Her words didn't make much sense to me then, but as I thought about them at her funeral, I thought I understood... Because wasn't she in heaven now... and I... poor boy... wasn't I alone, standing in the back of a church without her... alone in an earthly hell?

I uttered a prayer and asked God to take care of my beautiful red head and treat her like the angel she was. I had lost her; let her slip away. I had not listened to her. She had tried to teach me about love, about the importance of love above everything else. But I had been a fool. I had not listened. I had other issues, issues I thought were more important, but now knew they were not. I had forced her away, lost her for precious days and hours when we could have been together.

Those days are gone now, and I can never have them back.

After her funeral, everyone was invited to her parent's house. It was an unusually warm, sunny spring day. Their home was Early American, traditional architecture: a large, painted white wood exterior house with dark green shutters located in an older section of the city on a quiet, tree-lined street. The backyard was beautifully landscaped with flower gardens and large oak trees. Food and drink were provided inside on tables. The house and grounds easily accommodated all the people who came to mourn with her family. I stayed for a short time, standing mostly off to one side, leaning against a tree, observing her parents greeting friends and accepting condolences.

Charlie also attended her funeral, came on his own, and spent his time with law school friends. I saw him at their house after the funeral, but we did not talk. I didn't know what to say to him. It was not important to me.

I wondered instead about what it would have been like to have come to her parent's house under different circumstances, to be introduced to her family for the first time as her husband-to-be.

It was a stupid thought, I knew. I tried to put it out of my mind. And when I couldn't do it anymore, I walked away without saying goodbye and drove to the airport, where a chartered plane waited to fly me back to Charlottesville.

Weeks later, I received a kind note from her mother thanking me for coming and asking me to visit sometime. I didn't know how to respond. Should I tell them I loved their daughter? And that if she would have had me, I would have married her? Would this have made their sorrow easier to bear? I didn't think so. Instead, I sent a letter thanking her mother for her offer and saying I hoped to visit sometime when my schedule allowed.

The letter was a lie.

I knew I could never return. It would be too painful.

My board of directors reluctantly accepted my resignation at a delayed meeting. A brief report was circulated to them prior to the meeting, detailing reasons for the delay including a report from NYPD blessed by the CIA. Prior to the meeting, members expressed their sympathy and regret to me, each in their own way. Everyone knew the company would never be the same again. Lin and Arthur were gone. In their absence, the board nominated Bob to be the next Chairman and CEO before I departed. I knew he would fail, but I didn't care. I wanted to be anywhere except at that board meeting. When it was thankfully over, I left immediately and didn't stay to talk to anyone. As far as I was concerned, Gemstone International was now in my past, no longer important. It was time to move on. This chapter in my life was over.

I began to wonder if this was how I needed to view what happened as just another chapter in my life. Because wasn't I just another man, not unlike all other men who have some good fortune and some bad? Did I, any more than anyone else, did I have a special right or privilege to demand a higher level of God's grace? I think not.

And Nue, was he wrong? I'm not sure. Thailand and its people need industry and jobs as much as anyone. Why shouldn't they have them? And certainly, they have not been the first nation to seek economic advantage through the use of violence. There is a long tradition of appalling wars which have followed this logic.

Speaking of Nue, he had been traveling under a Thai diplomatic passport. Given his rights under international law, he was allowed to leave the US without being charged with a crime in the US. According to Charlie, he had sat upright in his chair the night Monica died, never flinched during gunfire, never moved. He had not been hit by a single bullet. I didn't understand how this was possible. Charlie said he didn't either.

Sometime after her funeral, I called David, my attorney friend in my hometown of Grand Haven, Michigan, and asked him if he had received a package in the mail with my name on it. He said he had. I asked him to open the package and call me after he had time to review the contents. He called a day later and said the documents were genuine and the money was mine as stipulated, as Nue told me, all five hundred million dollars in a Swiss bank account under my name, no strings attached, backed by a letter of credit. He asked me what I wanted to do with the money. I told him I didn't know. I needed time to think about it. The matter was complex. I still had my stock but never signed it away. And Nue never got the stock he wanted, but I had his money, money he paid me for the stock. Nothing was resolved. It was a mess.

And then there was Arthur, another messy business. Nue must have made promises to Arthur he never intended to keep. Arthur was probably just a short-term solution. He had a limited lifespan from the time he agreed to work for the Thai. He just didn't know it. Or perhaps Nue decided to eliminate him after he discovered Arthur was an interminable conniver.

Phillip had somehow disappeared in the chaos of that night. Charlie had no explanation for how he escaped. But I was not surprised. Phillip was a survivor.

Lin had not been so lucky. He had been shot and died en route to the hospital without uttering another word. That was unfortunate because I longed to ask him questions. I wanted a better explanation of how he could have worked so tirelessly for me when his first loyalty was to the Thai based on his birth. Obviously, he and his Thai friends had a plan, one only they understood. In the end they must have decided not to destroy my company after all. Kept it intact for their use after I was gone.

And M... I think of her every day.
Her smile lingers like a tear in my mind's eye, which never falls.

THE END

See below for excerpts from Book 3, PRETENDING TO BE ALIVE.

AMBERGRIS ISLAND, BELIZE, FRIDAY, APRIL 24, 1998, 9:10 A.M. ILANA

Ilana released the shoulder straps of her summer dress, permitting a warm breeze to gather the soft folds of cloth and remove the offending garment guilty of obscuring the beautiful curves of her tanned body.

Disguised now by only a rather skimpy white bikini, she lay, face down, on a towel near the far end of a wooden dock jutting out into the Caribbean Sea and removed her top. The morning sun quickly warmed her tanned skin. She was grateful for a breeze because, without it, she would have quickly become too hot. As it was, she was perfectly comfortable as she rested some distance from the shore at the end of the dock. Even though she was nearly naked, she did not care if someone saw her. She knew she was beautiful.

The morning was hers, free to do as she pleased, as were most mornings, just as she wished it.

A meeting with that unpleasant man who was paying her to keep an eye on an American was not until shortly before noon.

9:24 A.M. JOHN

The best time to be on my dock was in the morning.

By midday the sun often bears down from directly overhead out of a clear blue sky with torrid heat. But in the morning, the sun is low on the water, casting a warm glow over the Caribbean Sea.

More importantly, Ilana is usually on the dock in the morning, as was true this morning. The sight of her beautiful tan body sunbathing at the end of the dock made me smile. Another dark night filled with nightmarish memories of Monica's death temporarily evaporated under warm rays of bright sunshine and the natural allure of a gorgeous island girl. The Caribbean Sea stretched out in front of me as far as I could see in all its rippled blue-glass splendor. On the edges of the sea near the horizon, a rush of splashing white water broke over an offshore reef. Large sea swells driven by the wind over miles of open ocean could be seen curling up over the reef in a rush of cascading white water. With their strength now dissipated by the rocky reef, the waves completed their long journey by floating harmlessly toward shore as only weak replicas of their former grandeur, creating a gently rolling blue-green aquatic sanctuary between the reef and the shore.

I placed a folding chair next to Ilana on the dock, intentionally covering her body with my shadow. Pretending to be completely unaware of her lovely existence, I took a sip of hot coffee from a mug and waited quietly for her expected response. Eventually she opened her eyes and frowned when she saw I had taken her sun. But instead of complaining, she simply slipped over the edge of the dock into the warm water. I watched in wonder as she gracefully stroked out into the calm waters, swimming like a creature who belonged in the sea. And in a way, it was true; the sea was her home. A native of Belize, she lived on the island of Ambergris. She told me she had left the island only once to visit Belize City on the mainland. This was as far as she had ever traveled. Her mother and father were dead. Her brother was a local fisherman. He was her only family and she lived with him in their family home. She didn't seem to work very much, some waitressing when it was busy tourist season, but this was the extent of her ambition. She often came to my dock in the morning. I didn't mind. She was a very attractive woman with big brown eyes and jet-black hair typical of her Spanish heritage.

But ever since Monica died, I have spent very little time thinking about Ilana or any other woman. Monica's memory is still too close. The night she died continues to occupy my thoughts during the day and plague my dreams at night.

Her death makes my life very difficult, but I try, I try to get by, one hour, one day at a time.

11:45 A.M. ILANA

He waited for her patiently, sitting on a bench in front of a badly scratched old wooden table.

A plate of half-eaten enchiladas rested in front of him. Occasionally, he took a bite of the food to pass the time. He was old, but not too old. The truth was, it was difficult to tell just how old he was because although his deeply tanned face, badly wrinkled from too many days in the hot sun, made him look old, it was possible he wasn't old at all. A full head of curly black hair touched with a hint of gray at the temples did nothing to indicate his age. Intense dark eyes and thick black eyebrows complimented a bushy mustache above his thinly drawn lips. If it wasn't for his wrinkled skin, he might have looked almost attractive... Except, something unpleasant seemed to inhabit this man's body, something which spoiled a good impression and made him appear ugly. It was as if a sense of contained violence emanated from his strongly built torso. You immediately knew you did not want to make this man angry.

After leaving John's dock, Ilana went to her brother's house to change into a fresh, lightly colored street dress, which showed off the deep tan of her smooth skin. Locking the door behind her, she walked quickly down the dirt road that passed for the main street of her hometown of San Pedro.

The town was originally a fishing village. However, in recent years, it has become a resort destination, and it has now passed for the closest thing to civilization on the island. Newly painted old wood houses and tourist-trap shops lined both sides of its dusty-dirt main street, which ran parallel to a beach. An imposing structure of a Catholic Church dominated the town's main square. Old and tired looking, the church's faded pink, stucco exterior was little more than a pale, washed-out reminder of how it must have looked in the grandeur of its original deep red color.

Ilana hurried by the church ignoring a strong urge to go inside. Maybe, she thought. Maybe it would be good to go inside today and say a few prayers at the altar. Maybe this would be better than meeting with the ugly man at the jewelry shop. But she was already late for her appointment, and she needed money. Quickly ignoring her good intentions, she passed the church.

Nearby, a few male laggards leaned against the wall of a corner t-shirt shop while intently following the simple ballet of her slim body, street dust rising from her leather sandals as she hurried by their staring eyes.

Ilana's destination was a Mayan silver jewelry shop situated near the center of town. Stopping briefly when she arrived inside the door of the shop, she pretended to look at the displays of local jewelry under glass. Seeing no one in the shop, she quickly slipped behind a dark blue, floor length cloth curtain which hid a private back room.

The man with intense dark eyes and a wrinkled face was waiting for her there.

'Would you like something to eat,' he pointed to some burritos slowly cooking on a black wrought iron pan over an old metal stove.

'Yes,' Ilana replied with little hesitation.

Taking a fork from a drawer, she carefully lifted a burrito from the pan on the stove and placed it on a handmade ceramic dish. Sitting down on a chair across the table from the man, she began to eat.

Neither of them spoke for long minutes, eating in silence.

Finally, the man asked her. 'How is our friend, the American?'

Ilana looked up from her burrito as if she had forgotten the man was in the room.

'Oh, he is fine,' she replied nonchalantly. 'We are going sailing this afternoon.'

'So, nothing has changed?'

'No, nothing has changed.'

'You would tell me if it had.'

'I would tell you, signor.'

'Good,' the man took a small roll of bills from his pants pocket and slid them across the table to Ilana. He then stood without finishing his enchilada and quickly exited a back door.

Ilana put the money in her purse.

Words of a Reader

I have read Book 1, *Winds of Success*, and Book 2, *Living with Death* by Richard Jan. These are new first-time novels, and they are two excellent adventure stories that entice you to read the others in the series (Dying to Succeed). As a reader with a PhD in English literature, one who has published reviews, one who has taught college literature courses, and one who has read countless novels over the course of years, I am impressed with the quality of these two novels. They are packed with international intrigue and displace a convincing knowledge of business in general and the gem trade in particular. And they weave an engaging plot with well-developed characters. One of the strengths of both of these novels is the attention to detail as the author takes you around the world to such places as Bangkok, Thailand, Hong Kong, New York City, the mountains of Montana, Charlottesville, Virginia, the shores of Lake Michigan, and elsewhere. He knows these places intimately: the clubs, the restaurants, the hotels, the landscapes, and the people. His main characters are fairly well-developed and creditable. The Novels also hold interest and attention to the emerging power struggle, crimes, violence, and sex scenes. And how all of these are played out in the context of a very successful business being brought down by political forces and criminal actions. If you are looking for well-written adventure novels that keep you wondering what's next and in which you develop empathy for the two main characters, I highly recommend these books, and I plan the others in the series with eager anticipation.

    -   *Robert Van Dellen, Ph.D, former professor of English, November 14, 2012*

www.ingramcontent.com/pod-product-compliance
Lightning Source LLC
Chambersburg PA
CBHW060439310726
48977CB00001B/258